C000030164

Undeniably His

Ramona Gray

This book is a work of fiction and any resemblance to persons, living or dead, or places, events or locales is purely coincidental. The characters are productions of the author's imagination and used fictitiously.

Adult Reading Material

Cover design by The Final Wrap

ISBN-13:978-1-988826-12-7

Chapter One

"Jane? Do you have a moment?"

Jane looked up from her computer screen, her heart dropping into her stomach at the somber look on Maria's face. Maria was the human resources administrator for the office and Jane cast a guilty look at the half-eaten sandwich on her desk. She had stolen it from the tray of sandwiches delivered to the office for the executive's meeting. Dismay rippled through her. She was going to get fired over a damn sandwich.

"Jane? Can we speak in my office?" Maria prompted.

"Of course." Jane dropped her napkin over her sandwich in a futile attempt to hide the evidence of her thievery before following Maria to her office.

Maria closed the door and sank into the chair behind her desk. She rubbed delicately at her temples as Jane perched nervously on the edge of the chair in front of Maria's desk. Maria stared quietly at her for a moment.

"I'm sorry!" Jane blurted out as she twisted a hank of her light brown hair between her fingers. "I'm so sorry. Please don't fire me. I shouldn't have taken the sandwich, I know that, but I forgot my lunch and I skipped breakfast and I…"

She trailed off as Maria gave her a puzzled look.

"I'm so sorry," she repeated, "I'll pay for the

sandwich."

Maria's brow furrowed and she glanced at Jane's hands as if she half-expected to see a sandwich in them. "What are you talking about, Jane?"

Shit! She should never have opened her big mouth.

"Uh, I took a sandwich from the lunch tray that was delivered today for the executive's meeting," Jane said as her pale skin turned bright red. "I thought that's what you wanted to speak to me about."

Maria shook her head. "No. I wanted to speak with you about the position you applied for."

"Mr. Dawson's personal assistant?" Jane said. "It was posted internally so I thought I was allowed to apply."

"It is and you are," Maria replied. "I'm just curious as to why you want to leave the finance department."

Jane cleared her throat. It probably wasn't a great idea to tell Maria that she applied for the position only for the pay raise. "Well, I thought I would try something different."

"You've only been here three months," Maria said. "You're doing well in the finance department and neither Kyla nor Mark have any complaints with you."

"Oh, well, I really like working with finance. I just feel like I'm better suited to admin work," Jane said.

"You don't have any admin work on your resume," Maria pointed out.

"No, but I didn't have any finance experience either and I picked up my current job duties very quickly."

She wondered if Maria could hear the desperation in her voice.

"That's true but being Mr. Dawson's assistant is a little more demanding than inputting numbers into a spreadsheet," Maria said. "It's not always strictly work-related either. Mr. Dawson is a very busy man and there is an expectation that you will assist him with picking up dry cleaning, ordering his lunch and bringing him coffee."

"I don't have a problem with that," Jane said.

"Are you certain?" Maria said.

"Yes."

"Have you ever met Mr. Dawson?"

"I've seen him at the staff meetings," Jane replied.

"Have you spoken with him?"

"No, he doesn't usually come down to the finance department."

Maria sighed. "Jane, can I be honest with you?"

"Yes."

"Mr. Dawson isn't like your current supervisor, Kyla, or even like Mark the CFO. He's not unkind, but he does have high expectations of his assistant. He won't explain things a second time, he'll want everything done exactly his way and he does not give second chances. Do you understand?"

"I do," Jane said.

"I think you're too fragile to work for Mr. Dawson," Maria said bluntly. "I think you could do well here but I believe you would be better off staying in the finance department. There's room for advancement there in a few years."

"I appreciate the advice but I'm tougher than I look," Jane said.

"Are you?"

"I am," Jane said with a confidence she didn't feel. "If I don't get the position, will it affect my current job in finance?"

"No," Maria said.

"Then there's no harm in interviewing, right?"

"No, there isn't," Maria replied. She eyed Jane's cheap dress pants and shirt. "Well, if I can't talk you out of it, I would suggest you wear something a bit more professional and," she hesitated, "expensive. Perhaps something from one of our lines? That will go over well with Mr. Dawson."

"Um, okay," Jane said. She smoothed her hand over her pants self-consciously as Maria stood.

"Excellent. You'll be meeting with Mr. Dawson at eight-thirty sharp. Don't be late please. He abhors tardiness."

"I won't be late," Jane said.

"Good. If you'll excuse me, I have a conference call in three minutes."

"Thank you, Maria," Jane said. She left Maria's office, closing the door behind her before leaning against the wall. Her heart was thudding and she felt a little sick to her stomach. If the HR person was suggesting she not apply for the position, maybe she shouldn't. Maria said that Mr. Dawson wasn't unkind but she knew the rumours circulating the office. He was demanding and sometimes he shouted. Embarrassingly enough, she wasn't entirely certain she wouldn't just burst into tears if he shouted at her. She was always so tired and lack of sleep made her cry easily.

You won't, Jane! You can do this. Don't pussy out now - you need this job.

That was true. If she got this position, she might actually have enough money to rent a place that had working heat and didn't have mold growing on the walls. Hell, she could actually buy some damn groceries.

Her stomach growled and she hurried back to her desk. Feeling slightly guilty, she scarfed down the rest of the sandwich before clicking the link to the company's website. She scanned the suits, choosing the lowest price option and studying the prices with dread. Even the cheapest suit was way above her budget.

She twisted her hair anxiously. Maria had suggested a suit from the Dawson line but there was no way she could afford it. She'd have to stop at the thrift store tonight and see if she could find something that wasn't too cheap looking.

৵ ৻

"You missed the meeting, Amy."

Luke walked into his sister's office and studied the bean bag chairs with distaste. "What happened to the leather chairs I ordered?"

"I hated them," Amy said airily as she studied the sketches in front of her. "They were super uncomfortable. Just try sitting in one of the bean bag chairs, Luke. You'll love it."

He sighed and kicked at one of the bean bags before leaning against the wall. "No thanks. You missed the meeting."

"I didn't miss the meeting," Amy said with a grin. "I deliberately chose not to go."

"Amy, it was important that you be there. The Board members get nervous when the lead designer doesn't - "

"The Board members don't give a shit about me," Amy said. "They just want to talk about the business and the new lines and how much money is coming through and blah, blah, blah. That's your department, remember? I design the clothing and you run the business."

"You should still be there," he said. "Half the Board members don't even know what you look like. Christ, half the *employees* have no idea what you look like."

"What for? So I can listen to them blather on about meaningless numbers? The company is doing well and the new line is exploding off the shelves. That's all I need to know. Besides, you know I like my anonymity. I work better when I'm not disturbed. Hey, what do you think of this?"

She showed him the sketch and he studied the flowing skirt and the off-the-shoulder blouse. "It looks good but not marketable for us."

She laughed. "What do you know about women's clothing, Lukie?"

"I know we've made our fortune from selling women's work attire," he replied. "Not frilly shit like that."

Amy laughed again before throwing her pencil at him.

"Maybe it's time we branched out in a different direction."

"The Board would disagree," he said as he picked up the pencil. "Just because you dress like a hippie at the office doesn't mean other women want to."

She studied her long dress and the multiple bead bracelets wrapped around both wrists. "I would have fit in so well at Woodstock, wouldn't I?"

A grin crossed his face and she walked toward him and pinched his cheek affectionately. "Do you ever wonder if one of us is adopted? We look nothing alike. You're so conservative and proper and I'm…"

"A hippie?" He said.

"Watch it, mister, or I'll start wearing flowers in my hair and going barefoot in the office," she teased.

He rolled his eyes. "Do you even want to know what the Board had to say?"

"Nope," she said as she returned to her sketches. "I assume if they were unhappy you'd be a lot more fired up."

"They are pleased with this quarter's numbers," he said. "The new line has brought in the highest revenue since last year. They're open to my idea of expanding internationally. I'll probably book the Paris trip to meet with the investors."

Amy shrugged carelessly. "Whatever you want, big brother. I just make the pretty clothes, remember?"

Luke tugged at his tie as there was a knock on the door. It opened and Maria stuck her head into the opening.

"Amy, is Luke in here… oh, Luke, there you are. I've been looking for you."

"Hi, Maria," Luke said as Amy waved at the HR administrator.

"Maria, come in and try the bean bag chairs. They're sinfully comfortable."

"Thanks, Amy, but I've got a meeting in five minutes. Another time, okay?"

"Sure."

"Luke, you're meeting with two internal applicants for the PA position tomorrow. Lisa Moore at eight and Jane Smith at eight thirty. If neither of them is suitable, we'll do an external posting."

"Thanks, Maria."

"You're welcome," Maria replied. She disappeared, closing the door behind her. Amy arched her eyebrow at Luke.

"What?" He asked.

"Why are you getting a new personal assistant? What happened to Elaine?"

"Her mother isn't doing well and Elaine is moving to Florida to care for her."

"That's a shame. She was the only assistant you had who didn't burst into tears on a regular basis."

"That's because Elaine was competent," Luke said.

"Also, she was fifty-three and too old for you to scold her."

"I don't scold my employees," Luke said heatedly.

"Yes, you do."

"No, I don't."

"Yes, you do."

"No, I don't," Luke said. "I have to go. Will you be at dinner this weekend?"

"Oh probably," Amy said. "I missed last week's and you know how mom gets."

"All right. Later, Ames."

"Goodbye, young Skywalker."

He rolled his eyes again and left his sister's office.

⇜ ⇝

"Hello, Jane!"

"Hi, Tanya." Jane slowed down and paused at the front desk of the care home. "How are you?"

"Can't complain. How are you? You're a little late today."

"I had an errand to run after work. How is she?"

Tanya hesitated. "It's been a bad day for her. She's been confused for most of it."

Jane sighed. "Okay, thanks."

"Before you go, I have an envelope for you." Tanya handed her the envelope and Jane took it with a distracted smile and continued down the hallway to the last door on the left. She knocked on the door before opening it and stepping into the small room.

The old woman was sitting in a recliner chair by the window and a surge of love went through Jane. She hurried over and set her purse and the plastic bag on the floor next to the chair before touching the woman's hand.

"Mama J?"

The woman continued to stare out of the window and Jane smoothed the wisps of white hair back from her face. "Mama J, it's Janie. I'm sorry I'm late today."

The woman turned her face toward her and Jane smiled at her. "Hi."

"Do I know you?"

Sorrow shot through her and she blinked back the tears. "Yes, my name is Jane. I'm your daughter."

"You have me mistaken for someone else. I don't have any children."

"I'm your foster daughter."

"Foster daughter? I don't foster any children."

"You did, Mama J. You fostered lots of children."

"That doesn't sound like me."

Jane tried to smile at her. "It's true, I promise."

She studied the tray of food on the small wooden table next to her. "You haven't eaten your supper."

"I'm not hungry."

"You should eat. You need to keep up your strength." She pulled a wooden chair up to the recliner and shrugged out of her coat before picking up the plate of food. She held a forkful of potatoes to the woman's mouth. "Try a bite, Mama J. It's good."

The woman opened her mouth obediently and they sat in silence as Jane fed her. When there were only a few bites of food left, the woman shook her head. "I'm full now."

"You ate lots, that's good," Jane said. She glanced at the open door before quickly eating the last of the potatoes and chicken. She set the plate down and held both of Mama J's hands. "I have a job interview for a better position tomorrow. It's why I'm late – I had to pick up a new outfit. Would you like to see it?"

Mama J didn't reply but Jane rifled through the bag anyway and pulled out the suit. "Isn't it pretty? I work for a company that makes clothing for women and I found one of their suits at the thrift store. It's a line from a few years ago, but I think it'll help make a better impression at the interview. It's a little big and it has a small rip in the skirt but I can hide it with the jacket. See?"

Mama J was already looking out the window again and Jane touched her hand. "Mama J? Would you like me to read to you?"

"Who are you? Why are you in my room?" The old woman gave her a startled look.

"My name is Jane. I'm your daughter."

"I don't have any children."

A tear slipped down Jane's cheek and she wiped it away before stuffing the suit back into the bag. "Why don't you let me read to you for a while?"

"No thank you."

Mama J turned her face away and Jane reached into her purse for a tissue. She brushed against the envelope that Tanya had given her, and she wiped her face and blew her nose before opening the envelope. She read the single-page letter as her face paled.

"No, oh no," she whispered.

She chewed at her bottom lip before leaning forward and kissing Mama J on her wrinkled cheek. "I have to go but I'll be back tomorrow and I'll tell you all about my job interview, okay?"

The old woman ignored her and Jane kissed her again before gathering her things. She stopped at the nurses' desk and Tanya gave her a sympathetic look. "I'm sorry, Jane."

"Five hundred dollars. It's going up five hundred dollars a month?" Jane whispered. "Why?"

"It's gone up for everyone," Tanya said. "All the residents received the same notice."

Jane didn't reply and Tanya squeezed her arm. "My sister works for another care home on the west side of the city. It isn't as nice as this one but Josephine will receive good care. They have a waiting list but if you put your name in now, you might - "

"No," Jane interrupted. "I don't want to move her. I'll find the extra money each month." She gave Tanya a small smile. "I have to go. I'll see you tomorrow, okay?"

She hurried out of the nursing home and walked down the street toward the bus stop. There was a bitterly cold wind blowing and she zipped up her jacket and hunched her shoulders as she waited for the bus. The temperature had plummeted last week and her thin jacket did nothing to keep her warm. She should have bought the winter coat she saw at the thrift store tonight but she'd had just enough cash to buy the suit. She knew how lucky she was to have found it but it cost her twenty-three dollars to buy it. She had three dollars and thirty-seven cents left in her bank account and payday wasn't for another three days. The money she'd spent on the suit had been earmarked for some ramen noodles and maybe a package of ground beef. With it gone, she had nothing but a loaf of bread and half a jar of peanut butter to tide her over until payday.

You'll make some tips tonight.

Yeah, she would, but she needed the tip money to pay her cell phone bill and buy a bus pass. The phone bill was due tomorrow and her bus pass expired in two days. She couldn't afford to give up either. The care home needed to be able to contact her and she couldn't exactly walk to work. The office building was downtown and she lived in the section of the city the wealthy liked to refer to as the Badlands.

Hey, Janie? Not to interrupt but how exactly are you going to pay the extra five hundred a month? You're barely making ends meet as it is, her inner voice asked nervously.

The new job. She would ace the interview tomorrow, get the position as Mr. Dawson's assistant and the pay increase would cover the five hundred dollars. She wouldn't be getting ahead like she thought she would but that didn't matter. What mattered was keeping Mama J where she was safe and happy. She owed her that.

The bus stopped in front of her and she boarded it, feeling a numb gratefulness for the heat that washed over her. She chose a seat near the back, leaned her head against the window and closed her eyes. Her shift at the club started in half an hour and she was already tired. She rubbed at her forehead before sticking her hands between her thin thighs to try and warm them. Maybe it wouldn't be busy at the club tonight and she could go home early. She always let one of the other girls go home – she couldn't afford to leave early and miss out on potential tips – but she would need the extra sleep if she was going to ace that interview tomorrow.

Chapter Two

At exactly 8:13 the next morning, Jane stepped into the elevator. She pushed the button for the thirty-seventh floor and smoothed her suit jacket down. She could see her reflection in the shiny walls of the elevator and she cringed a little. The suit really was much too big on her and she supposed she should have chosen something that fit her. But to find a Dawson suit in a thrift store was a bloody miracle and Maria had said that wearing something from their clothing line would make a good impression on Mr. Dawson. She squared her shoulders and leaned forward to check her make-up. She was wearing a minimal amount - only a bit of mascara and a touch of berry coloured lip gloss. After the layers of make-up she wore at the club all night, she liked to give her skin a break. She was starting to second guess her decision though. Most of the women here wore tailored suits and their make-up was flawless. That's probably what Mr. Dawson was expecting.

It was too late now. The elevator doors were opening and she quickly checked for any stray strands of hair that might have fallen from the twist before stepping out of the elevator. As the president of the company, Mr. Dawson had an office on the top floor of the building. He shared it with a few other executives, including some of the designers and her own current boss Mark.

She smiled at the blonde woman sitting behind the desk in the reception area. "Hello, my name is Jane Smith. I have an appointment at eight-thirty with Mr. Dawson."

"Have a seat, please. He'll be with you shortly," the woman said without looking up from her computer screen.

"Could you tell me where the ladies' room is?" Jane asked.

The woman pointed down the hall and Jane quickly walked to the bathroom. She slipped into the handicap stall, hung the jacket on the hook on the door and used the toilet. She adjusted the two clothespins she was using to keep the waistband of the skirt closed around her waist and leaned against the wall for a moment. She took a few deep breaths before murmuring, "You can do this, Jane."

She stepped away from the wall, her eyes widening when she felt the resistance and heard the ripping noise. She peered over her shoulder and cried out with dismay. A second hook was positioned lower on the wall she was leaning on. It had caught in the rip in her skirt and tore it even more.

"Shit!" She muttered and unsnagged the fabric from the metal hook before hurrying out of the stall. She turned and peered at her ass in the mirror before groaning.

"No, no, no," she whispered. The rip was so large that she could see the edge of her underwear and the length of her nylon-clad thigh. There was no way the suit jacket would cover it.

"Think, Jane!" She said fiercely as she held the ripped edges together. Maybe she could ask the receptionist for some tape. She could tape it together.

Tape isn't going to stick to the fabric, you idiot!

"Oh God," she moaned. She checked her watch. It was 8:17. She had exactly thirteen minutes to fix her wardrobe malfunction.

"Stapler! I can staple it together!" She said loudly. "Just staple it and - "

"Honey, stapling isn't going to help."

She shrieked and whirled around. A tall, chubby woman with long blonde hair and light blue eyes was standing in the doorway of the bathroom. She smiled at Jane before crouching in front of her. She examined the rip as Jane gave her a look of panic.

"I – I have an interview with Mr. Dawson in," she glanced at her watch, "eleven minutes and I ripped my skirt! Could you do me a huge favour and ask the receptionist if I can borrow her stapler?"

"I told you, stapling isn't going to work," the woman replied. She was wearing an off-the-shoulder blouse with a long skirt and there was a tape measure slung around her neck. She rummaged in the pocket of her skirt and produced a small plastic box of pins. "Luckily for you, I have some dress pins with me."

"Oh, thank God," Jane breathed. "Are you – do you work in the design department?"

"Something like that," the woman replied with a grin. "Hold still, honey."

She knelt and stuck her hands up Jane's skirt. The bead bracelets around her wrists jingled as she pinned the skirt closed with practiced ease. She stood and studied her handiwork. "There, that should work. As long as you don't do jumping jacks in the interview."

Jane turned and stared at the rip. It was still obvious that there was a tear in the fabric but neither her underwear nor her thigh was showing and the jacket would cover the worst of it.

"Thank you so much, I really appreciate this," Jane said as she grabbed the suit jacket from the stall. The woman eyed the clothespins around the waistband of her skirt as Jane pulled on the jacket and buttoned it. It hung from her small frame and she tried to adjust it as the woman watched.

"Don't take this the wrong way, honey, but your outfit is way too big."

"I know," Jane said.

"So why are you wearing it?"

"It's my only suit."

"Did you order it online from the website? Because we have a super easy return policy."

"No, I bought it at a store."

"The sales lady really should have made you try on a smaller size," the woman said with a low laugh.

Jane blushed as dull embarrassment went through her. The woman frowned and touched her shoulder. "I'm sorry. I wasn't making fun of you. You look lovely, really."

"I don't," Jane said miserably. "I know I don't but I was told that wearing one of the Dawson suits would give me a better shot at getting the job. I really need this job. You have no idea how much I need it."

She stared at the floor in embarrassment. "Only, Dawson suits are so expensive and I really couldn't afford one but then I found this at a thrift store. I figured wearing a Dawson suit that was a little too big was better than not wearing one at all."

She gave the woman standing in front of her a despondent look. "I look stupid."

"You don't," the woman said. "A little pale, maybe, but not stupid."

She grasped Jane's shoulders and straightened her. "Now, chin up and shoulders back. Look confident, act confident and you'll do fine in the interview. Don't let him intimidate you. His bark is worse than his bite, okay?"

"Okay," Jane said. "Thank you again."

"You're welcome. Good luck, honey."

Jane smiled at her and walked carefully back to reception. A woman was standing next to the desk chatting with the receptionist and she looked Jane up and down. A flicker of amusement crossed her face and Jane blushed again. The woman was wearing a Dawson suit as well but it was from the latest line and fit her perfectly. The dark green complimented her tanned skin and blonde hair beautifully and she was tall with lush curves. Jane crossed her arms over her small breasts and tried to stand a little taller as the woman smiled at the receptionist.

"Will you please tell Mr. Dawson that it was a pleasure meeting with him today and I look forward to working with him?" She gave Jane another quick look before heading to the elevators.

"Follow me please, Miss Smith."

Jane followed the receptionist through the maze of hallways. At the end of one were two large double doors with an alcove in the wall just outside of them. A medium-sized desk and two filing cabinets were tucked into the alcove. The receptionist knocked before opening one door. Jane took a deep breath and walked into the office. She jumped a little when the door closed behind her and cleared her throat. Her palms were sweating and her knees were literally knocking together from fear.

Mr. Dawson stood up from behind his desk and she walked toward him and held out her hand. "It's nice to meet you, Mr. Dawson. I'm Jane Smith."

"Good morning, Ms. Smith," he said politely.

A shiver went down her spine when his large hand swallowed hers. She stared wide-eyed at him for a moment. He was handsome, she knew that from seeing him at the staff meetings, but this was the closest she'd ever been to him and a weird weakness was stealing through her limbs. His dark hair was cut short and he had clear blue eyes and tanned skin. Despite the earliness of the day, dark stubble covered his square jaw and his wide shoulders filled out his suit jacket perfectly.

She realized she was still holding his hand and dropped it, wincing when he discreetly wiped his hand against his suit jacket. They stood in awkward silence for a moment and she tried to remember to stand straight when his gaze swept down her body.

"Thank you for meeting with me, Mr. Dawson."

"Please, have a seat," he said.

She sank into the leather chair in front of his desk and made a loud squeal and jerked wildly when one of the dress pins holding her skirt together punctured her right ass cheek.

ॐ ৵

Luke frowned when the woman sat in the chair and squealed loudly. Her thin body jerked in her too-big suit and her pale face turned even whiter. She stared at him with wide eyes, her lower lip trembling and her hands squeezing the arms of the chair.

"Ms. Smith? Are you okay?"

"Fine. I – I'm fine," she gasped out. Sweat was beading up on her brow and she chewed at her bottom lip as he studied her.

"Are you?"

"Yes," she said. She shifted in the chair and a flicker of pain crossed her delicate features before she straightened her shoulders and sat perfectly still.

"Right," he said. There was a file folder on his desk and he opened it and produced her resume. He studied it for a moment before looking up at her. "You work in the finance department currently."

"Yes, that's right," she said softly. "Kyla is my supervisor."

"Why do you want to leave finance?" He asked.

"I feel I would be better suited to admin work," she said.

"You don't have any admin experience on your resume," he said. "Just waitressing. Did you graduate from college?"

She shook her head. "No."

"Graduate high school?" He asked even though he could see it on her resume.

She flushed deeply before nodding. "Yes, of course. I was planning on taking the administrative assistant program at one of the community colleges but, uh, circumstances happened and I, uh, needed to find a job rather quickly. I waitressed for a few years until I applied for the data entry job here at Dawson's Clothing."

"Why did you want to work for Dawson's Clothing?" He asked.

"Well, I'd been looking for an office job and I have an interest in fashion," she said.

"An interest in fashion," he repeated. His eyes dropped to her suit jacket. It drooped on her thin frame and the sleeves were so long they nearly covered her hands. He could see a flush rising up from her chest and she cleared her throat again.

"Yes, I follow a lot of fashion blogs and I – I try to keep up-to-date with the current fashions."

"Indeed," he said. The woman was wearing a Dawson suit but it was from a line they had discontinued and the drab grey colour did nothing for her. Sweat was starting to drip down her temple and she wiped it away as he continued to study her. She was much too thin with dark shadows under her eyes. The way her collarbone jutted out and the sharpness of her cheekbones indicated a possible eating disorder. Her hair was a mousey-brown colour but her eyes were a rich, dark brown and she had incredibly long lashes. Her skin was pale but flawless and she had nice, full lips. She was actually rather pretty, he mused inwardly, if you looked past the exhaustion etched across her face.

"I work long hours and can be demanding of your time as well. Are you prepared for that, Ms. Smith?"

She nodded. "Yes, absolutely."

"You'll be expected to do some personal errands for me as well. Will that be an issue?"

"No."

"Are you certain?"

"Yes. I'm ready to do whatever it is you need," she said. She shifted in her chair and another flash of pain flared in her eyes. "My time is flexible."

She cast her eyes to the left as she spoke and he sighed irritably. The woman was lying to him. Why, he didn't know, but did it really matter? She was obviously not suited for the job. She was a scared little rabbit and he needed an assistant who wouldn't cower in fear when he spoke to them. It wasn't in his nature to be nurturing or patient. He'd spend his valuable time handing the little bunny rabbit in front of him tissues for her inevitable bouts of sobbing instead of getting his work done. It was better to leave her in Mark's department. He had an easy-going nature and all the patience in the world. He glanced at his watch and decided to end the torture for both of them.

"Well, thank you for coming in to meet with me, Ms. Smith. It was a pleasure."

Her lower lip began to tremble again and he watched with mute horror as tears welled up in her eyes. "I – the interview is finished?"

"Yes," he said briskly as he inwardly prayed she wouldn't burst into tears. "Thank you for your time. Maria will be speaking with you in a few days."

He stood but she continued to sit, clutching at the arms of the chair as she stared up at him with a look of desperation that made his stomach clench oddly.

"Mr. Dawson," she said anxiously, "I know I – I don't have much experience but - "

"You have no experience," he interrupted.

"Yes, right, but I promise you that I'm a quick learner and a hard worker. If you hire me, I won't let you down. I'll do whatever you ask of me and I – I won't complain about the long hours or hard work. Please, Mr. Dawson, I'm asking you to give me a chance. I'll make a great assistant, I really will."

He was growing increasingly uncomfortable by her begging and he cleared his throat loudly. "Ms. Smith, I have a very busy day so…"

She slumped in her chair and then stood, wincing a little as she did. She blinked rapidly, holding back the tears with obvious effort.

"Of course," she whispered. "I'm sorry. It was a pleasure to meet you today, Mr. Dawson."

She held out her hand and kept her gaze on his chest as he gave her hand a brief shake.

"You as well, Ms. Smith."

She nodded and he watched as, limping slightly, she left his office.

❧ ❦

With her ass cheek on fire, her stomach rolling with nausea, and hot tears sliding down her cheeks, Jane hurried down the hallway. She had pooched the interview in the worst way and she desperately wanted to get to the washroom, pull the pin out of her ass and sob for the next twenty minutes. Kyla wasn't expecting her back from the interview until nine so she had plenty of time to fall apart before going back to work. She had no idea how she was going to pay for the increase in Mama J's care and she tried to ignore the panic that was fluttering in her chest. She would think of something. She'd get a third job if she had to.

How, Janie? You barely get four hours of sleep a night as it is. How are you going to work a third job? Face it, girl, this job was your only chance and you fucking blew it. Mama J is going to end up in some horrible nursing home and it's all your fault. After everything she did for you, you're going to let her die in some place where they won't even care about her, where they won't -

"Hey, how did it go?"

She stumbled to a stop, squinting through the tears at the woman from the bathroom. The woman's eyes widened and she touched Jane's shoulder.

"Oh, honey. What happened?"

"I – I didn't do very well," Jane stuttered before wiping

at the tears on her face. "He ended the interview after less than five minutes. When I sat down one of the pins poked me in the butt and it hurt like hell and was really distracting and I - I…"

She trailed off and covered her face with her hands. She wouldn't cry in front of this woman, no matter how kind she was.

"I'm sorry, honey," the woman said.

"Me too," Jane sniffed. "I should go. I need to pull a pin out of my butt, find a Band-aid, and get back downstairs. Thanks again for your help."

"Wait, just a minute. Let me - "

"I'm sorry. I have to go." Jane ducked around her and limped down the hallway, praying like hell she would get to the bathroom before she really started crying.

ತಿ ೂಂ

Luke looked up in surprise when Amy walked into his office without knocking. She sat down in the chair and stared at him.

"Ames? What's wrong?"

"How did the interviews go?" She asked.

"Terrible," he said. "The first one was Lisa from marketing. She has plenty of experience and would do the job well, but she also made it perfectly clear that she hoped we'd be more than boss and employee."

"Ooh," Amy said. "How deliciously naughty of her."

"Sleeping with the employees is not a good idea," Luke said.

"Probably not," Amy said. She waited a moment before saying casually, "What about the second one?"

"Even worse. A Jane Smith – what kind of name is Jane Smith by the way – from the accounting department. She nearly started crying during the interview."

"Were you mean to her?" Amy asked.

"What? Of course not," Luke said. "I barely said

anything to her. She just sat there in her too-big, discontinued suit, and tried to tell me that she had an interest in fashion and would be a great assistant despite her zero experience."

Amy scowled at him. "Maybe you should give her a chance."

"Why? Let her stay with Mark. He's all about giving people chances and I'm all about getting the job done, remember? This woman was so flustered and sweaty I'm surprised she even remembered her own name."

"You make people nervous, Luke."

"That's not my fault," Luke said.

"It kind of is. You could try being less brusque."

He gave her a puzzled look. "What's gotten into you, Amy? Why do you care who I hire as my assistant?"

"I met Jane in the bathroom before the interview. She had a rip in her skirt and was panicking. I pinned her skirt for her."

"Okay," he said. "So what?"

She crossed her arms over her chest. "She told me she knew her outfit was too big but that someone had told her if she wore a Dawson suit it would give her a better chance at the interview."

"She should have bought one that fit then," Luke said as he scrolled through his emails.

"I don't think she has a lot of money," Amy said. "She said she bought this one at a thrift store."

"I don't want an assistant who buys her clothing at thrift stores," Luke said. "I meet with potential investors all the time. I need an assistant who looks like she can afford to wear our clothing."

"You could give her a clothing allowance."

"Since when do we start giving out clothing allowances to employees?" Luke said.

"I liked her, Luke."

"That's nice," he said distractedly as he opened an email.

"I think you should hire her."

"Mm, hmm," he said.

"Luke!"

"What?" He gave Amy an exasperated look. "Ames, I'm really busy. I have a meeting at nine and I - "

"I want you to hire Jane."

"What the hell for?"

"Because she's sweet and I think she needs help."

"I already give to charity."

"Luke, I mean it. Give her a chance, will you?"

He shook his head. "She's not going to work out and then I'll have to fire her and she'll be out of a job completely. Is that what you want?"

"Mark will take her back."

"No, he won't."

"He will if you ask him to."

He sighed loudly and sat back in his chair. "I don't want to hire her, Amy. It's not going to work."

"I think it will," she said stubbornly. "Luke, please. Just give her a chance, okay? For me?"

She gave him a pleading look and he could feel his resolve weakening. He never could say no to his baby sister.

"Every time she cries, I'm sending her to your office," he said.

She grinned triumphantly. "That's fine."

"I mean it, Amy. And when she fails - "

"If she fails."

"*When* she fails, you have to ask Mark to let her have her job back."

"No way."

"Yes way."

"I hate Mark and he hates me. He won't do it if I ask him."

"He doesn't hate you and yes he will. You two used to be friends and now you won't even talk to him anymore."

She glared at him. "It's better this way."

"Is it? It's been over a month since you started fighting with him. Are you ever going to tell me what the fight was about?"

"We didn't fight and it's none of your business anyway. Are you going to hire Jane or not?"

"Yes, I'll hire her if you promise to talk to Mark when I fire her."

Amy hesitated before nodding. "Fine. But only because I know she's going to do a great job and you won't be firing her."

"Whatever, Ames."

He waited for her to leave and when she didn't, gave her an impatient look. "What?"

"Are you going to call Maria and tell her?"

"You want me to call her right now?"

"Yes."

"Why?"

"Because then she can tell Jane right away. She was really upset when she left your office and I want her to hear the good news today."

He sighed loudly. "You're not going to leave my office until I call Maria, are you?"

"Nope."

He picked up the phone and punched in Maria's extension as Amy gave him a delighted grin.

❧ ❦

"Hello, Mama J."

"Janie! How are you, dear?" The old woman gave her a warm look and Jane breathed a sigh of relief before kissing her cheek.

"I'm great. How was your day?"

"Oh fine. I watched a movie in the common room with some of the other residents and worked a little on my scarf." She stared at the knitting in her lap before stroking the soft yarn.

"You didn't eat," Jane said.

Mama J stared at the plate of food. "I was waiting for you. I thought we could eat together."

"I'd like that," Jane said. She moved the tray of food closer to Mama J and pulled out her peanut butter sandwich from her purse.

"That's not a very big dinner, dear," Mama J said as she ate her meatloaf. "Why don't we share mine?"

"No. This is more than enough," Jane said. She forced herself to eat her sandwich slowly. When she was finished, she filled her water bottle from the sink in the bathroom and drank all of it, hoping it would help to ease the hunger pains in her stomach.

"What did you do today?" Mama J asked.

"I have the most wonderful news," Jane said. "I got a promotion at work. I'm the new assistant for the president of the company. I start Thursday."

"Congratulations, honey," Mama J said. "I'm so proud of you."

"Thank you. I didn't make a very good impression in the interview so when Maria told me I got the job, I almost didn't believe it."

"I'm sure you made a terrific impression. You're such a sweet girl, Janie, and you deserve all the good things that come to you. I love you."

"I love you too, Mama J," Jane said. "This new job is just the thing I need to turn my luck around. I have a feeling that it's only going to get better from now on."

The old woman smiled at her and Jane leaned forward and hugged her. "Everything's going to work out, Mama J. I know it."

Chapter Three

"Hello, Jane."

Jane swallowed the mouthful of peanut butter sandwich and placed her napkin over the other half before smiling at the woman who had pinned her skirt together. "Hi there."

"How's the new job going?"

"Good, I think," Jane said. "It's only my second day though."

"I'm sure you're doing very well. I'm sorry, I didn't mean to interrupt your lunch," the woman replied.

"That's okay," Jane said. "I was just having a quick bite to eat at my desk. It's busy today."

The woman placed the potted plant she was holding onto Jane's desk. "I brought you this as a 'welcome to the 37th floor' gift."

"Thank you so much. It's beautiful," Jane replied.

"Ms. Smith, I need that letter!"

She jumped up at the sound of Mr. Dawson's voice and snatched the letter from the printer. "Please excuse me."

She hurried into his office and placed the letter on his desk, chewing worriedly at her bottom lip as he scanned it. He signed it and handed it back to her.

"It looks good. Can you add it to the package for the

lawyer and run it over to them? Their office is about three blocks away on 105th."

"Yes, Mr. Dawson."

"Also, stop at the deli on the corner and pick me up some lunch. Thai soup, turkey sandwich with no cranberry and extra mayo."

"Of course. Do you have a tab there or…"

She trailed off, hoping like hell he wouldn't ask her to buy it for him and expense it.

"Use the petty cash in the bottom drawer of your desk. Remember to put the receipt in."

"Yes, Mr. Dawson."

He finally glanced up at her. "When you're back, I'll need you to finish the document for…"

He trailed off and looked around her. "Amy? What can I do for you?"

Jane's eyes widened and she stared speechlessly at the woman who had saved her the day of the interview.

"Hey, Luke. Just popped by to say hello," Amy said cheerfully. She held out her hand to Jane. "We haven't formally met yet. I'm Amy Dawson."

Jane shook her hand as dismay filled her body. She had asked the head designer for the company to fetch her a stapler. The woman responsible for creating the clothing lines of the very large and very impressive company Jane worked for had stuck her hands up her skirt and then watched her cry in the hallway. "You – you're Amy Dawson?"

"I am," Amy said.

"I'm so sorry," Jane mumbled.

"For what?"

"I – I didn't know who you were earlier. I never should have asked you to get a stapler for me."

She gave Amy a look of panic before glancing at Luke. He was staring at them and Jane flushed before scurrying toward the door. "I'll take this to the lawyer now and get your lunch, Mr. Dawson. It - it was nice to meet you, Ms.

Dawson."

"Call me Amy," Amy called after her.

When she was gone, Amy smiled at Luke. "How's it going?"

"She asked you to get her a stapler?" Luke said.

"Long story," Amy replied. She checked to see that Jane wasn't at her desk before sinking into a chair. "So, how's she doing?"

"Fine," Luke said distractedly as he studied the spreadsheet on his computer screen.

"Just fine?" Amy said. "Give me some details, Luke."

Luke sighed and leaned back in his chair. "She seems intelligent and competent. I haven't had to repeat instructions and she has a good return time on documents I give her. She hasn't cried yet and she doesn't try to make small talk."

Amy studied him carefully. "But?"

"Nothing," Luke said.

"Spill it, Luke. You know you can't keep anything a secret from me."

Luke tugged at his tie. "She smells like peanut butter."

Amy gaped at him. "What?"

"She smells like peanut butter. For the last two days, she's eaten a peanut butter sandwich for breakfast and for lunch. Who does that past the age of ten?"

"Plenty of people. You don't like peanut butter but that doesn't mean everyone doesn't," Amy said.

"That's all she eats," he said. "I think she might have an eating disorder or something."

"Just because a girl is on the slender side doesn't mean she has an eating disorder," Amy said with a frown. "Don't be that guy, Luke."

"I'm not trying to be," he said. "I honestly think she might have a problem. Now that she's wearing clothes that actually fit she's even thinner than I thought."

"You're not firing her because you don't like what she eats," Amy said.

"I know that," Luke replied. "But for someone who works for a clothing design company, she wears terrible clothes. I meet with investors and buyers all the time, what happens when they walk by her desk and see her dressed like that?"

"Don't be so shallow," Amy said.

"Look, like it or not, how our employees are dressed is important in this company. It's why we don't do casual Fridays."

"If it bothers you so much, give her a clothing allowance," Amy said.

"Like I told you before, I've never done that for an employee and I'm not starting now," Luke said. "If she can't afford to buy nice clothes, that's not my problem."

"You're being a dick," Amy announced.

"Yes, well, if you're done insulting me, I have a lot of work to do."

Amy stood and blew him a kiss. "Be nice to her, Luke."

"I'm not the nice one – you are, remember?"

"You should try it some time, it feels good to be nice." She grinned at him and left his office before he could reply.

❧ ❧

"Here's your lunch, Mr. Dawson. I'm sorry it took so long – there was a line at the deli."

Luke looked up as Jane hurried into his office. The scent of snow and cold air clung to her and she was still wearing her thin jacket. Her hands and face were bright red from the cold and her lips were blue. He sighed inwardly. She wasn't even wearing gloves or a scarf for God's sake.

She set the brown paper bag on his desk and smiled tentatively at him. "The documents have been delivered to the lawyer's office."

"Your lips are blue," he said.

"It's a bit chilly out," she replied.

He studied her thin jacket. "You should dress more appropriately for the weather."

She touched her jacket self-consciously but didn't reply.

He opened the bag of food, took out the foil-wrapped sandwich and the container of soup and opened it. "Do you own any Dawson brand clothing, Ms. Smith?"

"I – uh, I have one suit."

He ate a spoonful of soup. Her stomach growled loudly and he raised his eyebrow at her.

"I'm so sorry," she said as she pressed her hand against her flat stomach.

"So, your suit is the one you wore to the interview?" He asked.

She nodded and he couldn't hide the look of distaste that flickered across his face. "I see. Most of your clothes are from Walmart then?"

Her face which had begun to pale turned a fiery red and she blinked rapidly. He groaned under his breath. Now the waterworks would start.

"Am I not dressed professionally enough?" She asked in a quiet voice.

"It's fine," he said. His tone of voice suggested that it wasn't fine and she chewed at her bottom lip before backing toward the door.

"Enjoy your lunch, Mr. Dawson."

"Thank you, Ms. Smith."

༃ ༄

Luke buttoned his jacket and handed a pile of papers to Jane. She took them and he glanced at his watch. It was past six and he would be late if he didn't get his ass moving.

"I'm leaving for the day, Ms. Smith. You should go as well. The rest of it can wait until Monday."

"Okay. Have a nice weekend, Mr. Dawson."

Luke nodded distractedly as he strode past her desk. He was halfway to the elevator when he clutched at his jacket pocket and muttered a curse. He had left his cell phone on his desk. He walked back toward his office. Jane wasn't at her desk and he stopped abruptly in the doorway of his office.

He had eaten his soup but only half his sandwich at lunch. He'd wrapped the other half back in the foil and tossed it in the trash can under his desk. Jane was holding the foil-wrapped sandwich in her hand and as he watched, she unwrapped it and studied the sandwich before carefully wrapping it up again and tucking it into her purse.

He backed away from the doorway and leaned against Jane's desk. He had just caught his assistant stealing his half-eaten sandwich from the trash. What the hell did he do now? Nothing, he decided abruptly. What could he do? Demand she throw his old food back in the trash? He started toward his office again as Jane came barreling out of his office with his cell phone in one small hand. She ran straight into him and bounced off his wide chest. He caught her around the waist before she could fall.

She stared up at him mutely, her hand clenched around his cell phone as he frowned at her. He could feel her ribs through her shirt and without thinking he blurted out, "You're too thin."

She pushed away from him, straightening her shirt and holding out his cell phone to him. "You forgot your cell phone."

"Thanks." He stuck it into his pocket. "Why are you still here?"

"I was just leaving," she replied.

She slipped into her jacket and zipped it up. "Good night, Mr. Dawson."

"I'll walk you to your car," he said. "It's late."

"Oh, I'm taking the bus," she replied.

He followed her to the elevator and they stood in

awkward silence as they waited for it. He cleared his throat. "Are you enjoying your new job, Ms. Smith?"

"Very much," she said without looking at him. "Thank you for the opportunity."

He sighed. She hadn't looked him in the eye since he'd made that wisecrack about her clothes at lunch and he could feel guilt creeping in. He ignored it. He didn't need to be friends with his assistant. Still, it was obvious that he had hurt her feelings and for some reason that bothered him.

"You're doing a good job," he said.

"Thank you," she said as the elevators opened. They stepped inside and she pushed the button for the lobby and the button for the parking garage.

"I mean it," he said. "I'm impressed."

"It's only been two days," she replied.

"True but I had an assistant once who downloaded a virus on her first day and nearly wiped out our entire computer system."

"You're kidding," she said. She glanced briefly at him before looking at the floor again. "What was she downloading?"

"Porn," he said.

Her mouth dropped open and she looked so shocked that he laughed. She blushed. "Are you serious?"

"Yes," he said. "She thought we wouldn't be able to trace it back to her and was completely surprised when we fired her for it."

She shook her head and gave him a timid look of amusement as the elevator doors opened. "Well, I'll try to wait at least a month before I start watching porn at work, Mr. Dawson."

He laughed again. "I appreciate that, Ms. Smith. Enjoy your weekend."

"Thank you, you too," she said.

He watched her walk across the lobby before the elevator doors closed. When they opened in the parking garage, he nodded to the security guard and climbed into his car. He pulled out of the garage and stopped for the traffic. His car rocked with the force of the wind and he glanced idly at the bus stop in front of their building. Jane was standing at the bus stop with her hands tucked deep into her pockets and her face buried in the collar of her jacket. Another strong gust of wind blew and she staggered on her feet before catching her balance.

He sighed loudly and turned right, pulling up in front of the bus stop and lowering the passenger window. "Get in, Ms. Smith."

She stared blankly at him. "I'm sorry?"

"Get in the car. I'll give you a ride home."

"Oh no," she said as she shivered wildly. "I don't live around here and - "

"It's fine. Get in before you freeze to death."

She hesitated and he made a harsh noise of impatience. "I don't have all night, Ms. Smith."

She glanced around before opening the door and sliding into the seat. Her hands were shaking heavily and she could barely buckle her seat belt. He turned the heat on high and pulled out into traffic.

"Where do you live?" He asked.

She recited the address. He cursed under his breath. "The Badlands? You live in the Badlands?"

She nodded and then said defensively, "It's actually not that bad of a neighbourhood."

"Wasn't there a murder out there last weekend?" He said.

She just shrugged and they drove quietly for a few minutes. "You need to get some gloves and a scarf," he said. "In case you haven't noticed, it's winter."

"I'll buy some this weekend," she replied.

"What are your plans for tonight?" He asked.

"Dinner and then relaxing," she replied.

His gaze dropped to her purse and she blushed guiltily and pulled it a little closer to her body. He suddenly had a very bad feeling that her dinner was half of a stale turkey sandwich.

"How about you?" She asked.

"Drinks with Mark," he replied.

"Mark Stanford?" She asked.

He nodded and she gave him a hesitant look. "Are you friends?"

"Yes. We've been friends since we were kids. He, Amy and I started the company together."

"I didn't know that," she replied. "I knew that you and Amy started the company but I didn't realize Mark was there from the beginning as well. He – he's a nice man. I only met him a couple of times but he was nice."

"He is much nicer than me," he said.

"Oh no, I didn't mean that you weren't a nice man. I mean that he was nice and, uh…."

She trailed off and he grinned at her. "I'm teasing you, Ms. Smith."

"Right," she said and then blushed again.

They drove the rest of the way in silence. When he parked in front of the building, he stared in disgust at it. "This is where you live?"

"Yes," she said as she unbuckled her seat belt. "Thank you for the ride home, Mr. Dawson."

"I'll walk you to your door. It isn't safe for you."

"No, no, that's fine," she said hurriedly. "It's much safer than it looks."

"Oh yeah?" He pointed to the two men huddled together on the street corner. "So that's not a drug deal going down?"

"Uh, I'm sure it isn't," she said.

"I'm walking you to your door," he said. "No arguments."

He got out of the car and locked it securely before taking her arm above her elbow. He walked her to the door of the building, frowning when he saw the lock was broken, and followed her into the foyer. It smelled strongly of urine and his hand tightened on her arm when a man wearing a dirty overcoat and swaying drunkenly stood up from the corner.

"Hey, pretty lady. You're early tonight."

"Uh, hi, Mickey," Jane said.

"You wanna come up to my apartment and have a drink with me?" He slurred. He moved closer and when he reached out to touch Jane, Luke shoved him back angrily.

He stumbled and fell back against the wall before blinking blearily at Luke. "Who the hell are you?"

"Stay away from her," Luke said.

"It's fine," Jane said quickly. "Mickey's my neighbour."

"Yeah, I'm her neighbour," Mickey said. "We're gonna have drinks tonight."

"No, we're not," Jane said. "Go sleep it off, Mickey."

"Why don't you sleep it off with me, pretty Jane?" Mickey wheedled. "You know you're dyin' to see what's in my pants."

"Shut the fuck up," Luke snarled at him, "or I'll knock what teeth you have left out of your goddamn head."

"Mr. Dawson, it's fine," Jane said. He ignored her and pulled her against his body. He wrapped his arm protectively around her waist when Mickey drifted closer again.

"Go anywhere near her, Mickey," he said in a low voice, "and I'll beat the hell out of you."

"Jesus," Mickey whined, "I was just being friendly."

He glared at the two of them before staggering toward the door. He disappeared into the dark and Luke grimaced. "This is not a safe place for you to live, Ms. Smith."

"Mickey is harmless," she said.

He realized he still had her pressed up against him. He released her so quickly she stumbled and nearly fell. He steadied her with a hand on her elbow and she gave him an embarrassed smile.

"Thank you again, Mr. Dawson. Good night."

"I'll walk you right to your door," he said. "Let's go."

She sighed but didn't protest when he followed her up the stairs. She lived on the second floor and he studied the dirty carpet and the stained walls with disgust as she pulled her keys out of her pocket.

"Good night," she said. "Thank you for - "

"Your cheque bounced."

They both turned at the sound of the gravelly voice behind them. The man standing behind them was wearing sweatpants and a stained and ripped t-shirt that barely covered his large beer belly. He scratched at the hairy band of flesh peeking below the shirt before picking his underwear out of the crack of his ass.

"Mr. Ranson, uh, hi," Jane said nervously.

"Rent was due yesterday and your cheque bounced," he said. "I want my rent money."

"I'm so sorry," Jane said. "I thought I had enough to cover it. I'll write you another cheque right now."

He shook his head. "Nope, gonna need cash from now on."

"I was paid today," Jane said. "The cheque will clear, I promise."

The man scratched his ass before sniffing at his fingers. He looked Luke up and down, his beady eyes studying the expensive watch around his wrist, before shaking his head again. "Nope. Cash only."

"Sure, no problem," Jane said. "I'll go to the bank first thing in the morning and - "

"Gonna need the cash tonight."

"The bank is already closed," Jane said with a hint of desperation, "and I'm not sure I can get the full amount out through a bank machine. I promise I'll bring the cash to you first thing in the morning."

"Cash tonight," the man said slowly, "or find somewhere else to sleep for the night." He studied Luke again. "Maybe you can stay at your fancy boyfriend's place."

Jane flushed miserably. "I'll get the money now. I'll bring it up to your apartment in - "

"How much is the rent?" Luke interrupted. Jane gave him a horrified look.

"No, Mr. Dawson, I can't - "

"How much?" He repeated.

Jane pressed her lips together and shook her head. Luke turned to her disgusting landlord. "How much?"

"Nine hundred," the man said. He watched greedily as Luke pulled a money clip from his pocket and counted out nine one-hundred-dollar bills. He handed the money to the landlord who clutched it and recounted it as Luke watched with disgust.

"Good night," Luke said pointedly.

The landlord stared at him for a moment before waddling to the stairwell. He let the door shut behind him with a loud bang and Jane jumped before giving Luke a look of shame.

"Oh God, I'm so sorry, Mr. Dawson. I'll go right now to the bank machine. My limit is five hundred but I can bring the rest to you Monday morning. Or," she chewed on her bottom lip, "if you give me your home address, I'll bring it by first thing tomorrow morning."

"You can bring all of it to me on Monday," he said shortly.

"Are you sure? I really don't mind. In fact, I'd feel better if you let me pay you some of it tonight and drop the rest off tomorrow. There's a bank machine a few miles from here. If you can give me a ride to it, it'll take less than ten minutes to get there."

He didn't reply and she chewed again on her lip. "Oh, right. You have plans with Mark. If you tell me where you're having drinks, I'll drop it off tonight. I can take the bus to the restaurant."

"It's cold and it's late."

"I don't mind," she said frantically. "I take the bus all

the time and I'm fine with the cold. Why don't you give me the restaurant name and I'll bring the five hundred dollars to you."

"No," he said. "Monday morning is fine."

"A-are you sure?" She whispered.

He nodded and backed away when her eyes began to water. "I'm positive. Good night, Ms. Smith."

"Good night, Mr. Dawson."

She turned away quickly and jabbed her key into the lock before slipping inside and shutting the door. He waited until he heard the lock turn before walking away.

෯ ๑

Her apartment was freezing but she didn't bother turning up the heat as she kicked off her boots. She could turn the thermostat up as high as it would go and it wouldn't make a difference. She had spoken to Mr. Ranson three times about the heat now and he still hadn't fixed it. She supposed she should be grateful that she had at least some heat trickling through the apartment.

Speaking of heat...let's talk about how Mr. Dawson put his arm around you twice today.

She tried to ignore her inner voice but it carried on happily.

He was warm, wasn't he? He smelled delicious and he held you a little longer than necessary. Did you notice?

He told me I was too thin, she snapped at her inner voice. *Besides, he was just saving me from falling on my ass the first time.*

Yeah but what about the second time? He didn't need to touch you the second time when he was protecting you from Mickey. How sweet was that, by the way? You should thank him. Maybe give him a blow job at work on Monday to -

Shut up! What is wrong with you? Don't you remember what happened the last time we slept with our boss?

Her inner voice fell silent. Jane stomped across her apartment and quickly changed into her flannel pajamas.

It wasn't even eight yet but she wasn't working tonight and it wasn't like she could afford to go out with the few friends she had.

She sighed heavily and grabbed her purse before sitting down on the couch and wrapping herself in a blanket. She pulled out the foil-wrapped sandwich and unwrapped it. Shame flooded through her but her hunger overrode it easily and she bit into the sandwich. The bread was a little stale but after three days of eating nothing but peanut butter sandwiches, it still tasted amazing. She forced herself to eat slowly. When it was gone, she considered making herself a peanut butter sandwich before curling into a smaller ball and staring out the window.

She was exhausted but she still wished she was working tonight. Friday and Saturday nights were the busiest at the clubs and good for tips but she never worked them anymore. She used to, she used to work every weekend in fact, but that had all changed three months ago. Now she worked Monday to Thursday at the club and the combined total of tips in those four nights was less than the tips she used to make on a Friday night.

She sighed again and closed her eyes. It was her own damn fault for being so stupid and naïve. She hadn't put two and two together that getting the best shifts was a direct result of sleeping with Jeremy. She hadn't seen - or maybe didn't want to see - who Jeremy really was. It had felt too damn good to be with someone, to have a warm body to curl up against and believe that it wasn't just her against the world. She thought that Jeremy cared for her, maybe even loved her. It was that belief and her relief at finally not feeling so alone that kept her in a relationship with her boss at the club.

She walked to the bathroom and brushed her teeth before climbing into bed. She curled up under the covers and tried to sleep. She didn't want to dwell on the past, it made her feel stupid and ashamed, but it kept crowding in.

The sex was okay with Jeremy, at least she thought it

was. He was her first and the fact that she was a virgin had appealed to him more than she cared for. She didn't always orgasm but she never complained. Jeremy liked to boast about his abilities in bed and she figured it was probably her nerves and insecurities that made it occasionally difficult. Jeremy found her attractive but he had hinted more than once that she would look even better with a boob job which didn't exactly help her confidence in bed. She had always been on the slender side with narrow hips and small breasts and she was a little envious of her coworkers and their lush curves. Of course, slender was twenty pounds ago and now her ribs stuck out and her breasts were practically non-existent.

She turned onto her back and stared at the ceiling. She was slowly starving to death and was now resorting to stealing her boss' garbage.

Don't forget that he paid your rent out of his own pocket. That's another first in humiliation for you.

Another wave of shame washed over her and she wiped at the tears that were starting to leak down her cheeks. She was feeling sorry for herself and her grumbling stomach but there was no point to that. Her life was what it was and she had to make the best of it. In the morning, she would buy a few groceries and –

You can't. You heard what Mr. Dawson said about your clothes. You need better clothing or he's going to fire you.

He wouldn't. He can't! She thought frantically.

Sure he could. You're on a three-month probation, remember? He can come up with another reason for firing you even if it is because of the way you dress. Tomorrow you need to get your ass into a proper clothing store and buy some Dawson brand clothes. Your job depends on it.

I'm starving! I need food.

You need this job.

She would try the Food Bank again, she decided.

You make more now than the last time you tried. They're not going to approve you. You make too much money and it's not their problem that most of it goes to caring for Mama J.

Suddenly overwhelmed and wracked with self-pity, she turned on her side and wept bitterly.

~ ~

"Sorry, I'm late," Luke said as he sat on the barstool next to Mark.

"No problem," Mark replied. He took a sip of whiskey as the bartender nodded to Luke before bringing him his usual. "I assume work was the usual culprit?"

Luke shook his head and sipped at his scotch. "No."

"Interesting," Mark said before raising his eyebrows at him. "Don't leave me in suspense."

Luke studied his best friend. Mark's dark hair was too long and there were dark circles under his eyes. "You look like shit. You need a haircut."

"Thanks, Mom. Don't change the subject. Why were you late?"

"I was driving an employee home."

Mark jerked in surprise. "You're shitting me."

"No," Luke said. "My assistant, Jane Smith."

"Ahh, the tiny Jane Smith – a perfectly good data entry clerk until you poached her from me. How's she working out?"

"Fine," Luke said. "She's smart and works hard. How well do you know her?"

"Honestly, not that well. She was only in my department for a few months and she mostly worked with Kyla."

"Is she in a relationship?"

"How the hell would I know," Mark said. "Why do you want to know?"

"Just curious," Luke replied.

Mark laughed. "It's more than just curiosity."

"No, it isn't."

"Sure it is. Don't tell me you've got a hard-on for your

PA. That's asking for trouble."

"I'm not attracted to my PA," Luke snapped.

"I'd be surprised if you were. She weighs, what, ninety pounds? You've always liked the ladies with curves."

Luke didn't reply and Mark took another drink of whiskey. "So, why were you driving your PA home?"

"Because she was standing at the bus stop in her stupid thin jacket and it was freezing outside. The wind nearly blew her over."

"So now you're a Good Samaritan?" Mark said with a grin.

Luke sighed. "She lives in the Badlands, Mark."

"Jesus. You're kidding me."

"I'm not. You should have seen her apartment building – it's filthy and dangerous. Her drunk neighbour tried to get her into his apartment while I was standing right there. He outweighed her by at least a hundred pounds. If I hadn't been there, who knows what the hell would have happened. Then her landlord showed up and told her that her rent cheque bounced. He demanded the rent in cash right then or he was going to kick her out into the street."

"Christ."

"I paid her rent for her."

"You did not!"

"Of course I did. What was I supposed to do? Just let her be kicked out of her apartment on the coldest night of the year?"

"Holy shit," Mark said. "You really do have a thing for your PA."

Luke downed his scotch in one large gulp before signalling the bartender for another. "No, I don't. She's paying me back on Monday."

"Well, that was nice of you."

"I thought she had an eating disorder but now I'm not so sure," Luke said slowly. "I didn't eat all of my sandwich at lunch and I saw her take it out of the trash and put it in her purse."

"Christ, Luke. You really should pay your employees more," Mark said with a frown.

"She's making more for me than she did in your department," Luke said.

"Maybe she's just bad with money," Mark said with a shrug. "That's not really your problem if she has a shopping addiction."

"She wears cheap clothing from Walmart."

"She doesn't have to be addicted to clothes shopping," Mark said. "Anyway, how is your PA's money problems any of your concern?"

"It isn't," Luke said abruptly. "Forget I said anything. Mom wants you to come by this weekend for dinner."

"I can't make it," Mark said immediately. "Tell her I'm sorry but I'll try and stop by one night during the week to see her."

"When Amy won't be there?" Luke asked.

Mark stiffened at the mention of her name and Luke sighed loudly. "What's going on with you and Amy?"

"Nothing," Mark muttered.

"Bullshit. We've been best friends for nearly thirty years and I know you better than anyone. A month ago, everything was normal and now you and Amy barely speak to each other and you've stopped coming for family dinners. What are you and Amy fighting about?"

"We're not fighting about anything," Mark said.

"Yeah, that's what Amy says. Why aren't either of you telling me the truth?"

Mark scowled at him. "Leave it alone, Luke."

"Leave what alone?" Luke said.

"Just mind your own business."

"She's my sister," Luke said. "I love you, man, you know I do, but if you've hurt her or – "

"Hurt her?" Mark said angrily. "You think I would hurt your sister?"

"No. I know you love her like a sister too but

sometimes siblings fight," Luke said. "You guys need to talk about whatever this is and fix it."

"No, you need to mind your own business," Mark retorted. "I'm gonna go. It was a long day at work and I'm tired. See you on Monday."

"Mark, wait. I'm trying to help."

"Yeah, well, you're not. Good night."

Mark threw some bills on the bar and stalked away as Luke stared in shock. What the hell was going on?

Chapter Four

"You have a beautiful home, Mr. Dawson."

"Thank you, Jane." Luke handed her a glass of wine and she sipped at it before smoothing her skirt nervously.

"Thank you for giving me a place to stay tonight. I can't believe my rent cheque bounced again."

"It's fine. Why don't I show you to your room?"

"Okay," she said. She set her wine glass on the island and followed him out of the kitchen and up the stairs. He opened the first door on the left and stepped back. She stood inside the room, staring silently at the king bed as he turned on the gas fireplace.

"This is, um, a very large guest room," she said.

He shrugged out of his suit jacket and took off his tie before beginning to unbutton his shirt. "It's not the guest room."

"It isn't?"

He shook his head and stripped off his shirt before standing in front of her. He unbuttoned her shirt as she stared mutely at him. "No, it's my room."

"Mr. Dawson," she whispered. "I – I can't sleep in your room."

"You're not going to be sleeping, Jane."

"What will I be doing?" Her voice was a low moan and as he pulled off her shirt he studied the way her nipples poked against her bra.

"I've been meaning to speak to you about your work duties, Ms. Smith." He leaned down and pressed a kiss against her collarbone. She moaned again, her tiny hands clutching at his waist. His cock hardened at her touch and he pressed his pelvis against her so she could feel how much he wanted her.

"Y-you have?" She stuttered as he reached behind her for the clasps of her bra.

"Yes." He undid her bra and pulled it from her body. "You've been doing very well and I think its time we gave you extra duties. Don't you?"

"Like what?" She whispered as he cupped one small breast. He kneaded it gently before leaning down again and sucking on her nipple. It swelled in his mouth and she cried out when he nipped the hard, little bud.

He straightened and took her mouth in a hard and possessive kiss as he worked his hand under her skirt. He skated his fingers over the smooth satin of her panties. "Spread your legs, Jane."

"Yes, Mr. Dawson."

His cock throbbed and he slipped his hand between her thighs when she opened them. He cupped her through her panties, lust coursing through him when he discovered how wet her panties were. Breathing heavily, he pulled them down her legs and she stepped out of them as she stared at him.

"Mr. Dawson, what are my new duties?" She asked as he reached under her skirt again.

He played with the soft curls between her thighs before moving his hand lower. He probed at her opening, sliding his finger into her smooth heat as she moaned in submission and leaned against him.

"Taking all of my cock in your tight little pussy," he murmured into her ear. He traced the curve of her ear with his tongue before sucking on the lobe.

"Sh-should I start right now?" She asked as she ran her

hands down his back.

"Brilliant idea," he said. He moved his hand away from her, smiling a little at her whimper of need, and lifted her easily. He carried her to the bed and laid her down on it.

"Lift your skirt, Ms. Smith," he ordered.

She obeyed immediately, shimmying it up over her hips until her pussy was exposed. He stared hungrily at it as she braced her feet on the bed and spread her legs. He could see her perfect clit peeking out from between the lips of her pussy and hurriedly unbuttoned and unzipped his pants. She rubbed her clit with the tips of her fingers and moaned as he shoved his pants down his legs. He kneeled between her open legs and her eyes widened when she glanced at his cock.

"Mr. Dawson, you're too big," she said in her sweet, soft voice. "I can't take all of that in my tiny pussy."

"Yes, you can," he said. He rubbed his cock against her clit and her hips arched up. "Be a good girl, Ms. Smith, and take my cock."

"Yes, Mr. Dawson," she said.

His cock twitched and he pushed the blunt head of it into her narrow opening. She was unbelievably tight and he knew he should wait and allow her to adjust but he couldn't stop. He pushed forward as she dug her fingers into his biceps.

"Mr. Dawson, it's too big!" She complained.

"It isn't," he replied. "Spread your legs wider."

She obeyed immediately and he pushed into the hilt, ignoring her small gasp of discomfort. Her fingers were digging into his back and he stared down at her. She was trapped beneath him and he reached between their bodies and rubbed her clit until she was moaning in pleasure. He made a few deep thrusts as her thighs pressed uselessly against his hips.

"Oh, Mr. Dawson, your big cock feels so good in my pussy," she moaned again.

He propped himself up on his hands and thrust again.

"You're being a very good girl, Ms. Smith," he rasped. "Do you like being stuffed full of my cock?"

"Oh yes," she cried. "Yes, Mr. Dawson. I've never had a cock this big before."

He closed his eyes and rocked back and forth. Her pussy gripped him so tightly that he could feel his orgasm starting almost immediately. The base of his spine was tingling and he grunted loudly as he plunged in and out. Her small body was shaking under his and he opened his eyes. She was staring up at him and he kissed her deeply.

"Mr. Dawson," she gasped. "You're not going to come in me, are you?"

He grinned at her and her eyes widened. "You can't!"

"Yes, I can," he whispered before pinning her slender arms above her head. "You're mine, Ms. Smith and if I want to come in you, I will. Do you understand?"

She didn't reply and he thrust even harder. Fuck, he was so close to coming. "Do you understand, Ms. Smith?" He gritted out between clenched teeth.

She opened her mouth and said, "This weather just isn't letting up, folks! Make sure you dress warmly today – it's gonna be a cold one!"

He blinked at her. "Jane?"

"Just got a text from a listener. He's on the freeway north of exit 120 and he says it is slow going. Three car crash and traffic is backed up all the way to exit 72. If you're headed that way for your morning commute, you might want to consider a different route. Stay safe and remember to - "

Luke jerked awake. He sat up and stared at the alarm clock next to his bed before groaning and slamming his hand down on the top of it. The radio host's voice was cut off and he groaned again before collapsing on his back. He stared up at the ceiling in confusion before staring at the left side of the bed. He almost expected to see Jane lying there. It was empty and with a low moan, he threw the covers off and grabbed his erect cock. His balls were throbbing with the need for release and his hips arched as he jerked his dick with harsh strokes. An image of Jane popped into his head and he came immediately, hot liquid spurting out from his cock to splash across his stomach as he squeezed and rubbed almost angrily.

Panting harshly, he stared wide-eyed at the ceiling as his cock softened in his hand. Holy fuck, he had a goddamn sex dream about his PA.

࿔ ࿓

Monday morning, Jane smoothed down her new skirt and straightened her suit jacket before knocking on Mr. Dawson's office door. On Saturday, she'd gone to one of the shops along 17th Avenue. She was a little afraid that the salespeople would be rude or scornful – she definitely didn't look like their usual clientele – but the woman who helped her was actually very nice. She had asked what Jane's budget for clothing was and didn't laugh when Jane told her. She spent more than two hours with her, bringing her outfits to try on and helping her figure out how to make the most out of the money she had. In the end, she had walked out with two suits, and a dress, a blouse and a pair of dress pants. All of them were Dawson brand clothing and she hoped like hell it would convince Mr. Dawson she was serious about her job.

She was happy with her new clothes but she had spent all of her grocery money as well as the money earmarked for electricity and heat. She was already behind on both bills but her heat wasn't working anyway so if they cut it off what was the difference? As for electricity – well, she had candles.

After shopping she had visited with Mama J for a while. On Saturday, she was bright and alert but when she stopped in again on Sunday morning, her foster mother was confused and withdrawn. She didn't remember her and became agitated when Jane tried to tell her who she was. Jane had stuck around for a while, visiting the other residents in the common room and hoping that Mama J's mind would clear. Unfortunately, even after her nap she was confused and belligerent. Jane had finally given up and left around two, stopping at the grocery store to purchase a loaf of bread, another jar of peanut butter and a bag of oranges.

Her stomach growled at just the memory of food and she rubbed it lightly. She'd eaten an orange for breakfast and despite her hunger, the thought of eating yet another peanut butter sandwich for lunch made her a little nauseous.

"Christ, come in already!"

She jumped and realized that she was still standing outside of Mr. Dawson's door. By the irritation in his voice, he had been calling for her to come in for awhile. Clutching the envelope in her sweaty hand, she opened the door and smiled at him.

"Good morning, Mr. Dawson."

He didn't look up from his computer screen. "Good morning, Ms. Smith."

She placed the envelope on the shiny surface of his desk. "I wanted to apologize again for Friday night and to, uh, bring you the money that I owe you."

"Thanks," he said.

He was still concentrating on the screen and she waited for a moment. Stupidly, she wanted him to see her in her new clothing. He didn't glance up and feeling like an idiot, she turned to go.

Amy was standing in the doorway and she gave Jane a wide grin. "Good morning, Jane."

"Good morning, Ms. Dawson."

"Oh please, I told you to call me Amy, remember?"

She stood in front of her and studied her outfit. "Don't you look lovely today."

"Thank you," Jane said.

"Luke, doesn't Jane look lovely?"

Her boss finally raised his head and she flushed when his gaze swept over her body. He didn't say anything and there was a moment of awkward silence that Amy rushed to fill.

"That's one of my favourite suits from last year's line. The colour really suits your skin colour," Amy said.

"Thank you," Jane said again.

"How was your weekend?" Amy asked as Luke sighed loudly behind them.

"It was good. How, uh, was yours?" Jane asked awkwardly.

"Quiet. Other than our family dinner last night, I didn't even leave the house. I hate this time of year. I'm much better suited to warm beaches and the hot sun," Amy said with a grin.

"Amy, is there something you need?" Luke asked. "I'm very busy today and so is Jane."

"I wanted to chat with you about something. I'll be quick, I promise," Amy said.

"Excuse me," Jane murmured. She left the office, shutting the doors softly behind her.

☙ ❧

As Jane hurried out of the office, Amy sat in the chair and stared at Luke.

"What?"

"Did you talk to her about her clothes?"

Luke shrugged and Amy narrowed her eyes at him. "Did you?"

"I might have mentioned something about her clothes being from Walmart," he said.

"You ass," Amy said.

"What? It worked, didn't it? She's wearing Dawson brand clothing this morning."

"Did you give her a clothing allowance?"

"Of course I didn't."

Amy sighed. "Luke, I don't think Jane has a lot of cash."

Luke shrugged again. "I thought so too at first. She lives in the Badlands and takes the bus. I drove her home on Friday night because she was standing outside in the freezing cold and ended up paying her rent for her so she wouldn't get kicked out of her rathole of an apartment."

"What?" Amy gaped at him.

Luke glanced at his watch. "Can we talk about this later, Amy?"

"Nope. Not after that little tidbit. Spill it, big brother."

He sighed, leaned back in his chair and told Amy the entire story, beginning with seeing Jane take his discarded sandwich from the trash can. She listened quietly and when he was finished, frowned at him. "So, if her rent cheque bounced, how the hell could she afford to buy Dawson brand clothing?"

"I guess she isn't as broke as I thought," Luke said. "She's probably just bad at managing her money."

"A woman who takes her boss' leftover lunch from the trash doesn't sound like she's bad at managing money. It sounds like someone who's desperate."

"Maybe she's one of those penny pinchers," Luke said. "Maybe she regularly digs food out of dumpsters and eats it."

"Be serious, Luke."

"I am being serious," he said. "You were the one who made me watch that stupid marathon of people who were extreme money savers. Most of them had money to burn but they lived like they were penniless."

"You really think Jane is like that?" Amy asked.

"I don't know, Ames, and I'm tired of worrying about it. I've got a lot of work on my plate and my assistant's personal life really isn't my problem or concern."

Amy gave him a thoughtful look. "What's wrong, Luke?"

"There's nothing wrong."

"There is. You were quiet and withdrawn at supper last night and you're super irritable today. Tell me what's wrong."

"I had a fight with Mark," he said.

"About what?" Amy asked cautiously.

"You."

She stood and moved toward the door. "I told you – stay out of my personal business, Luke."

"That's exactly what Mark said to me," he said. "Amy, please tell me what's going on. I can't help you if I don't know why you two are fighting."

"There's nothing going on," she said angrily. "Leave it alone, Luke."

"You're my sister and if Mark is - "

"Mark isn't doing anything," she snapped at him. "I get that you're protective of me but I don't need your help. I'm a big girl and can handle my own business. Butt out, Luke."

She stomped out of his office and Luke muttered a curse. Fuck, could this day get any worse?

≈ ≈

Jane looked up from her monitor as Luke set a box of papers on her desk. "I need you to go through these and highlight all of the purchases that coincide with the dates I emailed you."

"Yes, Mr. Dawson."

He jerked like an electric shock had gone through him. He glanced at her and she wondered why his cheeks were suddenly red. He raked his hand through his dark hair and snorted angrily when his cell phone buzzed. He yanked it from his pocket and read the message, muttering a curse under his breath. She gave him a cautious look as he began to text furiously. He'd been in a bad mood all day and she had kept her head down and worked silently through the piles of work he had given her. Until he brought this new stuff, she had finished the last of her work and was hoping she could leave soon. It was after seven and if she didn't get her butt to the bus stop in the next ten minutes, she'd miss her bus and be late for her shift at the club.

When he was finished texting, she cleared her throat nervously. "Mr. Dawson, I was going to head out. Can I do this work in the morning or - "

"No," he snapped. "I need it done before my eight o'clock meeting tomorrow morning."

She chewed at her bottom lip and he gave he an irritated look. "I told you there would be overtime working for me, Ms. Smith."

"I know," she said. "I have an appointment at eight tonight."

He made an annoyed little huff and she said, "But I can come back to the office when I'm done and finish it."

"Whatever," he said. "I don't care when you do it, as long as it's finished by eight tomorrow."

"It will be," she said. "I'm sorry, Mr. Dawson."

He waved off her apology and stalked back to his office. She released her breath in a soft exhale, gathered up her things and left before he could change his mind.

৵ ৶

Jane yawned and rubbed at her eyes as she placed the pile of papers on Mr. Dawson's desk. After her shift at the club was finished at two, she had gone home and slept for a couple hours before showering and getting ready for work. She had arrived at the office at six and worked furiously to finish the pile of work on her desk. It was five minutes before eight and she moved aside nervously when Mr. Dawson walked into his office. He pulled off his overcoat and tossed it on the leather couch before sitting behind his desk.

"Good morning, Mr. Dawson."

"Morning," he said shortly without looking at her.

He didn't seem to be in any better of a mood and she touched the papers on his desk. "Here's the work you needed."

"Thanks. Can you get me a coffee and bring it to the boardroom?"

She nodded as he picked up the papers, his laptop and a few file folders and left the office. She ran to the kitchen and made his coffee the way he liked it before taking it to the boardroom. He gave her a distracted thank you and she smiled politely at the two men and three women sitting at the table with him before making her escape.

Once she was at her desk, she pulled an orange from her purse and peeled it with shaking hands. She was feeling shaky and weak from lack of food and sleep and she drank some water before eating the orange. It made her feel a little better and she took a deep breath. She had her tip money from last night in her wallet and she was sorely tempted to take a few dollars and buy a bagel from the café in the lobby downstairs.

She ignored the temptation. It was slow last night and after splitting her tips with the bartender, she only had about thirty dollars in tips. She needed that money for Mama J. Tanya had left her a message on her cell phone last night that Mama J had ruined her only nightgown and would need a new one. She would have to stop tonight and pick one up before visiting her.

She took another deep breath, rubbed her aching temples and opened her email. Mr. Dawson had sent her half a dozen emails after she left last night and with a soft sigh, she started her work.

ॐ ॐ

"This is the third night in a row you can't stay. You said your time was flexible, Ms. Smith."

"I know and I'm so sorry," Jane replied. She tried to

smile at her boss but his look of anger stopped it before it really began. "I can come back after my appointment again and finish."

Mr. Dawson sighed loudly and glanced at his watch. "Are you going to have appointments every night at eight?"

"No," Jane lied. "It's just this week."

"Is it?" He asked.

She swallowed and glanced at the floor before nodding. "Yes."

She had a very bad feeling that he knew she was lying and when he continued to stare at her, she squirmed in her chair. It was almost seven thirty and she had already missed her bus which meant she would be late for her shift at the club. If she was really lucky, Jeremy would just dock her pay and not outright fire her for being late.

"I'm sorry," she said again. "Would it work for me to come in later tonight and finish it?"

"Fine," he bit out. "Better run, Ms. Smith. I wouldn't want you to be late for your appointment."

She flushed as he walked away but quickly shut down her computer and hurried to the elevator. She had worked late the last three nights and gone directly to the club after. She still hadn't picked up Mama J a nightgown and guilt coursed through her.

It's fine, Janie. Mama J can wear her robe for one more night. She won't mind.

As she ran outside and stood at the bus stop, her stomach growled and she felt so lightheaded that she thought she might faint. She grabbed the metal pole of the bus sign and held on grimly as she bent over and breathed deeply. She wished she had thought to bring two sandwiches to work with her. She should have planned for the possibility that Mr. Dawson would require her to work late again tonight. He had been in a bad mood since Monday and her inability to stay later than seven hadn't helped his mood. If this kept up, she would be forced to quit her job at the club.

You can't! You won't have enough money to pay for Mama J's care.

No, she wouldn't, but maybe she could get a weekend job at another restaurant or club.

If you can't? You're screwed, Janie. Worse – Mama J is screwed. After everything she's done for you, you're really going to let her wither away in some third-rate nursing home?

She blinked back the tears as she straightened and shivered in the cold. God, she was so tired. Over the last three days, she'd gotten a total of maybe seven hours of sleep and the exhaustion was setting in. It made her weepy and slow and she wondered grimly if she would even make it to the weekend without passing out or falling asleep at her desk. She'd had to redo a letter three times today – thank God, she had caught the mistakes before giving it to her boss. With the mood he was in the last few days, he probably would have fired her on the spot.

The bus pulled up and with a sigh of relief, she climbed the steps and found a seat at the back. Ignoring the smell of the man who was sitting in front of her, she closed her eyes and tried to doze.

ॐ ॐ

Luke stared out his office window. It faced the street and he watched as Jane approached the bus stop. His hands clenched into fists when she suddenly grabbed the metal pole of the bus stop and bent over. It was too dark and he was too high up to see if she was shaking but he had no doubt she was. The last day and a half she'd had a visible tremor to her entire body. Earlier today when she brought him coffee, her hand was shaking so badly that she'd spilled it on his desk. She had apologized profusely and quickly cleaned it up while he watched her furtively. Her face seemed even thinner than usual. Her pale skin was stretched over her cheekbones and she had dark circles under her eyes. She looked like she was on the verge of collapsing and he wondered if she had some type of illness. Maybe she was at doctor appointments all this week. Despite the heavy workload, he was about to tell her to go home and get some rest when she had finished mopping up the spilled coffee and hurried out of his office. She looked completely exhausted and he was oddly worried about her.

Are you? You've been a total dick to her for the last three days.

I've been busy and she hasn't exactly made it easier for me with her inability to stay late. Besides, I haven't been a dick.

You have, and we both know you're being a dick to her because of your dream.

He abruptly walked away from the window and sat down at his desk. He was not going to start thinking about that stupid dream again.

Why not? It was a good dream.

No, it wasn't. It was utterly ridiculous and came completely out of left field. He was not attracted to Jane. Okay, maybe he did find her pretty despite how obviously exhausted she was, but she was too much of a scared little mouse for him. Just because he'd had a very lengthy and very detailed dream about her didn't mean anything. It was a random piece of oddness seeping out of his brain. Lots of men had sex dreams about women they didn't find attractive.

Oh yeah? Do lots of men wake up from these sex dreams with their dick so hard and painful that they have to rub one out? Do you think they come all over their own damn stomach like a horny teenage boy?

He stared grimly at his computer screen. Just thinking about the dream was making his cock stiffen and he adjusted it roughly. Jesus, what was wrong with him? His workload, his fight with Mark and that stupid dream about his fragile little bird of an assistant had him acting like a total lunatic.

He needed to talk to Mark and apologize – that would

help to bring normalcy back to his life. Other than some short and terse work-related emails, they hadn't spoken since Friday night and it was getting to him.

"Luke?"

He looked up in surprise at Mark standing in his doorway.

"Hey."

"Hey," Mark said. He hesitated before walking into his office and sitting in one of the chairs. "Listen, I'm sorry about Friday night."

"No," Luke said immediately. "I'm sorry. I shouldn't be butting in on your personal shit. I'm just worried about you and Amy."

"You don't need to worry," Mark said. "Everything's fine. I've had the day from hell – you wanna grab a drink with me?"

Despite his mountain of work, Luke nodded. "Yeah. I could use a drink."

He stood and casually walked to the window. He peered at the bus stop. Jane was gone and he jumped when Mark spoke next to him.

"What are you looking at?"

"Nothing. Let's go," Luke said.

Chapter Five

Jane placed the files on Luke's desk and checked her watch. It was just after six but the office didn't technically open until eight and she was certain she was the only employee in the building. She studied the couch in Luke's office before sitting on it with a weary sigh. Her head was aching miserably and she felt sick to her stomach. As punishment for being late last night, Jeremy had docked her pay the half hour and made her give all of her tips to the bartender. Probably illegal but it wasn't like she could do anything about it. She had really needed her tip money and she fought back her urge to burst into tears. Crying wouldn't help.

She rested her head against the back of the couch. She didn't know how long it would take to finish the work that Mr. Dawson had left her so she came in at five thirty. She was terrified that she would be fired if it wasn't finished when he came in at eight. Unfortunately, the work hadn't take all that long and she was regretting losing even that extra hour of sleep she could have gotten.

She rubbed at her aching temples before lying on her side on the couch. She would rest her eyes for a few minutes and see if that helped her headache. If it didn't, she would eat another orange and grab some Advil from the staff room.

๛ ๛

Luke stared at Jane's empty desk. It was just before eight and normally she would be sitting at her desk already. A thin thread of worry went through him – she hadn't looked good at all yesterday – and he shook it off. She was fine. He headed into his office and hung his jacket on the coat hook before closing the doors. Jane wasn't his problem. He had enough on his plate. It was a relief not to be fighting with Mark anymore but he still had what felt like a thousand things to finish before -

He stopped in his tracks and stared silently at the couch. Jane was curled up on it and he hurried over. He squatted and breathed a sigh of relief when he realized she was sleeping. He reached for her shoulder to shake her awake but stroked her cheek instead. She didn't move and he grinned when she began to snore softly. He stroked her cheek again – God, she had soft skin – and then moved his hand to her shoulder to shake her awake.

Don't. She needs sleep.

He hesitated. His inner voice was right – Jane looked utterly exhausted. Her skin was too pale and the dark circles under her eyes almost looked like bruises. Still, he should wake her up and send her home. If she was too tired to work she shouldn't be here.

Let her sleep. You think she's going to get any rest at that shithole apartment? She probably spends most of her nights awake because she's worried she'll be attacked. You saw the lock on her door – it wouldn't keep out a determined toddler.

He stood abruptly and shrugged out of his suit jacket. He draped it over her thin body and smiled again when she sighed happily and burrowed her face under it. He walked to his desk as her soft snoring started again.

๛ ๛

"Hey, Luke?" Mark strolled into his office just before noon. "I know this is bad timing but I've got some financial statements you need to look at before Friday. Also – I'm starving and heading to O'Keefe's for lunch. Want to join me?"

"Keep your voice down," Luke said in a low voice as he glanced at the couch.

Mark followed his gaze. "Luke? Buddy? Why is your assistant sleeping on your couch?" He dropped into the chair. "Shit, tell me you didn't screw her right here at the office."

"Jesus, Mark," Luke said. "No, I didn't screw her. I came in this morning and found her asleep on the couch."

"So, you covered her up with your suit jacket and left her to sleep the morning away? You know, most employers fire their employees for sleeping on the job."

"I don't think she feels well," Luke said.

"Then send her home. Or are you hoping she passes her germs to you so you can get out of looking at these financial statements?"

Luke snorted and shook his head. "No. I'll take them home with me and look over them tonight. I need to pass on lunch though."

"You sure?"

"Yeah. I'll get something delivered from the deli and eat at my desk."

Mark stood and glanced at Jane again before giving Luke a considering look.

"What?" Luke asked.

"Nothing," Mark said. "See you later."

When he was gone, Luke looked up the number for the deli. Normally he would have Jane order lunch and pick it up for him but it was bitterly cold outside. Sending her out in her stupidly thin jacket would be cruel. He glanced again at Jane's pale face before ordering enough food for both of them.

෨ ෯

"Do you like it, Jane?"

Her boss's low voice saying her given name sent a tingle down her spine and she smiled up at him. "It's amazing. I love it."

He put his arm around her waist and pulled her back against his hard body before nuzzling her ear. "Good, I'm glad."

She studied the table in front of her. It was covered in all of her favourite foods and her mouth watered as she stared at the roast chicken and mashed potatoes. She would smother everything in gravy and eat and eat until the constant, horrible ache in her stomach finally disappeared.

Her boss nuzzled her ear again and the hunger pangs were overshadowed by something stronger and sweeter. Heat bloomed in her belly and she shivered in his arms when he placed a warm kiss on her throat.

"How are you going to thank me?" He murmured.

"Whatever you want," she whispered.

He made a low sound of approval as his hand moved from her waist to her breast and squeezed gently. "Whatever I want?"

"Yes," she moaned. His thumb was stroking her nipple into a tight little bud and she wished she wasn't wearing a shirt and bra. It would be so nice to feel his warm hand on her naked skin.

"A kiss," he said before rubbing the dark shadow on his jaw across her sensitive throat. "Will you give me that?"

"Yes."

"That's my good girl," he said before turning her around.

She stared up at him as he cupped her face and rubbed his thumb gently over her cheekbone. "One kiss and then you can eat as much as you like."

"Okay," she whispered. As hungry as she was, she suddenly wanted his kiss so much more.

"Jane?"

"Yes?"

"Jane, wake up."

She frowned up at him, wondering why he didn't just shut up and kiss her already.

"Jane, it's time to wake up."

She tried to ignore what he was saying. It didn't even make sense to her. She felt so safe and warm in his arms and he smelled really good. She wanted her kiss, dammit. Why did he keep talking?

∂ ∾

"Jane?"

Luke sat down on the couch next to Jane and gently shook her for a third time. Her eyes rolled back and forth behind her eyelids and she muttered something he didn't understand.

"Jane, wake up now."

She opened her eyes and blinked blearily at him. He breathed a sigh of relief. "Hey, how are you feeling?"

"I want my kiss," she whispered before lifting her head and pressing her mouth against his.

He stiffened in shock at the feel of her soft lips and she made a noise of frustration before whispering against his mouth, "Please, Luke. You promised. I want my kiss."

Her warm breath and sweet pleading did him in. She wanted to be kissed and damned if he didn't want to kiss her. Had wanted to kiss her since the moment he woke from his dream of her. He cupped the back of her skull and gave her what she wanted. She moaned into his mouth and wrapped her arms around his broad shoulders. She clung tightly to him and when he traced the seam of her lips with his tongue, she parted them willingly. He dipped his tongue into her mouth and pulled her closer at the taste of her sweetness.

Be gentle, he warned himself.

He sucked on her bottom lip and then slicked his tongue across it. She gasped and pushed her tongue into his mouth. He sucked firmly on it and slid his other arm around her slender waist. He pulled her into a sitting position and shifted back on the couch before lifting her into his lap. She weighed next to nothing and the heavy beat of his lust waned a little as worry crept in.

She pressed her chest against him and kissed him with a timid sort of sweetness that normally would have made him burn with desire but common sense was starting to kick in. He was making out with his PA in his goddamn office in the middle of a workday. What the hell was he doing?

Her stomach growled loudly and he tore his mouth from hers. She moaned unhappily and tried to kiss him again. He cupped her face and held her steady.

"Jane, stop."

She blinked at him and the desire in her eyes slowly turned to horror. She touched her swollen mouth before staring around his office.

"Oh my God," she whispered. "I – oh my God."

With a strength that surprised him, she scrambled off his lap and jumped to her feet. He stood and grabbed her arm when she weaved unsteadily. She raised a shaking hand and touched her mouth again. "Did you – why were you kissing me?"

"You asked me to," he said. He groaned inwardly at how stupid he sounded.

"I asked you to," she repeated slowly. She stared around in confusion before making a low moan of horror. "Oh God, I was dreaming. Wh-why was I dreaming?"

"You were asleep in my office when I came in this morning," he said.

"I was asleep in your... oh shit!" She gave him a terrified look. "I am so sorry, Mr. Dawson. I didn't mean

65

to do that. Please don't fire me. I'll never do anything like this again. I, uh, wasn't feeling well this morning and I thought if I rested my eyes for a minute, it might help. I'm so sorry. I finished the work you left for me. Just please don't fire me – I am begging you for a second chance. I know you don't give second chances but I promise if you -"

"Jane, stop," he said.

She trailed off and blinked back the tears as she gave him a look of pure misery. "I – I'll gather my things and leave."

She tried to walk away and he tightened his grip on her arm. "I'm not firing you."

"You-you're not?"

The look of cautious hope in her eyes made his stomach twist. "No, I'm not. How about this – I'll forget you fell asleep in my office if you forget that I was incredibly inappropriate and kissed you."

Her face flushed bright red. He had a feeling that her horror at realizing she was sleeping in his office had made her momentarily forget the kissing.

"Jane," he prompted when she didn't say anything. "Do we have an agreement?"

He released her arm as she nodded. "Um, yes. Thank you, Mr. Dawson. I promise it will never happen again."

He wondered if she meant the sleeping or the kissing and was a little dismayed to realize he hoped it was the sleeping. He shook off the little beat of pleasure that went through him at the thought of kissing her again. What was wrong with him?

"Good," he said briskly.

Her face still bright red, Jane said, "I'll grab your coffee for you."

"It's noon," he said.

"Wh-what?"

"It's noon. You've been sleeping all morning."

"Oh no," she said in a horrified little voice. "I slept all

morning?"

"Yes."

"Why didn't you wake me?" She asked.

He shrugged. "You looked like you needed the rest. If you're still not feeling well, you can go home."

"No, no," she said hurriedly. "I, uh, feel much better."

She didn't look much better – the dark circles were still under her eyes and her hands were trembling noticeably – but he nodded.

"All right. I don't have as much work for you today so I shouldn't need you to stay late."

"Okay," she said. She began to inch toward the door.

"But I will need you to work through lunch," he said.

"No problem," she said a bit frantically. "No problem at all."

She watched nervously as he sat down at his desk and opened the large brown paper bag the deli had delivered a few minutes ago.

"Sit down," he said.

She sat down and grimaced with embarrassment when he pulled out the soup and sandwich and her stomach growled loudly. "I'm sorry."

"It's fine," he said.

"Do you think, I mean, would you mind if I grabbed my sandwich from my desk before we get started?" She asked.

"Not necessary," he said before pushing the containers across the desk. "This is for you."

She stared at him in a mixture of surprise and confusion as he took out the second soup and sandwich and two bottles of water. He took the lid off his soup and unwrapped his sandwich.

"Eat up, Ms. Smith," he said.

ཚ ᷒

Jane studied the food in front of her. Shame and

hunger were warring within her but hunger won easily. She unwrapped the sandwich and took a large bite. It was a turkey sandwich with sweet cranberry sauce and she wanted to bury her face into it. She tried to chew slowly but she finished her sandwich before her boss had even eaten half of his. Her face burning with embarrassment but unable to help herself, she quickly took the lid off her soup and inhaled deeply.

"Careful, it's hot," her boss said.

She gave him a weak smile and made herself set the spoon down and drink some water. Mr. Dawson was studying her and she cleared her throat. "So, you found the work I left for you on your desk?"

"I did," he confirmed. "Thank you."

"You're welcome."

She waited for him to start talking about work and nearly choked on her sip of water when he said, "Did you grow up here, Ms. Smith?"

"Uh, yes, I did," she said. "Did you?"

"Yes. Do you have any siblings?"

She shook her head. "How about you? I mean, besides Ms. Dawson?"

"No, it's just Amy and me. Are you close to your parents?"

"They died when I was fifteen."

He stopped with his spoon halfway to his mouth. "I'm sorry."

"Thank you." She took her own bite of soup. Oh God, it was so good. It was cream of broccoli and although she normally hated broccoli, she decided she was incredibly stupid. Broccoli was as delicious as chocolate.

"How did they die?"

Her eyes widened at his bluntness. Not that she hadn't had people ask her about her parents' death but it was usually after they'd known her for a while. She opened her mouth to share her usual lie about their deaths but the way he was staring at her, as if he would see straight through her to the dark truth, made her blurt out the truth.

"My mother caught my father cheating on her. Three days later, she shot him while he was having a nap and then shot herself."

"Jesus Christ," he muttered.

She hurriedly ate more soup, hoping that he wouldn't ask her any more questions about her life. She hated talking about herself. Even before the murder/suicide of her parents she was shy and quiet, and after that trauma she became even more withdrawn. If it hadn't been for Mama J, she would probably be a complete recluse by now.

"Were you there?" He asked.

She jerked, spilling her spoonful of soup all over his shiny desk. She apologized profusely before mopping up the spill with her napkin. He handed her the paper bag to throw the napkin in and she busied herself with throwing her empty sandwich wrapper in the bag as well.

"Were you, Jane?"

"Was I what?" She hedged.

"Were you there when it happened?"

"No, of course not."

"Jane," he said softly.

She chewed at her bottom lip and avoided his gaze.

"Tell me the truth, please."

"Yes, I was there," she said. "I was in my room studying for my math test. I heard the first shot but didn't realize it was gunfire. I thought maybe someone had set off a firecracker in our yard. Stupid, huh?"

"No."

"Then there was the second shot and I heard a thud from my parents' room. I ran to their room and my dad was in bed and there was blood and brains all over his pillow. My mom was lying on the floor at the end of the bed. She had shot herself in the temple and blown off most of her skull. The thud I heard was her body hitting the floor."

He didn't say anything and without daring to look at him, she continued, "My mother left a note explaining that my dad tarnished their love with his affair, and he didn't deserve to live but that she couldn't live without him. I called 9-1-1 but they were both already dead. My mom had some mental health issues, I think. She would often spend days in her bedroom and she wouldn't eat or bathe. My dad called it her 'moods' but I think she might have had severe depression. Anyway, I didn't have any other family so the police called Child Services and they put me in foster care."

She finished her soup and resisted the urge to lick the Styrofoam container clean. Apparently reliving her parents' death hadn't done anything to diminish her appetite. Of course, this was the first food she'd eaten in days that wasn't a peanut butter sandwich or an orange.

"What happened then?" He asked quietly. Half his sandwich and most of his soup sat untouched in front of him and she looked longingly at them for a moment before drinking the rest of her water. She should never have told him the truth but it was too late to start lying now. He might as well hear the rest of her pathetic life story.

He's your boss! Stop telling him how pathetic you are. You'll get fired just for being so pitiful.

If he didn't fire me when I stuck my tongue down his throat, he's not going to fire me over my stupid life story.

Another wave of embarrassment went through her and she could feel her cheeks reddening. Oh God, she had made out with her boss. Why the hell didn't she learn her lesson the first time?

"Jane," he prompted.

She took a deep breath. "I lived with my first foster home for about three months before my foster dad was arrested for child pornography."

"Fuck," he said. "Don't they do some kind of interview process for foster homes?"

"Yes," she said. "I guess he was really good at hiding it. They moved me to a new foster home. They were an older couple and they were nice. They had been trying to adopt a baby for years and fostered kids while they waited. I had my own room and they treated me well. I lived with them for almost two years but then they finally got the chance to adopt a baby. They needed my room for the nursery so they asked my social worker to move me to a new home."

"Are you fucking kidding me?" He said.

She glanced up at him. To her surprise there was no pity in his eyes, just something that looked suspiciously like anger.

"You lived with them for two years and they kicked you out?" He said.

She shrugged. "They needed the space for the baby."

It was rather surprising to her how easy it was to share this part of her life's story. At the time, it was a devastating loss. She had grown to love both Judy and Karl and even thought they might adopt her. She had made sure to do well in school and to help around the house with chores in an effort to make them want her permanently. The night Karl and Judy sat her down and told her she was moving to a different foster home was horrible. She had cried and begged them to keep her, promised to help with the baby and offered to sleep on the couch in the basement. Judy and Karl cried with her and she believed their tears were genuine but the very next day the social worker had come for her.

"Where did you go then?" Mr. Dawson asked.

"I went to another foster home and it wasn't very," she paused, "nice."

"What happened?"

"They had other foster kids, six in total. One of them was a sixteen-year-old boy named David. One night he snuck into the girls' room and tried to rape me."

She watched as his hands clenched into fists and

another look of anger flitted across his face.

"He didn't," she said. "I fought back and managed to get his hand off my mouth long enough to scream. It woke up the other girls and he ran back to his room. I told the foster parents what happened but they didn't want to lose the money either of us brought in so they told me to keep quiet about it when the social worker came."

"Did you?" Mr. Dawson asked.

"No. They'd put a lock on the girls' room to keep David out but he was angry and he constantly threatened to try and rape me again or kill me. I – I was afraid that sooner or later he'd get me alone and hurt me. The social worker came by about a week after his first attempt, I told her what happened and one of the other girls was brave enough to back me up. They removed all of us from the home."

"Where did you go then?"

"Well, I was seventeen by then and only had a year left in the foster system. There was an older lady who had been a foster mom for a long time and she was retiring. They asked her to foster me. I guess they told her it would only be for nine months or so and she agreed. That's how I met Mama J."

Her face softened and a smile crossed her face. "Mama J was amazing. Her husband died quite young – I think Mama J said he was only fifty-two. They didn't have any kids of their own so they decided to foster. I lived with her until I was eighteen and was kicked out of the foster program."

"What did you do then?" He seemed oddly fascinated by her life story and she gave him a quick fleeting glance.

"Mama J didn't make me leave. She wasn't going to foster anymore and she asked me to stay with her. She didn't have a lot of money – her husband's illness had left her with a large debt in medical bills – but despite that she wanted me to stay."

A small smile crossed her face. "Mama J saved my life.

She really did."

"Where is she now?" He asked quietly.

Sorrow flitted across her face. "After I graduated high school, Mama J worked at Walmart and I waitressed for a few years to help with household bills and to save up for college. I applied and was accepted to the administrative assistant program but about a month after I started, Mama J got sick. She was starting to show signs of Alzheimer's. They did a bunch of tests and confirmed the diagnosis. She had to quit her job and I quit college so I could go back to waitressing full time to cover the bills. The first year or so wasn't too bad but then it got to the point where I couldn't leave her alone anymore. She had to be moved into a care facility."

"Does she remember you?" Mr. Dawson asked.

"Sometimes. The disease has started to progress more quickly in the last year though. More often than not, she doesn't know who I am."

She studied her hands before clearing her throat. "Sorry, I'm prattling on and on about my boring life when I should be working. What do you need done for this afternoon?"

He stared silently at her before saying, "I've sent you a few emails on what I need. If you have any questions, just ask. All right?"

She frowned slightly before standing. "Um, all right. Thank you for lunch, Mr. Dawson."

"You're welcome, Jane."

Chapter Six

"Mama J? I'm sorry it's been a few days. I've been so busy at work." Jane hurried into Mama J's room and pulled the pajamas she bought out of the bag. "I brought you some new pajamas."

Mama J stared blankly at her before returning her gaze to the window. Sorrow pierced Jane's heart and she set the pajamas on the bed before dragging a chair in front of Mama J's chair.

"Mama J?" She took her hands and squeezed them gently. "How are you today?"

"I can't find Walter," the old woman said. "I've looked for him for days and he's gone."

Jane squeezed her hands again. "You need to eat your supper."

"Maybe he's still at work," Mama J said. "I told him he works too hard but he wants me to have pretty things. Isn't that nice of him?"

"Very nice," Jane said. She pushed the plate that was sitting on the tray in front of Mama J, a little closer to her. "It's time to eat now."

Mama J stared at the food before scowling at Jane. "Who are you?"

"My name is Jane. I'm your daughter."

"Walter and I don't have any children."

"I'm your foster daughter," Jane said. "Eat up now."

"I don't have any foster children." Mama J gave her a suspicious look. "What have you done with Walter?"

"I haven't done anything with him, I promise," Jane said. She sat back and tried to smile at Mama J as the woman scowled again at her.

"I don't like you. I want you to leave."

Jane rubbed her aching stomach. "Why don't I sit with you while you eat. We can talk about whatever you want."

"No! I don't like you!" Mama J's voice was rising and Jane waved at Tanya when the nurse stuck her head into the room.

"It's okay, Mama J. It's okay," Jane said soothingly.

"Leave!" Mama J shouted. "Leave right now, you horrible girl!"

She grabbed the tray of food and threw it at Jane. It struck her in the chest and chicken, potatoes and gravy splattered across her chest and face. Jane winced and picked up the tray from the floor, as Tanya hurried into the room and stopped Mama J from getting out of her chair.

"It's okay, Josephine," she said softly. "Just relax."

"Tell her to leave!" Mama J shouted. "Right now!"

"Okay, I'll go," Jane said. She stood and grabbed her purse before hurrying out of the room. She used the washroom, wiping the gravy and food from the front of her t-shirt and silently thanking God that she had gone home and changed out of her work clothes before visiting.

When she emerged from the bathroom, Tanya gave her a sympathetic look. "You okay?"

"Yes. Is Mama J okay?"

"She settled down. I'll get a new tray of food brought up for her."

"Okay, thanks," Jane said. "Maybe I'll sit in the common room for a while and see if she's feeling better later."

"Jane," Tanya said, "go home. It's been a bad day for

Josephine and I don't think she's going to remember you tonight. Go home and get some rest – you look terrible."

Jane nodded as her stomach growled loudly. "Yeah, okay. I left her new pajamas on the bed."

Tanya nodded and Jane smiled gratefully at her before leaving the care home. The bus stop was two blocks away and she walked quickly, hunching her face into the collar of her jacket. She glanced at her watch as she waited for the bus. She should have been working tonight but as further punishment for being late last night, Jeremy had texted her this afternoon and told her they didn't need her to work. Thursday night was her best tip night and although she knew she needed the sleep, she needed the extra money more. She sighed as the bus pulled up in front of her. There wasn't anything she could do about it except hope that Mr. Dawson didn't need her to work late next week too.

ॐ ॐ

"You're kidding me," Jane groaned when she walked into her apartment an hour later. She flicked the light switch back and forth again. Her apartment was as cold as a crypt and they had cut off her electricity. Using her phone's flashlight, she hurried down the hallway. She pushed the heat to high but there was no familiar rattling as the heat started. Great. Her heat was cut off too.

Not that it matters. It barely worked anyway.

That was true but she was a little shocked by how cold it was in her apartment without any heat at all. Using the light on her phone, she changed into thick socks and her flannel pajamas and wrapped the blanket from her bed around her body. She rummaged in a drawer and found some matches to light the candle on the table. The sweet smell of apple pie filled the air and her stomach growled loudly in response. God, why had she bought the apple pie scented candle? Was she deliberately trying to torture herself?

Using the last of the bread, she made herself a peanut butter sandwich in the near darkness and ate it slowly. She had loved peanut butter for her entire life but if she ever could actually afford groceries, she'd never eat peanut butter again. She had one orange left and she stared for a while at it, debating whether to eat it now or save it for tomorrow.

Save it. You have seven dollars left to last until Monday night when you get your tips from the club and nothing but a jar of peanut butter and that orange to eat.

I'm still hungry.

You had a big lunch.

That was very true. Of course, eating a big meal had only seemed to make her even hungrier. After another moment of internal debate, she snatched up the orange and peeled it with shaky hands. She ate it slowly and then ate a few tablespoons of peanut butter before drinking a glass of water. Maybe Mr. Dawson would buy her lunch again tomorrow. If he did, she would only eat half of it and take the rest home to eat over the weekend. She could see her breath and the cold was seeping through her pajamas and her blanket. Her head aching and her limbs shaking from the cold, she put on her jacket before climbing into bed and pulling the covers over her head. She was so tired she wanted to cry but she staved it off grimly. She would catch up on her sleep and tomorrow she'd feel much better.

∂∾ ∾∂

"Jane? Are you feeling okay?"

Jane stared blearily at the woman standing in front of her desk. "Hi, Amy. Yes, I'm fine."

"Are you sure? You're very pale," Amy said.

"I'm good. How are you?"

"Fine." Amy shifted the bottle of juice she was holding

to her other hand before studying her closely. "Are you sure you're okay?"

"Yes, thanks. Mr. Dawson is in his office."

"Thanks." Amy gave her one last look of concern before disappearing into Mr. Dawson's office.

Jane rubbed a shaky hand across her forehead. Her head was throbbing miserably and she felt sick to her stomach. Why had she eaten that orange last night? She was so hungry she could barely think straight and her plan to catch up on her sleep last night had failed miserably. It was so cold in her apartment that she kept waking up, and she cringed at the thought of how awful it would be tonight. The weather had dropped another few degrees over night and they were calling it the coldest winter in years. She was going to freeze to death in her own damn apartment.

You can spend most of the weekend with Mama J. It's warm there.

Yes, she could if Mama J wanted to see her. She had called the care facility this morning and Bev the day nurse had told her that Mama J still wasn't doing well. She had told Jane to call before coming tonight, because if Mama J was acting like she was this morning there would be no point in stopping by to see her.

She printed off the document she had typed and grabbed it from the printer before walking to Mr. Dawson's office. He had been waiting for nearly an hour for it but she couldn't seem to get her brain to work right today.

She knocked and poked her head into the office. Amy was standing by the window and she smiled before beckoning for her to come in. Mr. Dawson was on the phone and he didn't look up as Jane placed the paper on his desk and turned to leave. The room spun crazily and a loud buzzing started in her ears. She groped frantically for the desk as her knees buckled and the room went black.

ào ´óô

"No, I understand that the – shit!" Luke dropped the phone into the cradle and jumped up as Amy made a soft gasp. Jane, her hand groping weakly behind her, was crumpling to the floor. He ran around the desk and caught her before she hit the floor. She was dead weight in his arms as he lifted her and carried her to his chair. He sat down and cradled her in his lap as Amy rushed forward.

"Luke? What happened?"

"She fainted," he said grimly as he felt for the pulse in her neck. It was weak but steady and he stroked her cheek. "Jane, wake up."

"Should I call 9-1-1?" Amy asked worriedly.

"Let's give her a minute," Luke said. He called her name again and shook her gently in his arms. Her eyes rolled beneath her eyelids and she made a soft little groan before blinking at him.

He leaned her against his chest and rubbed her back. "How do you feel?"

"F-fine," she stuttered. "What happened?"

"You fainted," he said.

"I did?" She whispered.

"Yes. Amy, can I have your juice?"

She opened the bottle of juice and handed it to him. He held it to Jane's mouth. "Drink, Jane."

She took a few sips and he held the bottle to her mouth again. "Drink some more."

She drank more and he breathed a sigh of relief when her harsh trembling eased a little.

Beside them, Amy gave her own sigh of relief. "She's starting to get some colour back in her face."

"I'm so sorry," Jane said. She tried to stand up and he tightened his arm around her.

"No, don't move yet," he said. "Finish the juice, please."

"I'm feeling much better," Jane protested. "Please, I'm so embarrassed."

"There's nothing to be embarrassed about," Amy said. "Drink the juice, honey."

Jane drank the rest of the juice and wiped her mouth with the back of her hand before giving Amy a shaky smile. "Thank you."

"Don't thank me," Amy said. "Luke was the one who caught you before you smacked your head on the floor and gave yourself a concussion."

Pale pink flooded her cheeks and she stared at his tie. "God, I'm so sorry, Mr. Dawson."

"It's fine," he said. "How do you feel?"

"Much better," she said. "Can you let me go now please?"

He didn't want to. He wanted to keep her in his lap until her shaking had stopped completely but she was giving him a pleading look. With a harsh sigh, he let go of her slender body. "Stand up slowly."

"I'm fine, really," she said.

She stood up and both he and Amy grabbed for her when she started to sway. She fell into his lap again and bit at her bottom lip as Amy felt her forehead.

"She doesn't have a fever but I think she should go to the hospital."

"I agree," Luke said as Jane shook her head fervently.

"No, I'm good now. I just stood up too quickly."

"I'm taking you to the hospital to be checked over," Luke said with a scowl.

"No, you're not," Jane said. "I don't need to go to the hospital. I was a little dizzy, that's all."

He gave her a look of exasperation. "You have two choices, Ms. Smith. You can walk out of this office with me or you can be carried out of this office by me. Either way – you're going to the hospital."

Jane gave Amy an imploring look and his sister shook her head. "Sorry, honey. I'm with Luke on this one. You need to go."

࿐ ࿔

"Mr. Dawson?"

Luke stood as the doctor entered the waiting room. For a Friday morning, the emergency room was surprisingly busy and Luke stepped past a wailing child and a man holding a bloody rag to his nose.

"Yes, I'm Luke Dawson." He shook the doctor's hand and followed him to a quieter spot. "How is she?"

"You're Miss Smith's…"

The doctor trailed off and gave him a questioning look.

"Boyfriend," Luke lied smoothly. "I'm Jane's boyfriend. How is she doing?"

"She's doing okay. We took some blood and sent it to the lab but I'm not expecting anything out of the ordinary from it."

"Did you do a CT scan?" Luke asked anxiously. "She fainted earlier."

The doctor shook his head. "No. I don't think Miss Smith's fainting was from a head trauma. She's dehydrated, exhausted and suffering from malnutrition."

He studied Luke closely. "Does Miss Smith have an eating disorder?"

Luke shook his head. "I don't think so. I've seen her eating."

"People with eating disorders can be very adept at hiding it," the doctor replied. "She's twenty pounds underweight, maybe even twenty-five. She needs to eat more than she currently is."

"I'll make sure she does," Luke replied. "Can I see her?"

"She's fallen asleep," the doctor said. "I'd like to keep her for the day, give her some IV fluids and allow her to rest. I'll discharge her around six if you'd like to come back and pick her up."

"I will," Luke said. "Thanks very much."

The doctor nodded and returned to the ER as Luke pulled out his phone. There were three texts from Amy and he sent her a quick text before tapping his foot anxiously against the floor. He wanted to see Jane before he left but if she was sleeping he didn't want to disturb her. The desire to see her was too strong to resist and he approached the woman at the admitting desk.

"Excuse me," he said, "my girlfriend is here and I wondered if I could see her quickly. I just spoke with the doctor."

"Name?" The woman asked.

"Luke Dawson."

"Your girlfriend's name," the woman said with an impatient sigh.

"Jane Smith."

She tapped at her keyboard before scanning the screen. "She's in room seven. I'll buzz you in."

"Thank you." Luke gave her his most charming smile. The woman rolled her eyes and waved him toward the door. She buzzed him through and he walked quickly into the ER. The rooms weren't exactly rooms, just areas sectioned off with curtains, but he found the one marked seven and stuck his head behind the curtain.

It was noisy in the ER but Jane was sleeping soundly. She was hooked up to a bunch of machines and he studied the screen that displayed her heart rate and blood pressure. He picked up her hand and squeezed it gently as a nurse ducked behind the curtain.

She gave him a curious look and he said, "I'm her boyfriend. She's my, uh, girlfriend."

"Okay," the nurse said. "I'm going to start an IV."

As she placed the IV in Jane's arm, Luke continued to hold her other hand. Jane didn't wake, not even when the nurse slid the needle into her hand.

"Boy, she's a sound sleeper, huh?" The nurse said.

Luke nodded. "Yes, she is. Sometimes she snores. I

know that because I'm her boyfriend."

The nurse gave him an odd look and he said, "I don't mind it though. It's kind of cute."

Jesus, what the fuck was wrong with him? He was babbling like an idiot.

The nurse taped off the needle in Jane's arm and adjusted the drip. "It looks like she's going to be asleep for a while so you might want to grab a coffee from the cafeteria."

"Right," Luke said. He hesitated before bending over and brushing his mouth against Jane's. "I'll be back at six, sweetheart."

❧ ❧

"How are you feeling, Miss Smith?" The doctor asked as he pushed past the curtain.

"Much better," Jane said. She wasn't exactly lying, she did feel better. She was still tired despite having slept for most of the day and she was stupidly hungry but the dizziness had passed. She didn't want to stay the night in the hospital so she pasted a large smile on her face. "I'm ready to go home now."

"Good, that's good," he said as he looked over her chart. "I'm going to go ahead and discharge you. I do have a couple of," he paused, "brochures I'd like you to look over."

He reached into the pocket of his lab coat and handed her the coloured brochures. She looked at them, her curiosity turning to embarrassment as she realized what they were.

"There are plenty of programs available for you to - "

"I don't have an eating disorder," Jane interrupted.

He gave her a patronizing look. "You're at least twenty pounds underweight, maybe more. This isn't something to be ashamed of. Many patients with treatment can - "

"I don't have an eating disorder," Jane said again. "I

don't, uh, have a lot of money right now for groceries."

The doctor patted her leg. "Of course. Well, I'm still going to encourage you to look over these brochures and think about speaking with a therapist, all right?"

"Sure," Jane sighed. She didn't know if she wanted to laugh or cry. She settled for grimacing as the doctor signed something on her chart and slipped it into the holder at the end of the bed.

"It was nice to meet you, Miss Smith. Take care."

He ducked behind the curtain as a nurse poked her head in on the other side. "Ready to have your IV out, Jane?"

"Yes," Jane said. She waited patiently as the nurse removed the IV.

"Your clothes are in that cupboard there," the nurse said as she threw the IV into the trash and stripped off her gloves.

"Thank you. Do you know if there's a bus stop close to the hospital?" Jane asked.

"There's one a few blocks away but I'm sure your boyfriend will be here any minute to pick you up," the nurse replied.

"Boyfriend?" Jane said.

"Yes, boyfriend," the nurse said. "That handsome dark-haired guy who brought you in. He said he'd be back at six."

"He's not my - "

"Jane?"

Her head snapped up and her mouth dropped open when her boss peered past the curtain. "Hi, how are you feeling?"

"Better, thank you. Um, what are you doing here?"

"I told you he'd be back to pick you up," the nurse said. She smiled at Mr. Dawson. "You're very prompt, I like it."

He grinned at her and she flushed a little before clearing her throat. "Have a good evening, you two."

She left and Jane stared at her boss. "You really didn't have to come back here, Mr. Dawson. I can take the bus home."

"It's freezing out," he said. "Also, I think you can call me Luke, don't you?"

"Uh, sure, okay," she said.

"Good." His gaze landed on the brochures and he plucked them out of her hand before she could try and hide them. He looked them over before staring at her and she shook her head.

"The doctor gave those to me but I don't have an eating disorder."

He didn't say anything and she bit her bottom lip. "I don't. I swear I don't."

"Okay," he said. There was an uncomfortable silence and she cleared her throat loudly.

"Uh, I was going to get dressed so…"

"Right, of course," he said. "I'll be outside the curtain. Shout for me if you need help."

She flushed bright red as he retreated. Jane swung her legs over and sat on the side of the bed for a moment. Why had he come back? It didn't make any sense.

Probably wanted to fire you in person.

Her stomach clenched and then gurgled and she pressed her hand against it.

He's not going to fire me, she thought desperately.

Don't be naïve. You spent most of Thursday morning sleeping in his office and today you fainted and he had to take you to the hospital. Your ass is so fired, girl.

Well, crap. She was getting fired. She grabbed her clothes and dressed quickly. She wouldn't cry, she told herself fiercely. No matter what, she wouldn't cry in front of him and embarrass herself further.

Chapter Seven

Luke parked in front of Jane's apartment building. He started to unbuckle his seatbelt and she gave him a startled look.

"You don't have to walk me to my apartment."

"Like hell I don't," he said.

"Mr. Dawson, I - "

"Luke," he reminded her, "and stop arguing with me. I'm walking you to your apartment."

He ignored her sigh and climbed out of the car. He took her arm and she smiled tentatively at him. "I don't feel dizzy anymore."

He didn't reply. He was a little ashamed to realize he had taken her arm because he wanted to touch her rather than to keep her upright if she fainted again.

There was no one in the lobby this time and he followed her up the stairs to her apartment. She unlocked her door and smiled again at him. "Thank you so much for your help today. I really appreciate it and I'm sorry I was so much trouble. Good night, Luke."

"Invite me in, Jane," he said.

"I – I'm sorry?" She stuttered.

"Invite me in please."

"Mr. Dawson," she said with a sigh, "if you're going to fire me, just say so all right? I know what I did today was terrible and I understand why you're firing me but I'd rather not drag it out."

"I'm not firing you," he said. "But I am going to come in and make sure you eat something."

She twisted a lock of her hair nervously. "I'll eat dinner. I promise."

"I know you will," he said, "because I'm going to cook it for you."

Before she could protest, he stepped around her and pushed open the door. He stepped inside the hallway and groped blindly for the light switch. He found it and flicked it up, cursing when nothing happened.

"Your power is out."

"It happens sometimes." She sounded nervous.

Luke, what are you doing? Of course she's nervous. She was almost raped as a teenager – do you really think she's okay with you coming into her apartment uninvited?

Fuck! He was a goddamn idiot. He really should leave before he made things worse but his need to make sure that she ate, as well as his weird desire to spend time with her, kept him from leaving.

"Jane, I'm not going to hurt you, okay?" He said. "I promise. I just want to make sure that you have some dinner."

She flicked on the flashlight on her phone and stared in surprise at him. "I know you won't hurt me, Mr. Daw – Luke."

"Why is it so cold in here?" He asked as she removed her boots. He followed her down the hallway to the kitchen.

"Uh, my heat isn't working very well. Mr. Ranson hasn't fixed it yet," she said. She chewed on her bottom lip. He was starting to recognize it as a sign of her anxiety and he studied her in the dim light.

"Is that right?"

"Yes," she replied. She lit the candle on the table. "Well, with the electricity out I guess you won't really be able to cook me dinner so…"

"I'm resourceful," he said. "Go and change and I'll start dinner."

He turned on the flashlight on his own phone and walked toward the fridge. "Go on, Jane."

He opened the fridge and held up his phone. It was empty and he muttered under his breath before moving to the cupboards. He opened the door of the nearest cupboard and shone the flashlight into it. It was empty as well and he opened two more. They were just as empty and he frowned at her. "Where's your food?"

She bit at her lip again and he sighed and opened the last cupboard as she said, "Luke, it's not - "

"Jesus Christ!" He jumped back and slammed the cupboard door shut before spinning around to face her. "There is a very large fucking rat in your cupboard, Jane."

A look of fear crossed her face and she took a few steps back. He started toward her as she backed up again.

"Your cupboards and fridge are empty – unless you count the cat-sized rat – and you have no power and no heat. What the hell is going on?"

"I told you," she whispered, "sometimes the power goes out."

"Don't lie to me," he said.

She pressed her lips together and he took her arm. "Tell me the truth."

"Fine!" She spat at him. She yanked her arm out of his grip. "They cut off my heat and my electricity yesterday and I can't afford food until payday. Okay?"

He stared dumbfounded at her. "Payday isn't until the end of next week."

"I'm aware of that," she said bitterly. "Can you please go? I'm very tired and I want to go to bed."

"I pay you a good wage," he said. "You need to learn how to manage your money better."

"Manage my money better?" She snapped at him. "Excuse me, Mr. Millionaire, but not all of us have money falling out of our butts like you do! I have responsibilities that you wouldn't even begin to understand so don't you dare lecture me about how I spend my money. Besides, I'd have electricity and heat and goddamn food if someone hadn't made snide comments about my wardrobe. I bought your damn Dawson clothing instead of paying my bills and buying groceries so that I wouldn't get fired. Now you have the nerve to come in here and tell me I'm not spending my money wisely? How dare you! Get out of my apartment, Luke Dawson. Right now!"

He stared at her, so taken aback by her sudden outburst of anger that he was momentarily speechless.

"Leave!" She snapped at him. She shoved at him but it didn't move him an inch. She made a low grunt of anger and hammered on his chest with her small fists. "Leave right now! Do you hear me? Leave!"

"Jane," he said, "I'm sorry, I didn't mean to upset you. I'll leave."

"I'm not upset! I'm angry and hungry and tired and I want to go to bed!" She burst into tears and he jerked in surprise when she leaned her head against his chest and sobbed. He put his arms around her as she buried her face in his jacket and flung her arms around his waist. She clung to him and cried brokenly. He stroked her back and murmured words of comfort until her sobbing had slowed to the occasional sniffle.

"Jane, you can't stay here," he said. "It's too cold and you have no food."

"I have no place else to go," she said.

"Pack an overnight bag and let's go," he said.

"Go where?" She sniffed.

He touched her soft hair before stepping away. "Pack a bag, please. You're not staying here tonight."

She sighed but nodded and left the kitchen.

❧ ❦

"Whose house is this?" She asked as he pulled into his driveway.

He shut the car off and grabbed her bag from the backseat. "Mine."

Her eyes widened. "I can't stay at your place, Mr. Dawson!"

"Yes, you can."

"No, I can't!" She said. "It isn't proper and if people at the office found out..."

She trailed off and he gave her an impatient look as he opened his door and cold wind blew into the car. "No one's going to find out. Besides, it's just for tonight. In the morning, we'll figure out something more permanent."

She continued to hesitate and he frowned at her. "Don't make me carry you into the house."

That got her moving and she followed him up the steps to the front door. His home was large and she studied the art hanging on the walls in the foyer. He took her jacket and hung it in the closet as she slipped out of her boots. Still carrying her bag, he walked toward the kitchen and flipped on the lights.

"Oh my goodness," she breathed. "This kitchen is amazing."

"Thanks," he said. He loved to cook and when he'd started renovations on the house, he'd spared no expense in the kitchen. He rummaged through the freezer section of his fridge as Jane ran her hand over the island top.

"Is this marble?" She asked.

"Yes. Sit down," he said as he popped something into the microwave. "I'll make you dinner."

"Oh, just a sandwich is fine," Jane said hurriedly.

"I don't have any peanut butter," he replied.

She flushed and he pointed to one of the stools at the island. "Have a seat, please."

"Let me at least help you," she said.

He shook his head. "No, you need your rest. Besides, I'm cooking dinner for myself and it's as easy to cook for two people as it is for one."

That seemed to appease her a little and she climbed onto the stool. Remembering what the doctor had said about her being dehydrated, he grabbed a bottle of water from the fridge and a bottle of beer. He opened the water bottle and set it on the island in front of her.

She drank some water as he took a large swallow of beer before putting a pot of water to boil on the stove. He grabbed another pot and began to make the tomato sauce for the pasta. While the sauce cooked, he took the meatballs from the microwave and set them on the counter. He heard the soft growl of Jane's stomach behind him and without speaking, he pulled a bag of fresh, raw veggies from the fridge and arranged them on a plate before adding a dollop of dip in the middle of it.

He set the veggies and dip on the island in front of her. "Eat up."

"Thank you." She reached eagerly for a carrot as he turned back to the stove. He stirred the sauce, tasting it and adding a bit more oregano before adding the meatballs. As they heated, he dumped the spaghetti into the boiling water. He took another swig of beer and turned toward Jane.

"Jane, are you…"

He trailed off, staring in surprise at the empty veggie plate. Jane was licking dip from her finger and she gave him a look of shame that made his stomach tighten.

"I'm sorry," she said. "That was rude of me to eat all the veggies."

"It's fine," he said. "Would you like more?"

"No, that's good," she said. "Um, dinner smells delicious."

"Thank you. It's pasta with my famous meatballs."

"Famous?" She said with a small smile.

"Well, not world famous you understand, but family famous," he replied.

She laughed. "You like to cook, huh?"

"Love it, actually. When I was younger, I almost went to culinary school."

"Why didn't you?" She asked as he set the island with plates and cutlery.

"Amy wanted to start a clothing line but had no interest in the business side of it. I saw her potential and wanted to help her achieve her dream so I went into business instead."

"That was very selfless of you," she said.

He shrugged, suddenly uncomfortable with the way she was looking at him. "Not that selfless. I've made a lot of money from Amy's dream."

"She really is very talented."

"Yes, she is," he replied. "I'm sorry about commenting on your clothes the way I did."

She shrugged and stared at the plate in front of her. "It's fine. My clothes are pretty awful and I should be dressing better for my job."

There was awkward silence as he finished making the pasta. He scooped some onto both their plates, ladled the sauce and meatballs over it and sat across from her. She inhaled deeply before giving him a tentative smile. "It smells delicious. Thank you."

"You're welcome."

They ate in silence. He had piled Jane's plate high with spaghetti but she only ate a little of it before pushing it away and giving him an apologetic look.

"It's very good. I'm just full and my stomach…"

She trailed off but he didn't need her to finish the sentence. He should have considered the fact that she probably hadn't eaten a real meal in who knew how long. Pasta wasn't exactly a great meal to give someone who was starving.

"It's fine." He started to put the leftovers away and waved her off when she jumped up to help. "No, sit and relax."

She sat quietly as he loaded the dishwasher and wiped

down the counters. He turned around just in time to see Jane yawning. It was only eight but she looked exhausted.

"Ready for bed?" He asked.

She blushed as he said, "Uh, I have a guest room for you to sleep in."

"Right, of course," she said.

"Okay, well, uh, follow me."

He grabbed her bag and she followed him out of the kitchen. "This is the living room," he pointed to the doorway to their right and waited as Jane peeked her head inside. He stopped at the next door. "My office." She checked it out as well and he pointed out the guest bathroom and the formal dining room before they went upstairs. His bedroom door was open and he paused. "This is my room."

He expected her to only glance into it like she had the others and his damn cock actually stirred when she stepped right into his room. Jesus, he was in trouble if just having Jane standing in his room made him horny.

He followed her in reluctantly and folded his arms across his chest as she studied the room.

"It's very nice," she said. "I like the fireplace."

"Thank you."

When Jane's gaze fell on his unmade bed, he suddenly wished fervently that he had made it. It was way too easy to imagine her crawling between the rumpled sheets, her body naked and ready for him.

His cock started to harden and he cursed under his breath. "Come with me and I'll show you the guest room."

"Yes, Mr. Dawson," she replied.

His earlier dream came roaring back to him and he turned around abruptly. There was no way he could hide the bulge in his pants after that. Fuck! Was she trying to kill him?

"I told you to call me Luke," he said more gruffly than he intended.

"I'm sorry," she said in a low voice.

He was beyond tempted to turn around and pick up from where they left off with that kiss yesterday. He clenched his hands into fists. Forgetting that she was his PA, she was also exhausted and probably scared. He was an asshole.

"Mr. Daw – I mean, Luke, did I do something wrong?" She asked.

"No," he said, "of course not."

He left his bedroom, hoping like hell she followed him. He breathed a sigh of relief when he heard her soft footsteps. He shoved open the door and stepped aside. There was no way in hell he was going into the bedroom with her. He didn't trust himself not to do something incredibly inappropriate.

She slipped by him and studied the room. "It's lovely," she said.

"That door leads to the bathroom," he said. "If you need anything in the night, just…"

He trailed off. What exactly would she need in the night? The only thing he wanted to give her was a slow fucking and that was the last damn thing on her mind. There was no way she felt the tension between them and even if she did, she would chalk it up to him being a jackass again.

"Okay, um, thank you again, Luke. I'll be out of your hair in the morning, I promise," Jane said.

"Good night, Jane."

"Good night."

He shut the door before he could do something really stupid like beg her to join him in his bed. His cock still hard and lust pulsing in his belly, he stalked down the hallway to his own bedroom. He stood in the master bathroom and contemplated having a cold shower before throwing his clothes in the hamper and brushing his teeth. He was climbing into bed when he heard the faint but unmistakeable sound of the guest bathroom shower. He groaned and flopped onto his back to stare blankly at the ceiling.

Jane was in the shower. She was in the shower and she would be very naked and very wet. Maybe she was running soap over her body at this very moment. Maybe she was sliding that soft hand of hers between her thighs and...

Fuck! He needed to stop this. He moved restlessly in the bed as forbidden images of a naked Jane flickered through his head. Maybe he should knock on the door and ask if her she needed help. He could wash her back and that small but delectable ass of hers. He threw back the covers and gripped his erect cock. He rubbed it roughly as he pictured Jane leaning back against him while the hot water flowed over both their bodies. He would cup her breasts and tease her nipples until she was begging him for more. When she was breathless and needy he would slide his hand to her pussy and caress her swollen clit until she cried his name and came all over his hand. He would lift her, brace her against the wall and make her take every inch of his cock until he was completely consumed by her hot, tight wetness. He would take her fully and leave no doubt in her mind that he was claiming her as his and his alone.

His hips arched and he came all over his hand and his stomach. He threw his arm over his mouth to muffle his loud groan as his orgasm swept through him. When the pleasure faded, shame took its place and he jumped up and hurried to the bathroom. He cleaned himself up fast, irrationally worried that Jane would come charging into the room and demand to know why he had masturbated to the sound of her in the shower. He threw the cloth into the hamper and climbed back into bed. Jesus, he was a pervert. A much more relaxed pervert but still a fucking pervert. With a loud sigh, he rolled onto his side and closed his eyes.

ॐ ॐ

The guest bathroom connected to her bedroom had a large walk-in shower. Jane hesitated only briefly before brushing her teeth, undressing and starting the shower. She was tired but also restless and she hoped that the hot water would help to relax her. She washed her hair and rinsed it before beginning to wash her body.

Her mind wandered to her boss. He had seemed tense and a little irritated with her and she leaned her forehead against the shower wall and let the hot water beat over her back. She shouldn't have gone into his bedroom but she couldn't resist. She wanted to see it, wanted to check out his bed like a horny teenager. Apparently having a full belly and a warm place to sleep had brought her libido roaring back to life.

Good. Let's talk about that kiss yesterday, her inner voice said.

God, had it really only been yesterday? It almost felt like a lifetime ago.

Once you're done your shower, why don't you accidentally wander into his bedroom? Tell him you got lost in his giant house.

She scoffed inwardly. Her boss already thought she was an idiot and despite the kiss they shared, he wasn't interested in her sexually. How could he be? She was too skinny and too poor and –

"Jane?"

She whirled around. Luke was a dark shadow through the foggy shower glass and she clapped her arms over her breasts.

"Mr. Dawson? What are you doing in here?"

The door opened and her eyes widened. Luke was as naked as she was and her eyes dropped to his cock. It was erect and standing proudly out from his body. She licked her lips and took a nervous step back as he crowded into the shower with her. It was a large shower but he was a big man and there were only a few inches of space between her naked body and his.

"Mr. Dawson?" She whispered.

"I told you to call me Luke, remember?"

"I'm sorry."

"Turn around, Ms. Smith," he said. "I thought you could use some help washing your back."

She hesitated before turning around. "Thank you. That's a very…kind offer."

"I'm a very kind man," he said. She jerked when his warm and soapy hands rubbed her upper back briskly. "Hold still please."

"Yes, Mr. Dawson."

He squeezed her right ass cheek making her twitch and moan. "Luke. Try not to be so forgetful, Ms. Smith."

She wanted to apologize but both his hands were on her ass now and his strong fingers were kneading and squeezing her flesh. It felt amazing and it took all of her willpower not to lean back and rub herself against his dick.

"Lower your arms," he demanded.

"Why?"

He made a snort of impatience. "Enough questions, Ms. Smith. Do as you're told, please."

She dropped her arms and gasped when he cupped both her breasts. He soaped them before tugging on her nipples. They beaded into hard points and this time she couldn't stop from leaning against him.

"Luke, please," she moaned.

"Ms. Smith," he chided, "behave yourself."

She forced herself not to rub against the very hard cock pressing against her ass.

"I'm simply trying to help you bathe but I get the feeling you're enjoying this more than you should," he said as he pulled on her aching nipples. "Are you wet, Ms. Smith?"

"Why don't you check for yourself," she said. She was shocked by how bold she was being but she needed him. Needed him in a way that she didn't understand but didn't want to ignore.

"Maybe I will," he teased before rinsing the soap from his hands. His hand passed over her flat stomach. "Open your legs."

She spread her legs with an eagerness that embarrassed her. His hand slipped between her legs and she moaned when he rubbed at her clit. She bucked her hips against his hand and his soft groan of approval made her shudder all over.

"Such a pretty pussy," he said before kissing her neck. "So wet and," he pushed one thick finger into her pussy, "tight."

She thrust her hips against his hand as he rubbed her clit with his thumb. "After you come, I'm going to take you back to my bedroom," he whispered hotly into your ear. "You're going to lie on your back in my bed and spread your legs so I can fuck you. Do you understand, Ms. Smith?"

"Yes," she whimpered as pleasure filled her entire body.

"Say it," he demanded.

"I – I'm going to spread my legs and let you fuck me," she moaned.

"That's my good girl," he said approvingly.

His thumb was rubbing against her clit, his finger thrusting in and out of her tight pussy and she clutched at his arm helplessly. Her orgasm was starting deep in her belly, her stomach tightening with pleasure as he sucked on her earlobe.

"Come for me, Ms. Smith. Right now."

His demand brought on her climax and she shouted his name as her back arched and pleasure rushed through her entire body.

Jane shook and shuddered, her fingers rubbing furiously at her clit as the last of her climax swept through her. Her eyes widened and she yanked her hand out from between her legs and made a low moan of dismay. She was alone in the shower and she stared blankly at her own hand before grabbing the soap and scrubbing at her naked body. Oh fuck, she had just masturbated in her boss' house while he slept in the next room. What was wrong with her?

She froze and clapped her hand over her mouth. Shit! Had she said his name out loud as she came? Had he heard her? What if he heard her? What if he knew that she was...

Jane! Snap out of it! He didn't hear you over the shower, for God's sake. Just chill out.

Her heart thudding in her chest, she finished soaping up before rinsing clean and shutting off the shower. She toweled herself dry, shuddering a little when she ran the towel over the sensitive flesh between her legs. Despite her orgasm, she was still feeling achy and unsatisfied. She needed Luke's hard body on top of hers. She needed his warm touch and his hot mouth and his dick. Maybe she could knock on his door. Maybe she could tell him she was having trouble relaxing and ask him to help her sleep by giving her a good, hard fucking. Maybe he would let her climb into his bed and spread her legs so he could -

Stop it, Jane!

Yes, she really needed to stop this madness. She forced the image of being naked and under her boss out of her head and dressed in her flannel pajamas before shutting off the bathroom light and climbing into the bed. It was deliciously comfortable and she curled onto her side. She was certain she'd never fall asleep, but within five minutes, she was sleeping deeply.

Chapter Eight

"What's so important that you had to wake me up on a Saturday morning and force me to drag my ass out into the cold?" Amy asked grumpily when Luke opened the door.

He glanced at his watch. "It's almost noon, Ames. Why were you still in bed?"

She kicked off her boots and hung her jacket in the closet. "Siblings for twenty-eight years and you still don't know I'm not a morning person? You suck as a brother."

She followed him into the kitchen and he handed her a coffee. "I don't suck that much. I know you need a coffee before you even resemble a human being."

"Bite me," she said before sipping at the coffee. "Seriously, what's wrong?"

"There isn't anything wrong," he said. "I need your help with something."

"What?" She asked. "And are you going to make me pancakes or let me starve?"

"I'll make you pancakes," he said. "Just listen to me for a minute, would you?"

She wrinkled her nose at him before drinking more coffee. "Fine, but you should know that I'm right on the edge of hangry over here."

"I'll keep it in mind," he said. He sat next to her at the island. "Jane is upstairs sleeping."

"Oh yeah?" She took another sip of coffee.

"Why are you not surprised by that?" He asked.

"I see the way you look at her. Although, sleeping with your PA is not the wisest idea, Lukie."

He glared at her. "I'm not sleeping with her, Ames!"

"Really?" Now she did give him a look of surprise and he stood and paced the kitchen.

"Do you really think I'm that kind of guy? She's starving to death, she fainted and spent most of the day in the hospital yesterday but you think I brought her back to my place for sex?"

Don't act so sanctimonious, buddy. You would have fucked her last night if she had given even the slightest indication that she wanted it.

He ignored his inner voice as Amy gave him an apologetic look. "Sorry, honey."

"Apology accepted," he grumped. "And what do you mean by the way I look at her?"

"Nothing," she said. "So, Jane is upstairs sleeping in your bed."

He gave her a look of exasperation. "She's sleeping in the guest room."

She grinned at him and he rolled his eyes. "After she was discharged from the hospital, I gave her a ride home. Both her heat and her electricity are cut off and she has no food. I mean, nothing, Ames. Unless you count the rat living in her cupboards."

Amy shuddered all over. "There was a rat?"

He nodded. "A big one."

"Oh God." Amy paled and he squeezed her shoulder. She was terrified of rats.

"I made her come home with me. She couldn't stay at her apartment. It was freezing and the doctor told me that she was malnourished and needed to eat more. I couldn't leave her there."

"She doesn't have any family she can stay with?" Amy asked.

He shook his head. "She grew up in foster care. She has a foster mom that she's close to but the woman lives in a care home after being diagnosed with Alzheimer's."

"God, that poor girl," Amy said.

"It's my fault, Amy."

"What's your fault?"

"That she doesn't have heat or electricity or food. I made that stupid comment about her clothes so she bought Dawson brand clothing with her last paycheque instead of paying her bills and buying groceries."

"Well, I bet you feel like the biggest horse's ass in the world right now," Amy said.

"Now you know why I brought her back here," he said.

"Do I, though?" She said cryptically.

"What's that supposed to mean?"

"Nothing. So, now what? You're going to let her live with you until she gets her heat and electricity turned back on?"

He shook his head. "She can't go back to that apartment. It's in the Badlands and the lock on her door is…pitiful. It's not safe for her there, Amy. I can't let her go back even if she does get her heat and electricity turned on."

"Guess you found yourself a roommate then," Amy said. "That's going to be awkward when the other employees find out your PA is living with you."

"Actually," he said, "this is the part where I need your help. You have a spare room at your place."

"You want me to invite Jane to live with me?" She said.

He nodded. "Yes."

"Sure."

He blinked at her. "Just like that?"

"Just like that, Lukie," Amy said.

"Thank you."

"You're welcome. Now, how about those pancakes you promised?"

❧ ❧

The smell of pancakes woke her. Her stomach grumbled and Jane sat up in bed. She stared at the strange room before remembering where she was. She checked her cell phone, dismayed to see that it was after noon and hurried to the bathroom. When she was finished, she brushed her teeth, dressed and called the nursing home.

"Hi, Bev. It's Jane. How is Mama J doing today?"

"Hi, Jane. Josephine's having another bad day, I'm afraid," Bev said. "She was restless through the night and became quite agitated this morning."

Guilt flooded through Jane. "I'll be there in an hour."

"Jane," Bev said, "why don't you take the weekend off? We sedated Josephine and she's sleeping right now. I don't think she's going to remember you today or tomorrow."

Jane chewed on her bottom lip. "Maybe if I drop by, it'll help her remember."

"Has it in the past?" Bev said.

"No, but - "

"We all know how much you love her but, sweetie, you need to take care of yourself as well. You've been looking awfully pale lately."

"I don't want to leave her all alone," Jane whispered.

"You're not. We're here and you know we care about her. Give yourself permission to live your own life for a couple of days, okay? I'll leave a note for Tanya to call you if Josephine improves. All right?"

"Okay," Jane said. "Will you tell her I love her though?"

"Of course I will. If you don't hear from Tanya tonight, call tomorrow."

"I will. Thanks, Bev."

"You're welcome, sweetie."

Jane stuck her phone into her pocket and checked her

hair in the bathroom mirror. It had dried fuzzy while she was sleeping and she wet her hands and tried to smooth it down. She applied a light layer of make-up to try and hide the dark circles under her eyes. She stared at the blush and her eye shadow, debating whether to fancy herself up a little more. She snorted in disgust. What did it matter what she looked like? Her boss wasn't attracted to her. She could have all the sexual fantasies about him that she wanted but he would never be attracted to someone as pathetic as her. Instead of worrying about what she looked like, she needed to be worrying about how she was going to survive the rest of the weekend without heat or food.

She cringed at the thought of returning to her apartment – Jesus, she'd never sleep again knowing there was a rat living with her – but she really didn't have a choice. Her stomach growled and she patted it soothingly. She would stuff herself full of pancakes this morning and maybe try and slip two or three into her purse when Luke wasn't looking. That would get her through today. As for tomorrow and Monday – she'd have to suck it up and drink lots of water. She could buy food after she got her tips on Monday night.

What if Jeremy is still pissed at you and cancels your shift on Monday too? Then what, Janie?

He wouldn't do that. If he did, well, there was always the rat living in her cupboard.

The thought of trying to capture, kill and eat a rat brought on only a mild sense of repulsion and she fought back the sudden wave of tears. Was this what she was reduced to now? Seriously considering trying to catch a rat and eat it? She was so fucked up it wasn't funny.

It won't come to that, Janie. Now, go downstairs and enjoy the food and the heat before you have to go back to your shitty apartment, okay?

She smoothed her hair again before leaving the bedroom. The scent of pancakes was stronger in the hallway and she hurried down the stairs and into the kitchen.

"Good morning, Luke. I'm sorry I slept so - "

She stopped and stared in surprise at Amy. Luke's sister gave her a cheerful grin. "Hi, Jane."

"Um, hi, Amy." Jane stood awkwardly in the doorway. Amy patted the chair next to her.

"Sit down and have some pancakes with me."

Jane sat down next to her as Luke put a plate with two pancakes in front of her. "How did you sleep, Jane?"

"Uh, very well. The bed in the guest room is very comfortable."

"Good. Would you like a coffee?"

"Yes, please. I can get it though."

He shook his head. "I'll grab it. Eat some pancakes."

Amy passed the syrup and the butter to her. "Eat up, Jane. My brother makes amazing pancakes."

Amy popped a forkful of pancakes into her mouth as Jane poured syrup over her pancakes before taking her own bite. They were light and fluffy and mouth-wateringly good and she shoved a couple more bites into her mouth.

Amy grinned at her. "See, told you."

Luke set a cup of coffee in front of Jane and added another stack of pancakes to the plate in the middle of the table before sitting down across from them. He sipped at his cup of coffee as Amy said, "Are you feeling better?"

"Yes, much better," Jane said.

"Good. Luke told me you were having problems with your heat and electricity at your place."

"Yes," Jane said. She gave Luke a grateful look. "He offered to let me stay at his place last night. It was very nice of him."

"That's my big brother – the nicest guy in town," Amy said.

Luke gave her a mock scowl and Amy laughed. "Sometimes, anyway." She finished her pancakes and sat back with a sigh. "God, those were so good, Luke. Thank you."

"You're welcome," Luke said. He reached across the table and transferred another pancake to Jane's plate. "Have some more."

"Thank you," Jane said.

"So," Amy said, "Luke also told me you live in the Badlands."

"I do."

"Well, that's horrifying."

Jane couldn't help but grin. "It's not as bad as everyone thinks it is."

"Says the woman whose roommate is a giant rat," Luke muttered.

Amy shuddered. "I would have screamed and wet my pants if I opened a cupboard and found a rat in it."

Jane shrugged. "I'll pick up a trap today."

"A trap isn't going to work," Luke said solemnly. "A sledgehammer might stop it long enough for you to make it to the fire escape."

Jane burst into laughter. "Okay, now you're exaggerating."

"I am not," Luke said. "You didn't actually see it, remember? I'm lucky it didn't drag me into the cupboard."

"It sounds to me like you need a new place to live," Amy said.

Jane pushed her plate away. It still had half a pancake on it and she nodded when Luke held his fork over the pancake and gave her a questioning look. He stabbed it with his fork and transferred it to his plate. He finished it as she said, "I'm good where I am."

"Really? With no heat or electricity and a giant dirty rat living in your kitchen?" Amy said.

"I'll get it all sorted out," Jane said with a cheerfulness she didn't feel. Desperate to change the subject she said, "So, do you have fun plans for the weekend?"

"A little bit of work, family dinner tomorrow night and

working on my ad for a roommate."

"You're looking for a roommate?" Jane said.

"I am. Just between you and me, I hate the process. You would not believe the weirdos that apply. I'm dreading it, to be honest."

Amy paused and gave Jane a thoughtful look. "Unless I found someone I knew who was looking for a new place to live."

Jane didn't reply and Amy nudged her. "Well, what do you say?"

"About what?" Jane gave her a bewildered look.

"About moving in with me."

"I – what – no, I can't do that."

"Why not?" Amy asked. "You need a new place to live and I need a roommate. It's a win-win."

"Why do you need a roommate?" Jane asked. "I know it isn't because of the cost of living."

"I hate living by myself," Amy said. "I'm a social butterfly. Come on, Jane. Live with me. My house is way nicer than your apartment and the rent is cheaper too, I guarantee it."

Jane stared into her coffee. She had just been handed the answer to all her problems. Why the hell was she hesitating?

"Yes," she said. "Yes, I'll be your roommate."

She didn't notice the way Luke slumped with relief as Amy gave her a hard and enthusiastic hug. "That's wonderful! Lukie, I have to go into the office this afternoon but you'll help Jane move her stuff to my place, won't you?"

"That's fine," Jane said. "I don't have very much stuff. I can do it myself."

"Are you going to move it on the bus?" Luke said with a raised eyebrow.

"It's only clothes and a few personal items," she mumbled.

"Then it won't take very long for us to move you into

Amy's place," he said. "Finish your coffee and I'll drive you to your apartment so you can pack up the rest of your things."

"If you're sure," she said.

"Positive," he replied.

ℒ ℒ

"Morning," Amy said as she wandered into the kitchen. It was nearly eleven on Sunday morning and she laughed when Jane glanced at the clock. "I'm not really a morning person. How did you sleep?"

"Really well," Jane said. "The bed is very comfortable."

"Good. Feel free to make any changes to the bedroom and bathroom that you want. If you want a different paint colour or different furniture, go for it. You do you."

"Amy, thank you so much. I can't tell you how much I appreciate this."

"You're helping me out, remember?" Amy said as she poured herself a cup of coffee. She sat down and sipped at the coffee as Jane joined her.

"You have a lovely home," Jane said.

"Thanks," Amy replied. "Oh, and help yourself to whatever food you want. We'll figure out grocery splitting later. What are your plans for today?"

"I don't really have any," Jane said. She'd called the nursing home this morning but Mama J was still confused and apparently even more combative today. "How about you?"

"I'm pampering myself and getting my nails and hair done," Amy said. She eyed Jane's hair. "You should come with me."

"Oh, that's really nice of you but I think I'll pass."

Earlier this morning, she'd reworked her budget. Living with Amy meant she had more disposable income but she couldn't waste that income on things like getting her hair done. She didn't even really have to work at the club anymore but she wasn't going to quit. If it didn't work out living here, she would need that extra money. For now, she would put the money from the club into her savings account. A nest egg would come in handy in case things went sour.

"C'mon, it'll be fun," Amy said. "It's my treat."

"No, definitely not," Jane said. "You don't need to spend your money on me."

"Pfft," Amy said. "I've got more money than I know what to do with. I like spoiling my friends. Say yes, Jane."

"Amy, I…"

She trailed off, torn between her desire to do something fun and her shame at being a charity case. She'd never had a manicure in her life and the only reason her hair was so long was because she hadn't gone to a hair stylist in years.

"You know you want to," Amy wheedled. "Please?"

"Okay, if you're sure?" Jane said.

"I'm positive!" Amy said. She took another few sips of coffee before standing. I'm going to have a quick shower and then I'll text Manuel and tell him there will be two of us at the salon today.

She squeezed Jane's arm. "This will be fun. I promise."

෴ ෴

"Amy, I can't go with you," Jane protested.

"Sure you can. Besides, I don't have time to drop you off at home."

"There's a bus stop right there. Pull over and I'll take the bus home."

"It's freezing cold and you're not even wearing a hat and gloves," Amy said. "You'll turn into a popsicle waiting for the bus."

"I can't go to your family dinner," Jane said.

"Why not?"

"Because your parents aren't expecting me and it's a *family* dinner."

Amy turned right and drove down a tree-lined street with craftsman style houses. "We always have random people at the family dinners. My mom believes the more the merrier. Stop worrying, Jane. Besides, I want you to meet my mom. She's going to love you."

Jane thought that was an odd thing to say but she stayed quiet as Amy made a few more series of turns until she pulled into a driveway and shut off the car. Like the others in the neighbourhood, her parents' home was a craftsman style.

"Oh good. Luke's here already," Amy said. "I wanted to talk to him about some work stuff. You'll have to distract mom while I do. She has a strict "no work talk during family time" rule."

Jane's stomach twisted nervously and she self-consciously touched her hair. Manuel had taken one look at her hair and nearly fallen over in his hurry to get her into the salon chair. She had thought she'd only get it cut but both he and Amy had insisted on a colour as well. Even she could admit that the dark brown with red highlights was a much better look for her than her natural mousey-brown. Manuel had cut three inches from her hair, adding a few layers to frame her face, until it just brushed her shoulders. She loved how light and bouncy it felt but she was suddenly wondering if Luke would like it.

"Your hair looks great, Janie," Amy said as they climbed out of the car. "I still can't believe you've never had a manicure or pedicure before. It's one of life's greatest pleasures."

"I did enjoy it very much," Jane said as she followed Amy up the steps to the porch.

Amy opened the door and they stepped into the narrow hallway. They hung their coats in the closet as a blonde-haired woman popped into the hallway. Amy was the spitting image of her and she gave the woman a hard hug.

"Hi, Mom."

"Hi, honey. How was your day?"

"It was good. Mom, I'd like to introduce you to Jane. She's my new roommate. Jane, this is my mom, Clara."

"It's nice to meet you," Jane said as Clara shook her hand and gave her a warm smile.

"Lovely to meet you as well. How do you know Amy?"

"Oh, well, I…"

Jane trailed off as Clara gave her a curious look.

"She works at the company," Amy said.

"Wonderful. What do you do there, Jane?"

"She's Luke's PA," Amy said.

"Delightful," Clara said.

"Jane and I pampered ourselves this afternoon and I told her she should come for dinner," Amy said as she pulled off her boots.

"Of course! The more the merrier," Clara said. "Your father and brother are in the living room. Take Jane in there and I'll bring you both a cup of tea to warm you up. Do you like tea, Jane?"

"I do. Thank you," Jane said. She followed Amy to the living room, biting at her bottom lip. She wished she had worn something a little more flattering than jeans and a t-shirt. She smoothed her hand over her hair as they walked into the room. Luke was sitting on a small loveseat with a beer in his hand and he didn't look up from the football game he was watching on TV.

"Hi, Dad," Amy leaned down and kissed the cheek of the grey-haired man sitting in the recliner.

"Hi, honey."

"Dad, this is my friend and new roommate Jane. Jane, this is my dad Gary."

Amy's dad tore his gaze from the TV and smiled at her. "Hi, Jane. Nice to meet you."

"Nice to meet you too," Jane murmured.

"Lukie? What's wrong?" Amy asked.

She realized that Luke was staring at her and she could feel a hot blush rising in her cheeks when he studied her hair.

"Nothing," he said hoarsely. "Uh, hi, Jane."

"Hi, Luke," she said.

She started for the armchair that was in the corner. Amy brushed past her and plopped her curvy body into it before grinning at her. "There's a spot next to Luke, Janie."

Feeling more self-conscious than ever, Jane sat next to Luke. The loveseat was small and she smiled nervously at Luke when her arm brushed his.

"Sorry."

"It's fine," he muttered before shifting away. He stared at the TV and took another large swallow of beer as Amy watched them with bright interest.

"How was your day, Ames?" Her father asked.

"Good. Jane and I went to Manuel's and had pedicures and manicures. We also got our hair done. What do you think?" She smoothed her hand over her blonde hair.

Her father smiled at her. "You look great."

"Thanks. Janie got a cut and colour. It looks fantastic on her. Don't you think, Luke?"

He didn't reply and Jane stared at her lap as Amy said, "Luke? What do you think of Jane's hair?"

He cleared his throat and without looking away from the TV said, "It looks nice."

"Nice?" Amy rolled her eyes. "It looks amazing."

Jane pulled at a loose thread on her jeans. Obviously, Luke hated her hair but why did that bother her so much? What did she care if her boss liked her hair or not? Luke shifted again on the loveseat. He was nearly hanging over the arm at this point and she tried not to take it personally. Her boss was very kind to her and had helped her out when she really needed it. But that didn't mean he liked her or that they were even friends. In fact, keeping a strictly professional relationship with him was very important. She needed to keep her job. Mama J *needed* her to keep her job. It was time to toss her dumb crush on him out the damn window and definitely stop thinking about how he might look naked. That was only asking for trouble.

∂∾ ∾∾

Jane washed her hands and peered at herself in the mirror over the bathroom sink. She touched her hair, thrilled all over again at how soft and smooth it was, before leaving the bathroom.

It didn't matter that Luke didn't like her hair, she told herself. What mattered was that she liked it. It was ridiculous to even wonder if he liked it.

Lost in her thoughts, she nearly ran into the very man she couldn't stop thinking about. She caught herself before she smacked into his broad chest and smiled at him.

"Sorry, I was woolgathering."

"That's fine," he said. He stood in the middle of the hallway with his big body blocking her path as he stared again at her hair.

She touched the ends of her hair nervously. "So, your mom is a really great cook."

"She taught me everything I know," he said with a ghost of a smile.

She chewed on her bottom lip. Luke hadn't spoken two words to her all evening and despite sitting across from her at the table during dinner, he hadn't looked at her either.

"I'm sorry for intruding on your family dinner," she blurted out. "I told Amy I shouldn't come, but she insisted. It won't happen again."

He didn't reply. She stared at his chest in awkward silence. She was close enough to feel the heat radiating from his body and she stifled her urge to lean against him. She was always so cold. Luke could easily warm her up.

Yes, he could. In more ways than one, her mind whispered slyly. *Why don't you ask him to show you his childhood bedroom? A little slap and tickle would really warm you up.*

She shot that thought down with grim determination. God, what was wrong with her? Luke didn't like her. Hell, his behaviour tonight clearly indicated he didn't even want to be in the same room as her.

"I won't be in the office for the next couple of weeks," he said.

"I know," she replied.

"I'm on a business trip to Paris," he said.

"Yes, I remember," she said, trying not to smile. "I booked your flights and hotel for you."

"Right," he said. "We're thinking of going international with the clothing line and I'm meeting with a couple potential investors."

This time she couldn't stop the smile. "Yes, I typed the proposal for you."

"Right," he mumbled.

Luke was acting so strange. She had never seen him this flummoxed before and it was a little adorable. As a flush rose on his cheeks, she said, "Have you been to Paris before?"

He nodded. "A few times."

"Oh. Two weeks seems like a long business trip."

"I'm taking a week vacation, as well," he said. "Paris is one of my favourite places so…"

He trailed off and she smiled at him. "Good for you. It's been so busy lately that you deserve a holiday."

"Thanks," he said. "I'll email you any work stuff I need done. Mark will be covering for me while I'm gone but I will be available by email and text even when I'm on vacation."

"Okay."

He didn't say anything else and she gave him another

awkward smile before trying to scoot past him. His hand closed over her arm, sending a jolt of adrenaline through her veins.

"I like your hair," he said in a low voice.

"Thank you," she whispered as pleasure pooled in her belly.

He lifted his other hand and she stood frozen when he threaded his fingers through her hair. "It looks really pretty."

She couldn't reply. The heat of his hand on her arm and the gentle tug of his fingers in her hair had rendered her speechless. She stared at him as he stroked her hair.

"So soft," he murmured. His hand left her hair and cupped her face. He stroked her cheek with his thumb and said, "Your skin is like velvet. Did you know that, Jane?"

She shook her head and he groaned when his thumb brushed across her mouth. He bent his head until his mouth was hovering over hers.

"Luke, please," she whispered.

"Please what, Jane?"

"Please kiss - "

"There you two are! Dessert is ready and Mom...oh, oops."

Luke let go of her so quickly that she staggered on her feet. He cursed under his breath and grabbed her arm as Amy grinned at them.

"Sorry to interrupt your moment."

"You weren't interrupting a moment," Luke snapped. "I was just telling Jane that I would be gone from the office."

"Right," Amy said. "Well, dessert is ready. Unless you two have something else in mind for dessert? I can tell Mom there was a work emergency so you can slip out."

"Don't be ridiculous," Luke retorted as he dropped Jane's arm. He pushed past Amy and stalked down the hallway. When he was gone, Amy wiggled her eyebrows at

Jane.

"So, what's new?"

"Nothing," Jane said.

"Didn't look like nothing," Amy said.

"I – nothing happened," Jane said.

"Because I interrupted you?"

"No because he's my boss and it's very inappropriate," Jane said. She was stupidly close to tears.

"Oh, honey, I'm sorry," Amy said. "I didn't mean to upset you."

"You haven't," Jane said.

"We don't have to stay for dessert," Amy said.

Jane shook her head. "No, that's fine. I don't want to make you leave early."

"I don't mind," Amy said.

"It's fine, really," Jane said.

She followed Amy down the hall and toward the kitchen. Amy stopped abruptly in the doorway and Jane nearly ran into her back.

"Amy, what's wrong?"

"Nothing," she said.

Jane peered around her. Her old boss, Mark, was being hugged by Amy's mother and he studiously avoided looking at Amy as Clara said, "Sit down, Mark. You're just in time for dessert."

Mark sat next to Luke who was staring at the table. Awkward silence descended and Clara said, "Amy, honey, look who joined us."

"I see him," Amy said. Her sunny disposition had disappeared and she continued to stand in the doorway. "Hello, Mark."

"Hi, Amy," Mark replied.

Clara frowned at her. "Honey, what's wrong?"

"Nothing."

"Well, sit down and have dessert with us."

"I'm full," Amy said. "Jane, would you mind if we left? I have a headache."

She gave Jane an almost desperate look and Jane shook her head. "No, of course not. Thank you for dinner, Mrs. Dawson, it was delicious."

"You're welcome, dear. Amy, are you sure you can't stay?" Clara asked.

"Positive," Amy said. She crossed the kitchen and hugged her mother before pecking her father on the cheek. "Good night. Thank you for dinner."

"You're welcome, honey."

☙ ❧

"Amy? Do you want to talk about it?" Jane asked.

They had just arrived home. Amy was sullen and quiet the entire way home and Jane wasn't sure what to say or do.

"Talk about what?"

"Why you're angry with Mark," Jane said.

"I'm not," Amy said with a scowl.

"You seem angry with him."

"Well, I'm not," Amy repeated. "I'm tired and I think I'll have a hot bath and go to bed. Good night, Jane."

"Night, Amy. Thank you for today. I had a lot of fun."

Amy's face softened and she smiled at Jane. "Me too. Thanks for coming with me."

Chapter Nine

"Are you kidding me?" Jane sighed with exasperation. She was adding another pile of paper to Luke's desk and her elbow had bumped one of the others. The papers dropped to the floor and floated under his desk as she sighed again.

It was her own fault. She was a bundle of nerves this morning and almost jittery with excitement. Luke was back in the office this morning after being gone for two weeks. She pushed Luke's chair back, dropped to her knees and crawled under the massive desk. As she gathered the papers, she tried to tell herself she wasn't excited about seeing Luke again.

Neither her head nor her body believed her and another little vibration of excitement went down her spine. She had spoken to Luke by email almost every day the first week but she hadn't heard from him at all the second week. Not surprising considering he was on holiday but a small part of her had hoped he would email her. The second week was very quiet and what little work stuff that had come up, Mark was able to answer all of her questions. She couldn't even use work as an excuse to email Luke.

She picked up the last of the papers and clutched them to her chest. She shrieked and reared up when something brushed her foot. The back of her head hit the top of

Luke's desk with a meaty thud and she groaned as she was pulled out from under the desk. Her head was ringing and little dots of light were flashing in her vision as she squinted at Luke. He was sitting in his chair, his face a mask of surprise and confusion, and he hauled her to her knees before touching her head.

"What are you doing under my desk?"

"I dropped some papers," she mumbled. She touched the back of her head and winced as Luke muttered a curse.

"Are you okay?' He asked.

"I hit my head a little," she mumbled again.

"Let me see," he instructed.

"I'm fine." She grabbed the arms of Luke's chair, keeping her head bowed, and tried to stand. The room swayed and she dropped back to her knees as Luke grabbed at her arms.

"Jane!"

"I'm okay," she repeated. "I just need a minute."

"Let me see your head," he demanded. He cupped the back of her neck and pushed her head down before parting the strands of her hair. When his fingers brushed over the bump, she winced and grabbed his thighs, squeezing them as he touched the bump again.

"There's no blood," he said, "but you have one hell of a bump already. Do you feel faint?"

"No," she said. "Not anymore."

"Take a couple of deep breaths," he instructed.

She did what he asked, staring at his firm thighs in his dress slacks as he rubbed the back of her neck. After a few minutes, she said, "Better."

"Are you sure?"

"Yes."

"You probably have a concussion."

"I don't," she said.

She lifted her head and smiled up at him. "Uh, welcome back."

His fingers tightened on the back of her neck.

"What's wrong?" She asked.

He didn't reply. His gaze roamed over her face and she licked her lips nervously. His gaze immediately dropped to her mouth and lust soared to life in her veins. The look on his face was one of pure hunger and she looked away at the intensity of it. She blushed when she realized she was on her knees between his legs.

Don't look at his crotch, she told herself fiercely as she stared at his crotch. His hand tightened on the back of her neck and his chest heaved as he gulped in a sudden rush of oxygen.

"I'm sorry," she whispered. She tried to stand, her eyes widening when he wouldn't let her. She stared up at him, her mouth going dry at the look of desire on his face.

"No," he said hoarsely. "Stay right where you are, Ms. Smith."

His other hand reached up and for one moment she thought he was unbuckling his belt.

Yes! Her inner mind crowed. *"Suck on his cock, Jane! Give him a blowjob and maybe he'll eat your pussy in return.*

She blushed at the shameless dirtiness of her inner thoughts. Disappointment rushed through her when he didn't go near the waistband of his pants. Instead, he brushed his fingers across her cheek before dragging his thumb along her bottom lip.

Without stopping to think, she closed her lips around his thumb and sucked. His low groan set her nerves on fire and she slid her mouth up and down his thumb, swirling her tongue around the knuckle as she stared up at him.

His nostrils flaring, he cupped her neck and pulled her forward. "Fuck, Jane," he muttered. "I want your hot little mouth on my dick."

She was still squeezing his thighs and he inhaled sharply when she reached for his belt buckle.

"Welcome back, buddy. How was the vaca – whoa!"

Luke yanked his thumb from her mouth and stood.

He grabbed her arms and dragged her to her feet. She spun around and stared wide-eyed at Mark as he stood in the doorway with a look of surprise on his face.

"I didn't mean to interrupt," he said as the surprise was replaced with a cheeky grin. "I can come back later."

"No!" Luke said as Mark turned to go. "Jane was, uh…"

He trailed off and with her cheeks blazing red, Jane said, "I dropped some papers under his desk."

"Right. She dropped some papers," Luke said.

When Jane went to bend over to pick up the papers, he grabbed her arm and said, "I'll get them. Could you, uh, grab me a coffee?"

"Of course, Mr. Dawson," Jane said.

The back of her head aching and her entire face bright red, Jane hurried past Mark. She shut the doors behind her as Luke sank into his chair.

இ ஒ

Mark strolled to the desk and collapsed in one of the guest chairs. "Hey, Luke?"

"Yeah?"

"If you're going to ask your secretary to give you a 'welcome back to the office blow job', you really should lock your office doors."

"She wasn't giving me a blow job!" Luke snapped.

"Really? Because from where I was standing, that's exactly what it looked like. I don't blame you. Now that she's gained some weight, she's a cute little thing."

"Stay away from her!" Luke snarled at him and Mark held up his hands.

"Calm down, dude. I'm not interested in your PA."

Luke groaned and rubbed his hand across his jaw. "She wasn't giving me a blow job, Mark. She really did drop some papers. I scared her when I came into the office and she hit her head on the desk. I was checking to make sure she wasn't bleeding."

"I believe you," Mark said. "How was your vacation?"

"Fine," Luke said.

"Fine?" Mark arched his eyebrow at him. "That's it?"

"What do you want me to say?" Luke asked in exasperation.

"I don't know, maybe that you got your rocks off with some saucy French maid."

Luke rolled his eyes before swiveling in his chair to stare out the window. There was no way he was telling Mark that he spent most of his week off wishing he was home. More accurately, wishing he was in Jane's bed.

He groaned again and closed his eyes. What the fuck was wrong with him? He was unbelievably eager this morning to see Jane. The moment he caught sight of her, his dick had gone to half-mast immediately. In the last two weeks she had gained weight and her skin glowed. The dark circles under her eyes were gone as were the sharp points of her cheekbones. She looked well-rested and healthy and…

Sexy as hell.

The way her pretty lips had pursed around his thumb and the feel of her soft tongue licking his skin was so fucking sexy. When she reached for his belt buckle, he had nearly come in his goddamn pants.

"Luke?"

"What?"

"What's going on with you?"

"Nothing," he said before turning around again. He pulled himself flush against his desk to hide his stiffy and turned on his laptop.

"So, did you find a lovely French lady and butter her biscuit?"

"Don't be crude and no, I didn't."

"Because you want to butter your PA's biscuit?" Mark said with a grin.

"Enough, Mark," Luke said. "Aren't you even going to

ask how it went with the investors?"

"You sent me an email and told me they were being assholes and waffling on it." Mark gave him a strange look. "You don't remember that?"

"Yeah, sorry. I'm still a little jet-lagged."

"Is that all it is?"

"Yes," he snapped. "Are you going to get me caught up to date on the last week or grill me about my sex life?"

"Non-existent sex life," Mark said. "Okay, okay," he held up his hands again at the look on Luke's face, "we'll talk work."

ᵔᵔ ᵔᵔ

Jane stared at herself in the bathroom mirror. Her lips and cheeks were red and her hair was mussed up from where Luke had gripped it. She smoothed it down, wincing a little when she touched the bump on the back of her head.

"Calm down," she whispered. "Just calm down. You were not about to give your boss a blow job in his office."

Bullshit.

"I wasn't!" She said frantically.

"Wasn't what?"

She whirled around, staring wild-eyed at Amy as the woman entered the bathroom.

"Jane? What's wrong?"

"Your brother is back," she whispered.

"I know. I'm on my way to see him."

"Mark is with him," Jane said.

A grimace crossed Amy's face. "I'll go later. Tell me what's wrong with you?"

"I...oh my God, Amy."

"What?" Amy asked in bewilderment.

"I was in Luke's office and I dropped some papers under his desk. I crawled under his desk to get them and he didn't see me when he came in. He sat down at his desk and scared the crap out of me and I hit my head on the desk. I was on my knees and he was, uh, looking at my head to make sure I wasn't bleeding. Mark came in and it looked like I was – was…"

She trailed off as Amy stared at her.

"Like I was giving him a blowjob," she finally whispered.

Amy burst into peals of laughter and Jane scowled at her. "It isn't funny!"

"It's hilarious," Amy said as she laughed harder. "You can't see it because you're too close to the situation."

"Oh God," Jane said. "Mark thinks I'm a whore."

"Who cares what he thinks," Amy said scornfully.

Like always, whenever the subject of the CFO came up, Amy was immediately tense and moody.

"Hey, Amy? Is there something going on with you and Mark?" Jane asked.

"Of course not," Amy said. "Why would you think that?"

Jane shrugged. "I know the three of you grew up together but you don't seem to like him very much."

Amy paused. Her cheeks were reddening and for a moment it looked like she was going to cry.

"What's wrong?" Jane asked. She hurried over and patted Amy's arm. "Tell me what's wrong."

"Nothing," Amy said. "Mark and I used to be friends and now we're not."

"Why not?"

"Because he's an asshole," Amy snapped before wincing. "Sorry."

"It's okay. Do you want to talk about it?" Between her day job and her job at the club, she didn't see a lot of Amy but even the couple of weekends she'd spent with her was enough to see that Amy wasn't the carefree, loving hippie she pretended to be. There was something wrong, just lurking under the surface of her happy façade that Amy couldn't quite disguise no matter how hard she tried.

"Not really," Amy said. "I'm making lasagna tonight for supper. I'll put the leftovers in the fridge for you when you're done at the club, okay?"

"You don't have to make me dinner every night," Jane said.

"I don't mind and besides, you cook on the weekend so it evens out. Speaking of, I'm going for a girls' weekend with Valerie and Monique so I won't be around this weekend. You're on your own, okay?"

Jane nodded. "When are you leaving?"

"Friday night. Are you still planning on painting your bedroom?"

"I was thinking I might if you're sure you're okay with me changing the colour?"

"Of course I am. Besides, it could use a fresh coat of paint so you're doing me a favour. Leave me the receipt and I'll pay you for the paint and the supplies."

"Absolutely not," Jane said. "I want to change the colour so I'll pay for it."

"Nope," Amy said. "It's on me."

"Everything's on you," Jane said.

Amy grinned at her. "It's why I make such an awesome roommate. Now, we both better get back to work. I know you and Luke are hot for each other but now that he's back from Paris try not to engage in any sexual shenanigans at the office."

"I'm not – we're not – I mean, there's nothing going on between us," Jane sputtered.

Amy grinned at her. "You know there isn't an actual rule here about coworkers boinking right? Technically, you can't be fired for any...sexual shenanigans you engage in."

"He's my boss!" Jane squeaked out as her face turned a fiery red.

"I know and normally I would caution against sleeping with your boss but there's something between you and Luke that's worth exploring. I've never seen him act this way before."

Despite her embarrassment, Jane couldn't resist asking, "What way?"

Amy shrugged. "So thoughtful and, caring, I guess is the word. My brother is usually pretty aloof. Even with the women he's been in actual relationships with."

Jane didn't know what to say to that so she stared at the floor as Amy squeezed her arm. "Give it a chance, why don't you, Jane?"

"Because sleeping with the boss is a mistake," Jane said.

"Are you speaking from experience?" Amy asked.

The bathroom door opened and a blonde woman gave them a curious look before slipping past them into the closest stall.

"I'd better get back to my desk," Jane said.

"Me too," Amy said. "I'll see you later."

∽ ∾

"Welcome back, Lukie."

Luke looked up from his computer as Amy walked into his office. She shut the doors and kissed his cheek before sitting down.

"Thanks, Amy."

"You look tired."

"Still a little jet lagged," he replied. He glanced at his watch. It was almost twelve-thirty and he was starving. He was reaching for the phone to ask Jane to order him lunch when there was a soft knock on the door and it opened. Jane, her cheeks red and the scent of snow clinging to her, carried in a large brown paper bag and set it on the desk.

"I ordered you lunch," she said.

"Thank you," he replied. He avoided looking at her and she did the same before giving Amy a brief smile and leaving the room.

"Well, that was awkward as hell," Amy said.

Luke frowned at her. "No, it wasn't."

"Whatever, big brother."

He leaned back in his chair and cleared his throat. "How is it, uh, going, living with Jane?"

"Really good," Amy said. "She's a real sweetheart and the perfect roommate."

"Are you two becoming, um, friends?" Luke asked casually.

"I think so," Amy said. "I don't actually see that much of her during the week. She usually goes from here to visit her foster mother and then goes to the club."

"The club?"

"Yes. She has a second job waitressing at some club on the west side. You didn't know that?"

"No."

She works there Monday to Thursday. She doesn't get home until after two usually."

"What?" Luke stared at her and Amy nodded again.

"I know, right? I don't know how she does it. I told her she could drive to the office with me in the morning so she doesn't have to take the bus anymore, but that still only gives her like four hours of sleep. I'd be a friggin' zombie. Anyway, we've been spending some time together on the weekends, when she's not at the care home with her foster mom, and I really like her, Luke. She's sweet and thoughtful. I've made her come to family dinner for the past two weekends and Mom and Dad like her too. Heck, I think Mom already considers her family. She clucks over her like a mother hen."

Amy suddenly laughed. "She made this giant casserole and sent it home with us because she thought Jane was too thin. We've been eating it for lunches for the past week."

"She looks like she's gained weight," Luke said.

"Yep, she has. Thank God. I was worried about her when she first moved in but a couple of weeks with a steady supply of groceries has done wonders. She looks so good now. Don't you think?"

Luke gave his sister a suspicious look before shrugging. "I hadn't really noticed."

"Bullshit," Amy said. "You couldn't keep your eyes off her ass when she was leaving your office a few minutes ago."

"Keep your voice down," Luke said. "What club does she work at?"

"I have no idea. She's weirdly vague about it."

"She shouldn't be out alone that late at night," Luke said.

"I offered to loan her the cash to buy a car but she refused," Amy said. "She said a bus pass is cheaper than gas and insurance. Maybe you should give her a raise."

Luke didn't reply and Amy picked at her bright pink thumbnail before smiling at him. "I'm glad you're home, Lukie."

"Thanks, Ames. I am too."

"Meet anyone interesting?"

"The investors were – "

"I'm not talking about the investors," Amy interrupted. "Did you meet any girls?"

Luke rolled his eyes. "We're not teenagers, Amy."

"Don't I know it. Did you meet anyone?"

"No. Why would I? I'm not looking to settle down and besides, a long-distance relationship never works."

"They don't," Amy agreed. "Which is why it's nice that you have a lovely, sweet woman just twenty feet away."

"I'm sure I have no idea what you're talking about," Luke said. He opened the bag and pulled out the sandwich and soup. Jane had ordered his favourite and he took the lid off the soup. "Is that it, Amy?"

"Almost," she said. "Are you going to family dinner this weekend?"

"Yes," he said before spooning soup into his mouth. "Are you?"

"No. I'm flying out for a girls' weekend on Friday

night."

"Oh." He tried to hide his disappointment. If Amy brought Jane to dinner at his parents', he'd have a perfectly valid excuse to be near her.

"Which is why I was hoping you would pick Jane up for dinner," Amy continued. "Don't let her tell you no, okay? Mom already told her she was welcome to come to dinner without me."

"Uh, sure, I can do that. No problem," Luke said.

"What are your plans for the weekend?" Amy asked.

"I don't know, why?"

"Well, Jane is painting her room on Friday night and I thought it would be nice if you went over and helped her."

Luke frowned at her. "Why would I do that? She's my assistant, not my friend."

"Just thought I'd throw it out there," Amy said innocently as she stood. "I've got some casserole with my name on it to heat up. Bye, Lukie."

"We need to talk about my Paris trip," he said.

She rolled her eyes and collapsed back in the chair. "You've got five minutes."

"I won't need five minutes," he said. "It was a bust. Neither Pierre or Julien would give me a firm yes on investing in the company. They like your designs, they're impressed with our distribution strategy but they think our digital storefront in a word - sucks."

Amy frowned. "It can't be that bad. We sell plenty of clothes online."

Luke shrugged. "Honestly, it's not that great. I think if we want international investors, we need to upgrade our digital presence. We could hire an in-house team that's dedicated to maintaining and marketing our digital channel."

"Fine with me," Amy said breezily.

Luke smiled a little. "We need to convince Mark it's worth the extra money. If you can meet with him and - "

"Nope," Amy said. "You meet with him. You have

more influence over him than I do, anyway."

"Bullshit," Luke said. "You've got him wrapped around your finger, Amy. You have since we were kids. He thinks of you as his baby sister and he - "

"I'm not his sister!" Amy snapped.

Luke blinked at her. "We grew up together. You're as much a sister to him as you are to me. Why are you pissed about that?"

"I'm not," she said.

"Okay," Luke said after a moment, "so, you meet with Mark and convince him to find money in the budget for an upgrade and I'll - "

"No," Amy said again before standing. "I've told you before, I don't want anything to do with the business side." She winked and smiled at him but both looked forced. "I just want to make pretty things, remember?"

"Amy, I'm really busy. It would help if you could meet with Mark."

"I said no," she retorted. "Either convince Mark yourself that this is a good idea or fire him and hire a CFO who does think it's a good idea."

Luke's mouth dropped open. "Ames," he said cautiously, "what the hell is going on with you? You want me to fire Mark?"

She sighed and rubbed at the back of her neck. "No, of course not. I'm just tired today. Let me know what you and Mark decide, okay?"

She reached across his desk and squeezed his hand before leaving the office.

ॐ ॐ

Jane added a final strip of painters' tape to the baseboard before standing and surveying her work. It was almost seven and she debated whether to start painting tonight or leave it for the morning.

She wandered out of the bedroom and down the stairs

to the kitchen. She poured herself a glass of water and grabbed some crackers to munch on. Even after three weeks of living with Amy, she couldn't get over her delight at always having food to eat. She suddenly smiled. She'd stopped to see Mama J after work and after nearly a week and a half of confusion, her foster mom was alert and actually knew who she was. She had exclaimed repeatedly about how good Jane looked and they had a good visit before Mama J started to tire.

She smiled again and drank some water. It was so good to have the old Mama J back. She was starting to worry that this was it, that the Mama J she knew and loved was gone forever. To have her back made her nearly giddy with happiness.

She grabbed some cheese from the fridge and cut a few slices to add to her crackers. She needed to feel happy right now. The last five days at work with Luke were nearly agonizing in their awkwardness. Every time she looked at him, she would remember the way he had stared at her, the low rasp of his voice when he said he wanted his dick in her mouth.

A little shudder of pleasure went through her belly and she scowled. God, she had to stop thinking about it. Luke was as uncomfortable and awkward around her– if not more – as she was around him. It wasn't until yesterday afternoon that he'd really looked at her for more than a few seconds.

She finished her food and drank the rest of her water before washing her hands. It wasn't that late. She'd try and get the first coat of paint on tonight and finish the rest in the morning before she visited Mama J.

She put her glass in the dishwasher, jumping a little when the doorbell rang. She walked to the front door and peered through the peephole. Her mouth dropped open and she pulled self-consciously at her t-shirt and yoga pants before opening the door.

"Hi, Luke."

"Hi, Jane."

"Um, Amy isn't here."

"I know. Can I come in?" He asked.

"Oh, of course," she said. He stepped inside and shut the door before taking off his jacket. He was wearing a t-shirt and worn jeans and she tried not to drool at the way his shirt clung to his broad chest.

"I'm here to help, " he said.

"Help with what?" She asked in confusion.

"Painting. Amy mentioned you were painting your room and asked me to help."

"Oh, well that's really nice of you but I can't ask you to give up your Friday night to help me paint."

He took his boots off and hung his jacket on the hook. "I don't mind."

"I'm sure you have better things to do," she said.

"Nope," he replied. He squeezed past her and started down the hall to the stairs. She stayed where she was and he glanced at her over his shoulder. "Ready to paint?"

"Um, yes, okay," she said before following him up the stairs.

She tried not to blush when they were standing in her room together. There was no need for it to be weird. Her bed was covered in furniture and pictures – it wasn't like they were going to start having sex or something.

She blushed at the thought and Luke gave her an odd look. "Are you okay?"

"Yes," she said. "I, uh, I finished taping."

"Looks good," he said. "Do you prefer to cut in or roll?"

"It doesn't matter," she said. "Honestly, I'm probably not great at either."

"Well, I happen to be an expert at cutting in," he said with a small grin, "so I'll do that. Okay?"

"Okay."

She watched as he pried open the paint can and stirred it before grabbing a brush and carrying it and the paint can to the step-ladder. He climbed the ladder and placed the paint can on the top of it before dipping the brush into it.

As he swiped the brush along the ceiling, she opened the second can and stirred the paint before pouring it into the tray and grabbing the roller. She began to roll the opposite wall, as Luke said, "I like the colour."

"Thank you," she said. There were a few moments of silence and feeling awkward, she said, "So, I never got the chance to ask how your holiday was."

"It was good," he replied. "I love Paris."

"Someday I'll go there," she said.

"You should," he replied. "It has amazing architecture and history."

"Do you travel a lot?" She asked.

He considered her question for a moment before nodding. "More than the average person, I think. How about you?"

"No. I've never been out of the state."

"You didn't travel with your parents before…"

He trailed off and she shook her head. "No, not really. We didn't have a lot of money for travelling."

"We didn't either," he said. "It's probably why both Amy and I like to travel so much now."

"I really want to go to Ireland," she said.

"I went there a few years ago," he replied. "It's worth a visit."

"I read online that you can stay in an actual castle," she said as she rolled more paint onto the wall. "How cool would it be to sleep in a castle?"

"Very cool," he said with a small grin.

She laughed. "You've slept in a castle in Ireland, haven't you?"

"Guilty," he said.

"Well, it's definitely on my bucket list," she said. "Some day I'll save enough money to make the trip."

"I was thinking I would give you a raise," he said.

She blinked at the rapid change in topic. "I'm sorry?"

"A raise," he repeated.

"For what? My job duties haven't changed."

He laughed. "Are you really trying to talk me out of giving you a raise?"

She flushed. "I don't want a raise that I don't deserve."

"You deserve it," he said. "I'll talk to HR on Monday about it."

"Well, thank you," she said.

"You're welcome. How is your foster mom doing?"

For a moment, she wondered if she was dreaming. Luke was being so friendly and downright chatty and she'd never seen this side of him before.

"Jane?" He prompted.

"She's good. She had a bad week but I visited her tonight and she was very alert."

"That's good," he said.

"I was starting to," she paused and he gave her an encouraging look, "I was starting to be afraid that she was lost forever. This was the longest stretch she's gone with being this confused."

"I'm sorry," he said. "That must be really difficult for – shit!"

He had knocked the paint can with his arm and she watched in horror as it tipped over and spilled down the front of his shirt. He grabbed at the can, light blue paint coating his arms and hands and spilling onto the drop cloth on the floor as he uttered another string of curses. He finally righted the paint can and dropped the brush on the floor as he jumped off the step-ladder.

Jane hurried forward, trying not to laugh as she stared at the paint soaking through his shirt.

"Fuck!" He said.

"Bend over," she said.

He bent obediently, more paint dripping from his shirt to the floor, and she reached over him and grabbed the back of his shirt. She pulled it over his head and dropped it to the floor with a wet plop.

He straightened and stared at the paint on the drop cloth. "Christ, what a mess."

She giggled as he held his paint-covered hands out in front of him. He gave her a mock scowl and she laughed harder. "It's just paint. A little soap and water and you'll be good as new."

"I look like a Smurf."

"Yeah, you do," she giggled.

He arched an eyebrow at her. "Be careful or I'll share."

"You wouldn't dare," she said as he took a step toward her.

"Wouldn't I?" He said with a wicked grin.

She started to back away. His grin widened and he quickly wiped his hand across her flat abdomen. She stared at the smear of paint.

"Jerk!"

He laughed and smeared more paint on the thigh of her yoga pants. She suddenly bent and dipped both hands in the pool of paint on the drop cloth before slapping her hands against his flat abdomen.

He growled at her, an honest-to-god growl that sent a little shiver down her back, before grabbing her around the waist and yanking her toward him. She stumbled over his paint-sodden shirt and fell against his hard chest as he wiped more smears of paint across the back of her t-shirt.

She laughed and squirmed against him. "Stop!"

"It's just paint," he said. "A little soap and water and you'll be good as new."

"Hey!" She squealed when he spread paint in a line across first her right cheek and then her left before making one on her forehead.

"Now you're an extra in *Braveheart*," he said.

She laughed and pushed at his chest, leaving more paint smeared across his skin. "I look terrible in a kilt."

She was still pressed against his body and he studied her mouth. Suddenly nervous, she bit at her bottom lip and watched as the playful look in his eyes was replaced with desire.

"Luke," she whispered.

"Ms. Smith," he rasped before bending his head and kissing her. She clutched at his broad shoulders as he traced her lips with his tongue.

"Open," he murmured against her mouth.

She parted her lips and he dipped his tongue between them, touching her teeth delicately before sliding past them to explore and taste. She moaned and returned his kiss. Her fingers dug into his warm skin as his big hand moved to her ass and squeezed it.

She rubbed her belly against the hardness she could feel pressing against it and he groaned harshly, his hand tightening on her ass. His other hand cupped her breast and she arched her back as he rubbed his thumb over her hardening nipple.

He kissed her throat before nipping it. She jerked against him and he licked his way to her ear and sucked on her earlobe.

"I want you so much, Jane," he whispered.

"I want you too," she gasped. She traced the dark hair on his chest as he squeezed her ass again and trailed kisses across the line of her jaw.

He slid his hand under her shirt and pulled the cup of her bra down. She cried out when he pulled on her nipple before teasing it with the pad of his thumb. He kissed her again, sucking roughly on her bottom lip before licking it with his warm tongue.

"Please, Luke," she moaned.

"I want to fuck you, Ms. Smith," he whispered into her ear.

She moaned again. Her panties were soaking wet and she couldn't stop rubbing her lower body against him.

"I want to find out how tight your little pussy is," he breathed. "I want to know what you look like coming all over my dick."

"Oh God," she moaned.

"Do you want that too?" He pinched her nipple and she arched her back again before nodding frantically.

"Yes. God, yes!"

"Good," he said. "Let's go to the shower and – "

"Well, that's the shortest girls' weekend of my life. Wait four friggin' hours in the airport just to have our flight cancelled because there's a blizzard two states over that's headed our – holy shit!"

Luke tore away from her so quickly that she nearly fell. He cursed and kept her upright with one hand on her elbow. Her face flaming, Jane turned around and readjusted her bra before taking a deep breath and turning back.

"Um, hi, Amy."

"Hey, you two," Amy said with a cheerful grin. "I'd ask how painting is going but from the looks of it – not so great. You guys know that the paint is supposed to go on the walls, not on your bodies, right?"

"I spilled the paint," Luke said. His face was red and he stared self-consciously at the smears of paint on his bare upper body as Amy leaned against the doorway. "What are you doing here? Aren't you supposed to be on a plane?"

"I am but it was cancelled due to poor weather," Amy said. She studied the both of them. "I'm so sorry I interrupted your painting. I'll head to my room and leave you two alone."

"No!" Jane and Luke both shouted.

Luke cleared his throat. "Uh, no, that's fine. I'll clean this mess up and then head home. I'll come back in the morning and help you finish, Jane."

"That's okay," Jane said as she stared at the floor. "I can clean it up myself and it won't take me long to finish tomorrow."

"No," Luke protested. "I made the mess, I'll clean it up."

"It's fine, really," Jane said. "Thank you but it's

probably, uh, better if you go home now."

"Nonsense," Amy said. "I was thinking of heading to a movie anyway."

"It's fine," Luke said. "Jane's right. I should get home and shower."

"You can shower here," Amy said.

Luke glared at her and she smiled sweetly at him. "You don't want to get paint on your car, Lukie."

"I'll risk it," he muttered. "Bye, Jane. I'm sorry I made such a mess."

"It's fine, really. Bye, Luke."

Without looking at either of them and leaving his shirt on the floor, Luke brushed past Amy. They stood silently until they heard the front door slam. Jane cleared her throat. "Well, I'd better get this cleaned up."

"I'm so sorry, Janie," Amy said. "I feel awful."

"For what?" Jane said. "You didn't do anything."

"Like hell I didn't. You and my brother were about to get busy and I ruined the whole mood."

"We weren't," Jane protested. "We were trying to, uh, clean up the paint mess."

"With your mouths?" Amy said.

"You didn't see what you thought you saw," Jane said. "We weren't doing anything."

Amy snorted laughter before grabbing Jane's arms. She steered her across the room, skirting around the puddle of paint, and stood Jane in front of the mirror mounted on the back of the door.

"This," she pointed to the blue handprint on Jane's right breast before spinning her around and pointing to the handprint on her ass, "and this looks like you were doing something. Unless you like grabbing your own boob and butt for fun?"

Jane turned scarlet before slapping herself in the forehead. "Oh, God. I'm an idiot."

"You're not," Amy said. "I keep telling you there's something between you and Luke. Hell, the sexual tension practically seeps from both your pores whenever you're in the same room together."

Jane sighed. "I keep telling you it's a bad idea."

"Yeah, I know. But for what it's worth, I think you should just go for it."

"I know you do," Jane said. "Listen, I'd better get this cleaned up before the paint seeps through the drop cloth."

"I'll help," Amy said. "Just let me change."

"You don't have to help."

"I know," she said. "I want to. Give me two minutes."

Chapter Ten

"Janie, did you know you have blue paint in your hair?" Mama J asked as Janie wheeled her down the hallway.

Jane laughed. "Yes. I was painting my room this morning."

"You're painting your room?" Mama J gave her a look of alarm as Jane wheeled her into her room. "But I loved the colour of your room. There was nothing wrong with it!"

Her voice was rising and Jane rubbed her arm soothingly. "Not at your house, Mama J. Remember, I don't live there anymore."

Mama J frowned before nodding slowly. "Right. We don't have a home anymore."

Tears spilled down her wrinkled cheeks and Janie squatted next to the wheelchair and took her hand. "Don't cry. We have each other, that's all that matters."

"You're a good girl, Janie," Mama J said before stroking her hair. "Your hair looks very pretty, even with the blue."

"Thank you," Jane said. "Are you ready for bed now?"

"I am. Will you read to me for a while?"

"Of course I will," Jane said. She helped Mama J change into her pajamas before tucking her into the bed. She sat on the side of it and reached for the book.

"Janie?"

"Yes?"

"Are you happy?"

"Yes," Jane said. "I'm always happy when I'm with you."

Mama J smiled before closing her eyes. "You're such a good girl, Janie."

She began to snore almost immediately and Jane sat with her for a few minutes longer before leaning down and kissing her forehead. "I love you, Mama J. I'll see you tomorrow."

She was just leaving the care home when her cell phone rang.

"Hi, Amy."

"Hey, sweetie. Listen, you really need to consider getting a texting plan. No one calls anyone anymore. I can't be limited to texting you only twice a day. Things happen that I need to share."

Jane laughed. "What happened?"

"Actually, nothing. I called to see what time you would be home."

"I'm just leaving the care home," Jane said.

"How is Mama J?"

"She was good today," Jane said.

"Good. Someday I'd like to meet her," Amy said.

"I'd like that," Jane said.

"So, are you heading straight home?"

"Yes, where else would I go?"

"My brother's house," Amy said bluntly.

Jane sighed. "The only reason I would go there is to apologize for my inappropriate behaviour last night."

"Good idea. You really should pop by and apologize," Amy said. "Have fun apologizing, Janie. I won't wait up for you!"

"Amy, no, that isn't - "

Amy hung up and Jane sighed and stuck her cell phone in her pocket before walking to the bus station. Maybe she should go and apologize. It wasn't that late and she didn't have any other plans. She was planning on apologizing Monday morning but was work really the place to be saying sorry to her boss for molesting him?

No, it wasn't, she decided. It was best to get it out of the way. If she didn't apologize, if she tried to pretend that it had never happened, Luke might not give her a raise and she really could use the extra money.

Don't be stupid, Jane. He wouldn't do that.

He might. She didn't know him all that well, did she?

You know him well enough. Get your ass to Luke's house. Maybe offer him a blow job as an apology.

Not helping!

Her inner voice remained silent and she shoved her phone back into her pocket. She would stop by, apologize and leave. Easy peasy.

ॐ ॐ

Nearly an hour later, she was standing on the doorstep of Luke's home and cursing her decision. This was a very bad idea but there wouldn't be another bus for half an hour and she was already freezing her ass off. She had bought a thicker coat last week at the thrift store as well as a hat, scarf and mittens but the wind was bitterly cold and her entire body was numb. She took a deep breath and shivering, rang the doorbell.

She waited a few minutes and was about to ring it a second time when the door opened. Luke was wearing a t-shirt and pair of shorts and he stared at her in surprise. Just the sight of him sent her desire into overdrive and she tried to think past the lust-induced cloudiness in her brain.

"Uh, hi, Luke. Can I - "

She squealed in surprise when Luke grabbed her arm and yanked her into the house. He pushed her up against the wall and kissed her as he fumbled at the zipper of her jacket.

"Luke, wait," she gasped as he pulled down the zipper and tugged her jacket off. It took her mittens with it and he muttered a curse when she touched his back.

"Your hands are freezing," he grumbled as he pulled off her hat and dropped it to the floor.

"Luke!" She clutched at him when he picked her up and carried her down the hallway. "What are you doing?"

"Taking you to my bedroom," he said.

"I – that's not why I'm here," she said as he wrestled her boots off with one hand and left them at the foot of the stairs.

"Why are you here?" He licked her collarbone and she jerked against him.

"I came to apologize for last night," she said as he carried her into his bedroom.

"You could have just called," he said.

"I thought you deserved an apology in person."

"Is that really why you're here?" He asked as he set her on her feet. "Or did you come here to finish what we started last night?"

She stared wide-eyed at him as he unbuttoned her shirt and shoved it down her arms. "Well, Ms. Smith? Do you want to apologize or do you want to be fucked?"

He flicked open her bra and pulled it off her body before cupping her breasts and kneading them lightly. "Which is it?"

"The second one," she whispered.

"Say it," he demanded as he reached for the button on her jeans.

"I want to be fucked," she said in a low voice.

He paused with his fingers on her zipper and said, "Try again please, Ms. Smith."

"I – I want you to fuck me, Mr. Dawson."

He kissed her, then whispered, "I want that too, little Jane."

"We really shouldn't," she said. "You're my boss."

"I won't tell anyone if you don't," he said before

tugging her jeans down her legs. He lifted her and placed her on the bed before pulling her jeans off and dropping them to the floor. He stripped off his t-shirt and shorts and she stared at his erect cock as he lay on his side next to her. He was big. Maybe even a little worrisome big. She ignored her sudden trepidation. It would be fine. Luke wouldn't hurt her.

"Please," she whispered. She was already soaking wet and she wanted his too-big cock with a desperation that embarrassed her.

"Patience, Ms. Smith."

He kissed her again, tasting and teasing her mouth with slow licks as she moaned and dug her fingers into the sheets. He licked her upper lip before kissing his way down her chest. He studied her small breasts and she could feel herself flushing self-consciously. She wished suddenly that she'd had the money for implants. Jeremy's words echoed in her head and she tried to cross her arms over her breasts. Luke grunted in disapproval before pinning her arms above her head with one large hand.

"I love your breasts," he said. "You have the prettiest nipples. Are they sensitive, Jane?"

He stared at her as she stammered, "I – I think so."

"You think so? Let's find out," he said with a small grin.

She cried out when he licked the right one before sucking it into his mouth. He teased it with his teeth and tongue as she arched upward.

"Very sensitive," he murmured appreciatively.

He sucked on her left nipple then flicked at it with his tongue as she rocked her hips against him. When both of her nipples were taut and throbbing, he traced his tongue along her collarbone. She moaned and squeezed his biceps, panting harshly when she felt his warm tongue dip into the hollow of her throat.

His hand cupped her pussy through her panties and she bucked upward, her fingers digging into his flesh.

"Jane," he said hoarsely, "you're so wet. I don't think I can wait any longer."

"I know I can't," she said. "Please, Luke."

She lifted her hips in a silent plea and he pulled off her panties and dropped them over the side of the bed. He cupped her pussy again, his fingers gliding across her wet lips before he rubbed delicately at her clit.

"Oh God!" She grabbed his arm and arched her back. "Please don't tease."

He rubbed her clit with firm, fast strokes and she writhed against the bed as tension coiled in her belly. She was embarrassed at how close she was already but Luke seemed to know exactly how to touch her.

One thick finger slid into her and the combination of his finger and the way his thumb rubbed against her clit, threw her over the edge. She arched into his touch and tried not to scream as the pleasure flowed through her.

"You look so beautiful when you come," Luke murmured into her ear when she'd finally collapsed against the bed.

His earlier need to hurry seemed to have disappeared and he propped his head up in his hand as he lay on his side next to her. He explored her trembling body with the tips of his fingers, circling around each of her nipples before tracing her ribs. He touched the small triangle of curls at the top of her pussy and made feather light brushes against her hips.

"Luke," she whispered, "I want to – I mean, it's your turn."

Her gaze dropped to his erect cock. The tip of it was rubbing against her hip and she must have had apprehension on her face because Luke's roving fingers stilled next to her belly button.

"What's wrong, Jane?"

"You're very big," she said.

An odd look came over his face and she said hurriedly, "I'm a little nervous. I'm sure it will be fine. I'm really wet so, you know…"

She trailed off as a hot blush lit her face and chest on fire. Oh my God, could she be any more awkward?

He still wasn't saying anything. Anxious to make up for her stupid comment, she wrapped her hand around his cock and stroked him firmly. He groaned and immediately pulled her hand away.

"Luke? Did I do something wrong?" She was making a complete fool of herself.

"No," he said. "I'll come all over your hand if you keep doing that."

"Oh," she said. She tried to act casual but secretly she was thrilled. Did he really want her that much?

"I had a sex dream about you," he said.

"You did?"

"Yes."

He didn't say anything else and she traced her fingers over his broad shoulder. "I had one about you too."

He sat up and opened the nightstand drawer. She watched as he opened the condom package and rolled the condom over his dick before returning to his side next to her.

"Will you tell me about your dream?" She whispered.

"Tell me about yours first," he said.

"It was the day I fell asleep on the couch in your office. I dreamt that we were in a room together and you had all this food for me on a table. It was all my favourite foods and I was so hungry. You said I could eat as much as I wanted but I had to give you a kiss first as a thank you."

She blushed softly. "It's why I kissed you when I woke up. I – I thought I was still dreaming and I was really hungry and wanted the food."

He laughed and she could have slapped herself in the head. "I also really wanted to kiss you too, though."

"I wanted to kiss you as well," he said. He nuzzled her neck and she lifted her head so he could press a kiss against her soft skin.

"Tell me about yours," she said.

He paused before leaning over her and sucking at her nipple. She moaned as desire and need blossomed in her belly again.

"It's not sweet like your dream," he said before nipping at the soft underside of her breast.

She jerked and clutched at his head. "T-that's okay. Tell me."

His hand circled her belly button again before moving lower. "You needed a place to stay. I brought you to my house – to my bedroom - and told you that you had new job duties."

His fingers tugged at her curls before slipping lower. She spread her thighs and moaned when his fingers brushed against her clit. "Wh-what were they?"

"Taking my cock into your tight pussy," he whispered into her ear as his finger slid into her throbbing core.

"Oh God," she whispered.

He eased a second finger into her. "In the dream, you said it was too big and that you couldn't take all of it."

He gently stretched her pussy with his fingers as he kissed the curve of her ear. She arched her hips upward before moaning, "What did you say?"

"I told you to be a good girl and take all of my cock."

She shuddered all over and for a moment she thought she might climax again from just Luke's hot words and the pressure of his fingers in her pussy.

"Was I a – a good girl?" She asked.

"Yes," he whispered before pushing his fingers deeper.

"Oh God! Please," she moaned.

"Do you want to be my good girl again, Ms. Smith?" He sucked on her earlobe.

"I do," she said eagerly.

"Say it," he murmured before biting gently on her lobe.

"I want to be your good girl," she said. Inspiration struck her and she clutched at his thick forearm. "I want to be your good girl, Mr. Dawson."

He groaned and she could feel his hips jerking against the bed. He pulled his fingers out and she made an embarrassingly loud whine of protest.

"Spread your legs wide," he rasped as he moved between her thighs.

She did what he asked, gripping his biceps when he guided his cock to her entrance. A small trickle of apprehension returned and her hands tightened around him. He stopped immediately and gave her a look of reassurance.

"I'll go slow, sweet Jane."

She nodded and he watched her face as he pushed in slowly.

"Christ, you're so tight," he muttered. "Am I hurting you?"

"No," she reassured him.

He pushed a little deeper. Her walls stretched to accommodate his width and she reminded herself to breathe as he pushed steadily forward. When he was fully sheathed, she felt stuffed full of his cock.

"Don't move yet, okay?" She said.

"Trust me," he muttered, "if I move right now, I'm going to seriously embarrass myself."

That made her giggle and he groaned a curse. "Don't squeeze like that."

"I'm sorry," she said.

He took a few deep breaths before propping himself up on his hands. "Are you good?"

"Yes," she whispered.

"Thank God," he said almost to himself.

As he began a slow slide and retreat, Jane braced her feet on the bed and slipped her hands around his narrow waist. She met each of his strokes with a thrust of her hips and he made a low groan. "You feel so good, Jane."

He started to move harder and faster and she bit her bottom lip as every nerve ending lit up with a crackling snap. Her fingers dug into his hard flesh as he pressed his mouth against her ear.

"I want you to come on my cock. Do you need your clit rubbed?"

She shook her head, unable to catch her breath long enough to form words. The thickness of his cock, the grind of his pelvis against her clit with every down stroke was more than enough to make her come.

She clamped her legs around his hips as her orgasm began a slow build in her belly. He was pounding her into the mattress now, making her small cries of pleasure cut out with every thrust. Her entire body trembled and then suddenly stiffened as she arched beneath him and her pussy clamped around his cock. Her climax shook her body and she clung to Luke as his long strokes turned short and erratic.

He made a hoarse shout, slamming into her and pinning her against the bed as his head fell back. He ground his pelvis against hers and shuddered wildly. She watched as a look of bliss crossed his face before he pressed his body against hers and buried his face in her neck. She stroked his back and kissed his shoulder as his hot breath washed over her throat.

After a moment, he rolled off of her. He disposed of the condom and then collapsed on his back before yawning.

"Should I go?" Jane asked.

He turned on his side and scowled at her. "No. You're staying the night."

"I can go," Jane said. "I'm not expecting - "

He made a loud grunt of displeasure before tugging her into his arms. She rested her head on his chest, listening to the steady thud of his heart beneath her ear. His big hand rubbed her back in slow circles.

"Go to sleep, Jane," he said before yawning again.

"Good night, Luke."

He muttered a goodnight in return and within seconds his hand had stopped circling her back and his breathing was deep and even. She continued to listen to the beat of his heart as contentment washed over her. It was so nice to be with someone again, so nice to have a warm body to sleep against and a –

Don't Jane. Don't start thinking that way. He's your boss not your boyfriend. In the morning, you tell him this was great but you can't do this again. Remember what happened the last time you dated your boss.

Cold tendrils of fear licked at the base of her spine. Her inner voice was right. She had to stop sleeping with Luke. It was dangerous and stupid of her. In the morning, she would tell him this was a one-time thing and he'd be fine with that. What guy didn't like to sleep with a girl with no strings attached?

In the morning, all this would end and she'd be alone in her bed but for now she would take advantage of the situation and snuggle her ass off. She curled in closer to Luke, putting her arm around his trim waist and kissing his broad chest. His hand moved to her hip and squeezed lightly.

"S'okay?" He muttered.

"Yes," she whispered. "Go to sleep, Luke."

∂৵ ৵৹

He woke up to an empty bed. Trying not to be frustrated, he used the bathroom, brushed his teeth and yanked on a pair of shorts before walking downstairs. He was surprised at his level of disappointment. He couldn't keep sleeping with Jane and he'd planned on telling her that this morning, so why was he wishing that she hadn't left?

He wandered into the kitchen and made an embarrassingly girlish scream when he saw Jane. She was sitting at the island and she immediately jumped up and gave him a look of chagrin.

"I'm sorry, I didn't mean to scare you."

"You didn't," he said as he placed his hand over his thudding heart.

She stared disbelievingly at him and he couldn't help but grin. "Was it the screaming that gave it away?"

She smiled and sank back into her chair but knotted her hands together nervously. "It might have been. I made coffee. I hope you don't mind."

"Not at all," he said. He poured himself a cup and brought it to the island. Jane was staring at the top of it and didn't look up when he slid onto the stool next to her.

"How did you sleep?" He asked.

"Good," she said, "really good."

"Did you? You look tired," he replied.

She grimaced and he could have kicked himself. "Sorry, I didn't mean – that is, you look fine."

"Thanks," she said.

There were a few minutes of excruciating awkwardness. It was time to tell Jane that as much as he enjoyed their night together, they obviously couldn't do it again. So, why couldn't he seem to get the words out?

"Luke," Jane said, "we can't do this again."

Disappointment coursed through him and he shook it off. This was a good thing. They were on the same page and that made everything much easier.

"Luke?" Jane said timidly. "I'm sorry."

"You don't have anything to be sorry about," he said. "I was going to say the same thing."

Relief crossed Jane's face and he bit back his feeling of hurt. Did he want her to be disappointed? Christ, what the hell was wrong with him? He wanted to sleep with Jane and he had. End of story.

"Okay, good," she said. She slid off the stool and grabbed her purse. "I should get going. I'll see you at work tomorrow, okay?"

"Are you not going to family dinner tonight?" He asked.

"No, I can't make it."

"Why not?"

Luke, let it go! The less time you spend with her, the better.

"I have other plans," she said. "Anyway, thank you again. Bye, Luke."

"Let me get dressed and I'll give you a ride home," he said.

"I'm going to see Mama J," she replied.

"I'll drive you there."

"No, that's okay. I don't mind taking the bus."

"Jane," he said in exasperation. "It's freezing cold outside and I would feel much better about how we're leaving things if you would let me give you a ride."

Or, she could ride you. Why don't you coax her back upstairs for the morning? You didn't exactly put on a good show last night. Tell me, did you last three minutes or four minutes before you were coming? Hell, you didn't even get to eat her pussy last night. I bet she tastes delicious. I bet she'll scream your name when she comes all over your face.

God help him, he wanted to do just that. Despite knowing it was a mistake, despite what Jane had said, he wanted her back upstairs and naked in his bed with a desperation that alarmed him.

"Luke? Are you okay?"

He drank the hot coffee in four large gulps, burning his tongue and his throat. But it had the desired effect of cooling his lust and softening his cock. He nodded and slid off the stool. "Yes. I'm fine. Give me five minutes and then I'll drive you to see Mama J."

"Okay," she said in defeat.

He stopped in the doorway of the kitchen. "Don't leave, Jane."

"I won't," she promised.

He nodded and hurried out of the kitchen.

৵ ৵

"What are you doing?" Jane gave Luke an alarmed

look when he shut the car off and unbuckled his seatbelt.

"I want to meet your Mama J," he said.

"What? Why?" She grabbed his arm when he started to open the door.

"Because she sounds like a lovely woman and I'd like to meet her." He arched his eyebrow at her and shook free of her hand like she was a bothersome fly before stepping out of the car.

She chewed on her bottom lip for a moment before getting out of the car. God, could this be any more awkward? Why the hell did she sleep with Luke last night? As amazing as it was, she'd barely slept last night as regret wormed its way in deeper. She'd slept with her damn boss. What if he fired her for sleeping with him? What if he fired her for refusing to keep sleeping with him?

Her stomach curdled and she didn't realize she was hesitating until Luke tugged on her arm. "Jane? Let's get inside. It's freezing."

She followed him numbly toward the care home. She needed to stop freaking out. Luke wasn't going to fire her. Yes, it was a mistake to sleep with him but he seemed to realize that as well so it was all good. Neither of them wanted to sleep together again so there was no problem. No problem at all.

Except for the fact that you actually do want to keep sleeping with him.

No, dammit, she didn't. She was just on a high from the unbelievable orgasms he gave her last night. She had limited experience but she was pretty certain that her boss was damn good in bed. He was way better than Jeremy anyway. It wasn't surprising that she was feeling a bit of disappointment over not sleeping with Luke anymore.

Are you sure he's better? Maybe last night was a fluke. You should probably sleep with him a few more times just to be certain. You didn't even get to suck his dick, for God's sake. C'mon, Janie, once more...for me?

She flushed bright red at her inner thoughts. She was

acting like a sex addict. What was wrong with her?

"Jane? What's wrong?" Luke took her arm and pulled her to a gentle stop.

They were standing in the foyer of the care home now but she took no notice of the residents that were sitting in wheelchairs or on the couches, or the way Bev was staring at them from behind the front desk. She stared up at her boss, her gaze planted on his lips. An image of them sucking on her nipple, of his teeth biting her pale skin, flickered through her and she made a low moan.

"Jane," he said, "stop looking at me like that or I'll take you back to the car right now and fuck you. I swear I will."

She chewed on her bottom lip and he made his own low groan. "Christ, stop that too."

"We agreed that last night was it for us," she whispered.

"We did," he said in a low voice. "So, stop looking at me like you want to be fucked."

She wanted to say she wasn't but she couldn't seem to spit out the lie so she settled for staying silent.

He held her arm when she tried to step away. "Stay here for a minute."

"Why?" She asked. She needed some distance from him. It was safer that way.

"Because I have one hell of a goddamn stiffy and I'd prefer not to have the senior citizens with heart conditions catching a glimpse of it," he muttered.

That made her laugh and also set off fireworks of need in her belly.

"Yes, real funny," he said through gritted teeth, "until I give some old lady a heart attack."

"Oh, please," she said, "your dick is big but it's not heart attack inducing big."

He gaped at her and she burst into giggles. After a few seconds, he grinned and said, "Why, Ms. Smith, I had no idea you could be so crude."

She didn't object when he dropped his arm around her shoulders and gave her a friendly squeeze. "I highly approve."

"Thank you," she said. Keeping her eyes above his belt line, she said, "Can I move now?"

"Yes," he said. "Although knowing that you think my dick is big almost caused a problem again."

She hesitated and then said, "Last night was very nice, Luke. I should have told you that earlier."

He winced and dropped his arm from her shoulders. "Very nice? Okay, mission accomplished in losing the stiffy. Let's go meet your Mama J."

She stared at him in puzzlement. What was wrong with saying it was very nice? Sure, it didn't exactly portray what she was thinking but it wasn't like she could tell him that he had the biggest dick she'd ever seen, that she'd never come as hard as she did last night and she wished she could fuck him again and again. That was rude and coarse and besides, they weren't going to do this anymore.

"I'm sorry," she said. "I – that was a compliment. Really."

"Sure," he said. "Let's go, Jane."

He was irritated with her, she could see it in his face and in the stiff way he walked. She sighed and stopped at the front desk. "Hi, Bev. How's Mama J this morning?"

"She's good," Bev said. "She just finished breakfast." Her gaze shifted to Luke's face. "Hi, I'm Bev."

"Sorry," Jane mumbled. "Bev this is my, uh, friend Luke. Luke, this is Bev."

"Nice to meet you," Luke said. He shook her hand and Bev giggled like a school girl.

"It's nice to meet you too."

As they headed down the hallway, Jane took a quick glimpse behind her. Bev was leaning over the desk and staring at Luke's ass. She gave Jane a look of unabashed glee and a thumbs up. Jane bit back her grin. She couldn't really blame Bev. Luke did have an amazing ass.

She stopped in front of Mama J's room. She was suddenly nervous and she gave Luke a quick glance. "Listen, you really don't have to do this. I know you're busy and - "

"I want to meet her," he said impatiently.

Before she could stop him, he had knocked on the door and opened it. Jane scooted past him and hurried to the window. Mama J was sitting in her chair next to it and staring at the falling snow.

"Mama J?"

"Janie! Hi, sweetheart. What are you doing back here so early?"

Jane breathed a sigh of relief and kissed Mama J's wrinkled cheek. "I missed you. I thought we could spend the morning together."

"Aren't you the sweetest thing," Mama J said. "But I worry that you spend too much time with me. You should be out having fun and..."

She trailed off as she caught sight of Luke standing behind Jane. "Hello, I'm Josephine."

"Hello, Josephine." Luke took Mama J's hand and shook it gently. "My name is Luke."

"You're a handsome fellow, aren't you?" Mama J said.

Luke grinned at her. "You're rather beautiful yourself, ma'am."

Mama J laughed. "Charming too, I see. Are you the new nurse?"

"No," Jane said, "Luke is…."

She trailed off, suddenly flustered by what to tell Mama J. Mama J would find it strange that her boss was visiting. She was just deciding to say he was her friend when Mama J's eyes lit up.

"Is he your boyfriend, Janie?"

"What?" Jane shook her head. "Mama J, no, he - "

"Oh, I'm so happy!" Mama J reached out and grabbed Luke's hand again. "You have no idea how happy I am! I was so worried about my little Janie being all alone. She's such a sweet girl and I love her so much. She's been much happier lately and now I know why. She's in love!"

"Mama J," Jane said as her face flamed with embarrassment. "Luke and I aren't - "

"You know, my Janie is a real catch," Mama J said to Luke. "You're treating her right, aren't you?"

"Mama J!" Jane said.

"What, honey?"

"Luke and I aren't, I mean we're not…"

She trailed off as she took a good look at her foster mother. For the first time in months, Mama J's face beamed with happiness and her pale cheeks were flush with colour.

"What is it, sweet Janie?" Mama J said with another happy smile at Luke.

Jane sighed. She was about to ruin Mama J's good mood and it made her feel terrible. "Luke and I aren't - "

"We haven't been dating very long," Luke broke in smoothly.

"Oh, I'm so happy for you both," Mama J said. "What do you do for a living, Luke?"

"I work for a clothing design company," Luke said.

"How nice," Mama J said. "Do you enjoy it?"

"I do," Luke replied.

Mama J pointed to a chair in the corner. "Pull up a chair, Luke. I want to hear everything about you."

"Mama J, he was only dropping me off," Jane said. "He doesn't have time to stay for a visit."

"Of course, I do," Luke said.

"No, you don't," Jane said pointedly. "You have that *thing* remember?"

"The *thing* was cancelled," Luke replied. "Besides, what better way to spend a Sunday morning than with two beautiful women?"

Mama J giggled and took Jane's hand. "Oh, he really is quite charming, Janie. I like him very much."

Luke grinned at her as he dragged the chair over. "I

like you too, Josephine."

∂◦ ◦∂

"Jane?"

Jane groaned and closed her eyes for a moment. She wondered if she could shut off the bedroom light and hope that Amy thought she was sleeping.

"I know you're awake, Jane. Can I come in?"

She sighed and sat up in the bed. "Yes."

Amy opened the door and immediately climbed into the bed beside her. She leaned against the headboard and stared at Jane. "So."

"So, what?"

"So, what happened with my brother?"

"Nothing happened," Jane said.

"Bullshit. You spent last night with him, didn't you?"

Jane picked at a thread on the quilt. "Fine. Yes, we had sex."

Amy grinned and held out her fist. "It's about damn time."

Jane rolled her eyes and fist bumped her. "I'm pretty tired, Amy. Can we talk another time?"

"Nope," Amy said cheerfully. "It's not that late and if I don't get all the details from you now, I never will. Why are you looking so depressed?"

"I'm not," Jane said. "I'm tired."

"Ugh. Yeah, I know why you're tired," Amy said. "Seriously though, what's going on? When you didn't come home today, I assumed you were with Luke but he showed up to family dinner without you. He said he spent the morning with you and Mama J but you told him you had other plans tonight."

"I did," Jane said.

Amy stared at her and Jane sighed. "Last night was amazing and I enjoyed myself immensely but both your brother and I agreed that last night was it. We had sex, got

158

it out of our systems and now we're back to the way it was before."

"It's not going to work."

"It'll work," Jane said.

"It won't," Amy replied. "Trust me, Janie. Once you sleep with someone you work with, it never goes back to normal."

"Are you speaking from experience?" Jane asked.

Amy jerked like she'd been touched by a live wire.

"What's that supposed to mean?" She snapped.

"It means that I think you and Mark slept together."

"Why would you think I slept with him? I told you I hate him!" Amy said before bursting into tears.

Feeling terrible, Jane put her arm around her and squeezed tightly. "Honey, I'm sorry. I shouldn't have been so nosy."

Amy continued to sob and Jane pulled her closer. She reached for some tissue from her bedside table and handed it to Amy before holding her and rubbing her back. When Amy's sobs had slowed to sniffles, she sat back and gave Jane a watery smile.

"Better?" Jane asked.

Amy shrugged and blew her nose before leaning back against the headboard. "I'm sorry."

"Don't be," Jane said. "Do you want to talk about it?"

Amy stared up at the ceiling. "No, I don't."

"All right," Jane said.

Amy gave her a surprised look. "Thanks, Jane. I appreciate that."

Jane shrugged. "If you don't want to talk about it, I'm not going to push you."

"Yeah, maybe you could mention that to Valerie. She's my best friend and I love her but the woman's like a dog with a bone. She won't stop asking me what's wrong."

"She's worried about you and so am I," Jane said.

"I'm fine," Amy said. "Are you really going to try and go back to acting like you never slept with my brother?"

"Yes," Jane said. "I don't regret it but it wasn't the smartest thing I've ever done. Sleeping with the boss is a quick way to finding yourself unemployed."

"Luke wouldn't fire you for sleeping with him," Amy said. "If he even tried, I'd kick his ass and hire you as *my* assistant. So, don't worry about that."

"Thanks, Ames," Jane replied.

"You bet, Janie. But for what it's worth – I think you should consider finding another job and having a relationship with my brother. He's a good guy and he really likes you. I know he does."

Jane smiled at her but didn't say anything. Despite what Amy thought, Luke wasn't interested in anything more than sex with her. Even if he was, she wasn't ready to give up the best paying job of her life for a relationship. She wouldn't find a job that paid as well as this one and what happened if she and Luke broke up? She wouldn't be able to live with Amy anymore and she'd be right back to where she used to be, only with a lower paying job and a lot less money. Mama J would be kicked out of the care home. Her stomach clenched at the thought and she must have been pale because Amy touched her arm.

"You okay?"

"Yes. Just tired," Jane said.

"I'll let you go to bed. Listen, will you promise to still come to family dinners at least? My mom and dad really like you and if you stop coming, mom will harass you until you tell her why. It's easier if you just come to dinner."

"I'll try to come at least once a month. How's that?" Jane said with a smile.

Amy laughed. "I'll let you work out the schedule with mom. Good night, Jane."

"Night, Amy."

When Amy was gone, she clicked off the light and curled up in the middle of the bed. For a moment, she allowed herself to imagine that she was with Luke and in his bed before pushing the image out of her head. She'd had her night with him and it was best to forget it ever happened. Of course, that was easier said than done. She was already feeling nervous about tomorrow. What if he treated her differently? What if he –

Enough, Jane! Luke will be fine. You'll be fine. Everything will be fine. Go to sleep.

She blew her breath out in a harsh rush and closed her eyes. Everything would be fine.

Chapter Eleven

"Ms. Smith! My office now!"

Jane straightened her skirt and pasted a smile on her face before walking toward Luke's office. She paused with her hand on the door handle. God, she did not want to go in there. The day had started off fine, Luke was a bit distant but perfectly polite and he'd made no mention of Saturday night. She had found it a little disappointing that there wasn't even a hint of his lust for her when he looked at her but reminded herself fiercely that it was for the best.

However, as the day wore on, Luke became more and more impatient with her. Just before lunch, he snapped at her about a missing email and then was pissed off with her when she took too long to get his lunch. He was in a meeting from one until two and he hadn't even looked at her when he returned. He had stomped by her desk, staring grimly at his cell phone before slamming the door to his office.

"Ms. Smith!"

His angry shout got her moving and she opened the doors and slipped inside.

"Shut the doors," he said.

Her stomach flip flopped but she shut the doors and gave him a bland smile. "What can I do for you, Mr. Dawson?"

"Amy's latest drawings are missing from the computer system. Last week, I specifically asked you to make sure the scans were on the F drive."

"They should be there," she said. "I remember moving them over."

"They're not," he said impatiently. "I've wasted the last half hour looking for them."

He scowled at her and her temper snapped. "Then you should have asked me earlier."

She stomped across his office and stood beside him before pushing on his shoulder. "Move please, Mr. Dawson."

He huffed angrily but rolled his chair back. She stood in front of him and used the mouse to click to the F drive and locate the files. It took her less than a minute and she tried to keep the irritation from her voice. "The files are right here."

There was no reply and she looked over her shoulder. Her face flushed. She was slightly bent over his desk and Luke was staring intently at her ass.

"Mr. Dawson," she said. God, why was her voice suddenly so hoarse?

"Yes, Ms. Smith?" He replied without lifting his gaze.

"I said the files are right here."

He rolled his chair forward, his knees hit the back of hers with enough force to buckle them and she fell backwards into his lap. His arm descended around her waist like a band of steel and stopped her from scrambling away.

"Mr. Dawson, you're acting," she paused, "inappropriately."

His hand tightened on her hip as he leaned forward and studied the computer screen. "I'm working, Ms. Smith. You're the one being inappropriate and rubbing your ass against my crotch."

"I am not rubbing my ass against your…"

She trailed off as she realized that she was, indeed,

rubbing her ass vigorously against his erection.

He groaned into her ear and cupped her right breast, kneading it gently as he tasted the side of her neck before inhaling. "You smell so good, Jane."

"We said we weren't going to do this again," she said unsteadily.

"You don't want me?" He unbuttoned her blouse with deft fingers and slipped his hand inside the cup of her bra.

"You've been a jerk all day and – oh God!" She couldn't stop her moan when his fingers tugged on her nipple.

"I have been a jerk," he murmured into her ear. "I'm sorry. Let me make it up to you."

"H-how?" She arched her back when he pulled on her nipple again.

"I think a transgression as egregious as this requires a pussy eating as an apology. Don't you?"

"Oh hell, yes," she said before she came to her senses and shook her head. "I mean, no."

"No?" He sucked on her earlobe before sliding his hand to her other breast and playing with her nipple. "You don't like having your pussy eaten, Ms. Smith?"

"It's not appropriate," she said before grinding her ass against his dick. "We said we wouldn't do this again."

"No, we said we wouldn't fuck again," he said. "I don't remember anything about pussy eating."

She opened her mouth and then shut it as he grinned at her. "Come by my house after work and I'll eat your pussy until you feel I've adequately apologized for my behaviour today."

Oh, God. Her panties were so wet she was afraid she was going to leave a damp spot on her skirt and his pants. She wanted desperately to say yes. She wanted to forget about what a terrible, horrible, no good idea it was to sleep with her boss and go for it. Only, she had responsibilities and as much as she wanted Luke, she couldn't go to his house tonight. She had a shift at the club and she couldn't miss it.

"I can't," she said. "I have plans."

"Your second job?"

She stiffened and he squeezed her breast before rubbing her thigh with his other hand.

"How do you know about that?" She asked.

"Amy mentioned it to me," he replied.

Now he would ask her what club it was and she would have to lie to his face. There was no way in hell she was telling him what club she worked at. He'd fire her for sure. He surprised her when, instead of asking her where she worked, he said, "I guess I'll have to apologize right now."

He had her legs spread and his hand stuck up her skirt before she knew what was happening.

"Stockings," he said appreciatively as he stroked the top of her thigh. "Very nice, little Jane."

She flushed and tried to close her legs but he was faster than her. His hand cupped her pussy through her silk panties and he rubbed at her clit through the wet fabric.

"Oh God," she hissed out as she squeezed the arms of his chair. "Mr. Dawson, we cannot do this in the office."

"You've left me no choice," he murmured. "Since you can't come by tonight, I have to make my apologies here."

"The weekend," she gasped out as his finger slipped under the crotch of her panties and rubbed at her clit. "You can apologize on the weekend."

"I can't wait that long," he said. "I don't think you can either."

"I can," she whispered. "I – I can wait until…"

She trailed off into a low groan as Luke slid his finger into her.

"Don't lie to me, Ms. Smith," Luke said as he slowly finger-fucked her. "You need your little pussy eaten right now. Don't you?"

"Yes," she said shakily. "Yes please, Luke."

He withdrew his hand and she made a whimper of

need. He nipped at her neck before pushing her into a standing position. She stopped him when he started to push her skirt up.

"The door," she said. "We can't do this – the door is unlocked."

He reached into a desk drawer and brought out a small silver remote. He pushed the top button and there was a low click as the doors locked.

"Problem solved," he said before pushing her skirt up around her waist. He tugged her panties down her legs. "Lift your foot."

Like she was in a dream, Jane lifted first one foot and than the other. Luke left her panties on the floor and she whimpered with pleasure when he kneaded her bare ass.

"Such a beautiful ass," he said before lightly biting her right ass cheek.

She squealed and he laughed before squeezing her ass. "Quiet, Ms. Smith."

"Maybe you should stop biting me then," she said.

He laughed again before standing. He moved his laptop to the far left of the desk and pushed his phone to the far right and then patted the shiny, empty space on his desk. "Hop up, Jane."

She blinked at him. "You've got to be kidding me."

"You have a better idea?" He said.

"Yes. The damn couch," she said before pointing to the leather couch in his office.

"Maybe next time," he said. "This time I want you spread out on my desk while I eat your pussy."

"There won't be a next time," she hissed as she stared at the doors. "We can't do this again. If we get caught – "

"Don't scream when you come and we won't get caught," he said before turning her and boosting her onto his desk. He unbuttoned her shirt the rest of the way before pushing her bra up around her collarbone. He stared at her breasts then leaned down and sucked on one throbbing nipple.

She moaned and clutched at his head as he nipped and sucked before pulling away. She pouted at him and he grinned before pushing her flat onto her back. "As much as I'd love to take my time and kiss every inch of your sweet body, little Jane, I have a meeting in half an hour. You're going to have to be happy with a quick but satisfying pussy eating."

She blushed and his grin widened. "God, you're so fucking adorable. Remember – no screaming my name when you come."

"Someone's full of himself, isn't he?" She said tartly as he took off his suit jacket and his tie. He unbuttoned his shirt and slipped out of it before draping it over the back of his office chair. "I never scream and I'm not about to start now in your office where anyone could – oh God!"

Luke had spread her thighs wide and buried his face in her pussy. Her hips arched, inviting him to lick her harder and deeper. He obliged, sucking on her already swollen clit as her hands clutched his head and pushed him into her. He teased her clit with his tongue as she moaned.

He lifted his head and slapped her lightly on her nylon-clad thigh. "Quiet, Ms. Smith."

"Luke, don't stop!" She hissed in a fierce whisper.

He grinned at her before tracing the top of her thigh high with his fingers. "Who's the boss here?"

She scowled at him and pulled on his hair. He winced before bending his head and kissing her flat abdomen. "I love the way you taste, little Jane."

"Please." Her tone turned to begging and she wasn't the least bit ashamed.

He trailed kisses along the bunched-up waistband of her skirt before pushing on her thighs again. "Nice and wide, honey."

She let her legs drop open to an obscene width. She no longer cared that she was lying on her boss' desk with her bare ass smudging his desk and her juices dripping onto its shiny surface. Just a few seconds of his mouth on her pussy had sent her lust into overdrive. It was never like this with Jeremy, she thought dimly as Luke kissed her inner thighs before licking the crease between her thigh and her pussy.

"Please," she repeated.

He took pity on her and parted her wet pussy lips with his thumbs before licking and sucking on her clit again. To her surprise and shame, she was immediately on the verge of coming. The muscles in her stomach tensed, her nipples tightened and her back arched again when he nuzzled her clit with his mouth and then sucked firmly. She barely had time to throw her arm over her mouth before she was screaming and coming all over Luke's face.

He held her down and pressed soft kisses against her inner thighs as she moaned and quivered against his desk.

"Do I need to point out that you screamed, Ms. Smith?" He asked.

"A gentleman wouldn't," she mumbled. "Apology accepted, by the way."

His low laugh sent shivers down her spine. She knew she should be sitting up, she was sprawled across Luke's desk in a very unladylike position, but her entire body was still trembling and she felt weak and disoriented. She cracked open an eye when she heard the foil wrapper. Luke's pants and briefs were around his ankles and he was rolling a condom onto his dick.

"What are you doing?" She tried to sit up but Luke grabbed her calves and hauled her forward until her ass was on the edge of his desk.

"Luke! We can't have sex in your – oh God!"

Her voice cut out and she made a low squeal of pleasure as Luke sunk his dick deep into her wet core.

❧ ❦

He hadn't meant to fuck her. He really planned on only eating her sweet pussy until she screamed his name.

But she looked so fuckable sprawled out on his desk and his cock was rock hard and begging him for mercy. He had rolled on the condom and plunged himself into that tight warmth he'd been dreaming about since Sunday.

Her squeal of pleasure made his balls tighten and he held her hips as he thrust deep and bottomed out in her. She was just as tight as Saturday night but being eaten out had made her soaking wet. She clutched at his forearms, her hips reaching up to meet every one of his strokes despite her small murmurs of protest.

She hooked her thighs around his waist, squeezing tightly as he moved in and out with hard strokes. He rubbed her thighs, feeling the soft rasp of her nylons against his hands as she stared up at him.

"We shouldn't be doing this," she moaned.

"I have to prove I can be better than very nice," he muttered.

"That – that was a compliment," she gasped when he made two rough thrusts.

"Very nice is not a compliment," he said with a low groan.

She made a low cry of pleasure when he rocked his body against hers. "It is."

"Agree to disagree," he gasped out.

He was already on the verge of climaxing when she whispered, "We have to hurry."

"Sadly, that's not a going to be a problem," he said before squeezing one firm breast. He rolled her nipple between his thumb and forefinger and pulled on it. She moaned and her pussy tightened around him in response.

He swore under his breath before renewing his pace with a desperation that bordered on embarrassing. He dropped over her, resting his hands on either side of her head and kissed her hard on the mouth. She opened to him immediately and he deepened the kiss as he fucked her with a hard and steady rhythm.

"Fuck," he muttered against her mouth. "You're so

fucking hot, Jane. You're so tight and wet and…"

He trailed off, his back arching as Jane clamped her hand over his mouth. He shouted into her palm as he climaxed deep inside of her. Panting loudly, he rested his forehead against Jane's. Her warm breath washed over him and she rubbed his back.

"You all right?"

"Fucking amazing," he mumbled. "You?"

"Incredible," she replied. He grinned at her and pressed a kiss against her mouth.

"Get up," she said before patting him on the back. "We need to get dressed before someone catches us."

He didn't want to. He wanted to carry Jane to his couch, strip her naked and spend the rest of the afternoon making her climax repeatedly. Instead, he forced himself to straighten and pull out of her warm pussy. He disposed of the condom then helped her off the desk. She rearranged her clothing and yanked her underwear on as he pulled up his briefs and pants. He followed Jane's gaze when she made a groan of embarrassment.

"Oh God, your desk," she whispered. It was wet and shiny with her sweet cream and her cheeks flushed bright red.

He shrugged. "I'll grab some paper towels and clean it up."

"And disinfectant," she said so primly that he snorted loud laughter.

She wrinkled her nose at him. "You go to the bathroom and wash your face and hands. I'll grab the paper towels and disinfectant."

"You might want to, uh, fix your hair first," he said.

She touched her hair. "What's wrong with my hair?"

He grinned at her and she hurried to his private bathroom. He heard her gasp of dismay from the desk. He walked to the bathroom and stood in the doorway, watching as she tried to smooth her hair down.

"I look ridiculous," she muttered.

"No. You look like you've just been fucked," he said.

She glared at him and gathered her hair into a pony tail before pushing past him and snagging an elastic band from his desk drawer. As she wrapped it around the ponytail, she said, "We can't do this again, Luke. Do you understand?"

"Not entirely," he said with another grin. "Do you mean we can't have sex again or we can't have sex at the office again."

She paused and then said, "Both."

"You hesitated."

"I didn't."

"You did."

"Did not."

"Did too."

She huffed in annoyance and said, "I'll be right back. Go get cleaned up before your meeting."

"Yes, ma'am," he said before giving her a small salute.

She rolled her eyes and slipped out of his office. He returned to the bathroom and washed his hands and face before staring at himself in the mirror. If Jane thought that he could stay away from her after this, she was wrong. The way she responded to his touch, the feel of her tight pussy was now an obsession.

Sleeping with your assistant is stupid and dangerous.

Yeah, it was. But it wasn't going to stop him from taking sweet little Jane every chance he got.

ॐ ∾

"Why are you so distracted?"

Luke stared blankly at Mark. "I'm not."

"Bullshit," Mark said. "You haven't heard a word I've said about this quarter's numbers."

"I've heard it."

"No, you haven't."

There was irritation in his best friend's voice. It wasn't

like Mark to be irritated so easily and Luke studied him for a moment. "What's wrong?"

"Nothing," Mark said.

"Now who's bullshitting?" Luke asked.

Mark rubbed his jaw. "I'm tired. I haven't been sleeping well."

"Why not?" Luke asked.

There was a knock on the door and Jane stuck her head into the room. "Mr. Dawson? I have the documents you – oh, I'm sorry, I didn't realize you were in a meeting."

"It's fine," Mark said as he stood. "Luke, take a look at the numbers and get back to me by the day after tomorrow, okay?"

Luke nodded as Mark slipped past Jane and shut the office doors. Vaguely, he realized he should have made Mark stay so he could find out what was wrong with him but the moment Jane had walked into his office, she was all he could think about. He'd tasted her pussy and fucked her on his desk just yesterday and already he wanted her again.

As she placed the documents on his desk, he tried desperately to think of a reason to keep her in his office. "Ms. Smith, there was a problem with the letter you emailed to me earlier.

"What was wrong with it?" She asked.

"Errors, multiple errors," he replied.

She stared at him in disbelief and he opened up the document before rolling his chair back. "Come see for yourself."

She hesitated and he tried to look calm and indifferent about her decision. Truthfully, he was dying to get her close to him. He didn't think it was his imagination that she'd been avoiding him today. But if he could touch her and kiss her soft mouth even once, maybe he could concentrate on his damn job.

She gave him a suspicious look before walking behind his desk. She kept her body straight and stared at the screen. He tried not to grin and failed miserably as he stared at her ass. She might think not being bent over made a difference but the way her skirt hugged her ass made him instantly hard.

"I don't see anything," she said.

"Third paragraph," he replied. Her skirt ended just above the knee and as she studied the screen, he slid his hand under her skirt and stroked her thigh. She stiffened and turned her head to glare at him.

"Behave, Mr. Dawson."

"I am, Ms. Smith," he said innocently as he nudged at her closed thighs. To his surprise, she shifted her feet apart as she turned her head to stare at the screen again. He caught a whiff of her body wash as he slid his hand up her inner thigh. She was wearing stockings again – God, that made him so fucking hard for her – and he stroked the soft skin of her thigh above the top of them.

"Th-there aren't any mistakes," she moaned.

"There are," he said as his hand inched higher. "Keep looking."

"I don't see any – oh, God…"

His hand had reached her panties and she widened her thighs as he touched the damp fabric.

"Keep looking, Ms. Smith," he said sternly as he ran his fingers back and forth over her panties. He pressed experimentally against her clit through the silk material and she moaned before plastering her hand over her mouth.

She dropped her hand and said, "There's one misspelled word."

"Like I said, an error," he replied.

"You said multiple errors." She turned her head to stare down at him.

He shrugged and withdrew his hand. She couldn't mask the disappointment that flashed across her face as she turned to face him.

"Regardless, I think there should be some sort of punishment for your error. Don't you, Ms. Smith?"

Her breath hitched and her eyes dropped to the tented crotch of his pants. A slow grin crossed his face. He had planned on tasting her sweet pussy again but now he had a better idea. She watched as he reached into the desk drawer and removed the silver remote. He locked the door, the click was very loud in the silence, and waited for her to protest.

When she didn't, he leaned back in his chair and said, "Remove your shirt and bra."

She chewed at her bottom lip as she considered his demand. "Ms. Smith," he prompted, "your punishment is not up for discussion."

Her face flushed and she unbuttoned her shirt before placing it on the desk. Her bra was white with a lace trim and her nipples jutted out against the silk fabric. He resisted the urge to stand and suck on them through the material. Instead he cocked an eyebrow at her and made a lazy flicking motion with his fingers. "The bra as well."

She reached behind her and unclasped it. As she pulled down the right strap he said, "Slowly."

She flushed but slowed her movements, easing the other strap down her arm before letting the bra slide slowly from her slender body. She placed it on the desk with her shirt and left her arms at her sides. He drank in the sight of her small breasts topped with delectable pink nipples. They were beaded into hard points and he smiled at her. "Come here."

He spread his legs and she stepped forward until the outside of her thighs pressed against his inner thighs. Her lovely breasts were directly in his face and she arched her back a little in silent supplication.

Unable to resist her plea, he slid his hands around her tiny waist and splayed them against her lower back before pressing a kiss between her breasts. She moaned and he pulled her closer before licking a circle around her nipple. She made a low sound of need and he sucked hard on her nipple before releasing it and blowing on it. Her body shuddered and he squeezed her ass before sucking on her left nipple.

"That feels so good," she moaned.

"Time for your punishment," he said before kissing her nipple.

She shivered all over again and he cupped her hips and pulled. "On your knees."

She licked her lips and glanced behind her at the door before kneeling between his legs. He stroked her hair before smiling at her. "My pants, Ms. Smith."

Her hands trembling, she unbuckled his belt before unbuttoning and unzipping his pants. She spread open his pants and licked her lips again when she saw his cock pressing against his briefs.

He pushed the front of his briefs down and freed his cock. The head of it brushed against Jane's chin and he groaned harshly. He cupped the back of her neck and tugged her head down.

"Open," he rasped.

Her lips parted and he groaned again when her tiny pink tongue darted out to wet her bottom lip.

"Open and suck my cock," he said as he kneaded the back of her neck.

"Yes, Mr. Dawson," she said.

"Fuck," he muttered and pushed her mouth down over his cock.

She sucked hard as he smoothed her hair back from her face and gathered it in a loose ponytail. "Look up at me, honey."

She stared at him as she sucked and he smiled at her. "That's my good girl. Keep sucking with that hot little mouth of yours."

He reached down and cupped her breast before pinching her nipple. She squeaked in surprise around his cock and he held her firmly by her hair when she tried to draw back. "No, honey. Keep sucking."

Her nostrils flared with the effort to breathe as she

sucked on the head of his cock. She traced around the ridge with her tongue and sucked again.

"More," he said hoarsely. "I want you to take more, sweet Jane."

She slid her mouth down his cock, her lips stretching around him and his hand tightened in her hair as his hips thrust upward. Her eyes widened as he hit the back of her throat and when she tried to pull back, he released her.

"I'm sorry, honey," he said as he petted her hair.

She stared wide-eyed at him before licking her swollen lips and plunging her mouth over his cock again. He groaned and held her head, pushing her mouth up and down his cock as she sucked and licked.

Her tiny hands gripped his thighs as she leaned forward and continued to bob her head up and down his dick. The feel of her hot, wet mouth around the thick length of his cock made his balls tighten. Christ, he wasn't going to last much longer.

She sucked harder and when her tiny hand fisted around the base and stroked him, he nearly came in her mouth. He muttered a curse and pulled her away from his cock.

She whined in protest and tried to take his cock into her mouth again.

"Honey, stop," he almost begged. "I'm close."

She pushed his hand away like it was an annoying fly and sucked him into her mouth again. He gripped the arms of his chair until his knuckles turned white.

"Jane," he gasped, "I'm so fucking close."

She released him with a soft pop and gave him a sweetly seductive smile. "I want you to come in my mouth, Mr. Dawson."

She lowered her mouth over his cock and sucked hard.

"Fuck!" His breath exploded out of his lungs and his hips arched up out of the chair as he came with a low hoarse grunt. She swallowed his warm seed as he groaned with pleasure. She gasped in surprise when he pulled her mouth away from his dick and pumped himself with his hand, splashing the last of his seed onto her upper chest.

He stared at her, his chest heaving for air before leaning forward. He kissed her hard on the mouth, sliding his tongue in deep as he used his hand to smear his come into her soft skin.

He pulled his mouth away and stared down at her. She blinked at him before studying her chest. "What are you doing?"

He kissed her again, trying to ignore his caveman satisfaction at seeing his come all over her skin. He lifted her to her feet and tucked his cock away before zipping up his pants and buckling his belt.

He took Jane's hand and led her to his private bathroom. He filled the sink with warm water and using one of the towels and the hand soap, he washed away the smears of sticky seed on her upper chest and breasts. He rinsed her clean and used a second towel to dry her before pulling her into his arms and cupping her breast. He rubbed his thumb over her nipple and pressed a light kiss against her mouth.

"That was amazing," he said in a low voice.

She smiled shyly at him. "I liked it a lot."

"Me too," he said. "So, um, I just wanted you to know that I'm clean. But I'll show you my medical records so you don't have to worry."

Jesus, he sounded like an awkward teenage boy.

She smiled at him. "I'm not worried, Luke."

"Okay." He kissed her again. "C'mon, it's your turn."

He brought her back into his office as she said, "Not a good idea."

"Yes, it is," he said. "Lie down on the couch."

"I really can't," she said. She pulled free of his grip and pulled on her bra and shirt. "I've been in here too long already. You know that."

He sighed with frustration. "Tonight, then. You can - "

"I'm working tonight," she reminded him.

He scowled. "I'm not the kind of guy who takes and doesn't," he paused, "give."

"I know," she said. "It's fine, Luke. Really. Besides, we can't keep doing this at the office."

He didn't reply and she combed her hair with her fingers. "How do I look?"

"Good," he said.

"Thanks. I'd better go," she said.

"Jane - "

"I've got some filing to do," she said.

She hurried to the doors, unlocked them and slipped out of his office. He stomped over to his desk. He sat in his chair and swivelled around, staring out the window. He enjoyed having Jane suck him off but if he'd known she wouldn't let him give her pleasure after, he would have made damn sure she came first. He sighed again and turned around to face his computer. He needed to remedy what happened this afternoon.

Chapter Twelve

Jane slipped into her bedroom. Without bothering to turn on the light, she padded to the bathroom. She shut the door and stripped off her clothes before brushing her teeth and taking a quick shower. Work at the club was busy tonight for a Tuesday and she'd done well in tips. Even Jeremy hadn't been nearly as annoying. She supposed it helped that he was dating the new girl. He tended to be less of an asshole when he was getting sex on the regular.

Speaking of which… you need to bang Luke tomorrow.

No, she most definitely didn't. She slipped her nightshirt over her head, shut off the bathroom light and walked toward her bed. Despite her long day and the fact that it was two in the morning, she was oddly restless.

Yeah, because you need to get laid!

Her inner voice probably had a point. She'd loved giving Luke oral sex today, it had seemed so decadently naughty to give him head in his office, but she was left feeling achy and unfulfilled all day. She was tempted to take the bus to Luke's place after work tonight but that was about the stupidest thing she could do. He would be sleeping and…

She cocked her head and took a step back from the bed. Why could she hear soft snoring? She flicked on the bedside lamp and her mouth dropped open. Luke was sleeping in her bed.

"What the hell?" She said.

He didn't stir and she reached out and poked him in the shoulder. He snorted and rubbed at his face before blinking sleepily at her. "Jane? What are you doing here?"

"What am I doing here?" She said. "You're in *my* bed."

He glanced around before giving her a sweet little grin. "Oh yeah, right." He threw back the covers. He was deliciously naked and she tried not to drool as she stared at his long, lean body. "Climb in, Jane."

"Luke," she said, "what are you doing here? Does Amy know you're here?"

"Yeah. She was still awake when I let myself into the house at eleven. Get into bed. I'm freezing my ass off."

Her gaze dropped to his crotch and he groaned when she licked her lips. "If you don't get into bed right now, I'll drag you into it."

She climbed into bed, lying awkwardly on her back. "Why aren't you at home?"

"Because I told you," he snuggled up to her and curved his arm around her waist, "I don't take and not give. Why are you wearing clothes? I'm naked, you should be naked too."

"Because I – I didn't expect my boss to be in my bed when I got home," she sputtered.

"Surprise," he said.

"This is a very bad idea," she said as his hand slipped under her nightshirt and cupped her breast. "Now Amy knows and - "

"You're telling me she didn't know before?" Luke tweaked her nipple until her back arched.

"I – all right fine, she knew but I told her it was just a one-time thing," Jane gasped out. "Now she knows that... oh God, stop doing that!"

"Stop what? This?" He sucked on her nipple through

the cotton material of her shirt and she gripped his hair before pushing his mouth away.

It's late and we both have work tomorrow."

"Yes, it is late," Luke said. "So, stop talking and let me fuck you."

"Luke," she whispered as his hand made circles on her bare abdomen.

"Unless you don't want me to fuck you. Is that it, Ms. Smith? You don't want to be fucked?"

His hand slipped between her thighs and cupped her wet pussy. "It doesn't feel like you don't want to be fucked."

She chewed on her bottom lip. "I – I want to be fucked."

"Good," he said. "Now, you're right that it's late and I worry that you don't get enough sleep so this is going to be on the quick side. But I promise I'll take my time on the weekend."

She wanted to tell him that she wasn't going anywhere near him on the weekend but his fingers were rubbing her clit and it was hard to think straight. The tension and aching she'd felt all day ratcheted up to an almost unbearable level and she moaned and grabbed his arm.

"You're so wet, sweet Jane," he murmured as he slid his finger easily into her aching warmth.

"I've been wet all freaking day," she muttered.

He laughed and nuzzled her throat before kissing her slowly and thoroughly. She sucked at his tongue and thrust her pelvis back and forth.

"Do you think you can be quiet, Ms. Smith?" He asked. "We don't want to wake your roommate."

"Yes. Just – hurry, Luke."

"Take off your nightgown," he said.

She sat up and pulled it over her head before tossing it on the floor. "Shit, I don't have a condom," she said in an angry mutter.

"All taken care of," he said. She turned to face him.

He was already rolling one on and he said, "I brought my own. Always be prepared, is my motto."

"That's the Boy Scouts motto," she said stupidly.

He burst into laughter and she hushed him before glancing at the closed door. He pushed her onto her back and kneeled between her legs as she stroked her hands across his broad chest. His cock probed at her pussy and she moaned, her nails digging into his hard chest.

"I've barely touched you and you're already wet enough to be fucked," he said. "Do you have any idea how goddamn hot that is, Ms. Smith?"

"Then shut up and fuck me, Mr. Dawson," she snapped at him.

He grinned and rubbed the head of his cock against her clit, watching as she squirmed and panted beneath him. "Did you like giving me head at the office?"

She refused to answer and tried to squeeze her hand between them. Her questing fingers brushed against his cock and he inhaled sharply before taking both her hands and pinning them above her wrists. "Answer me. Did you like being on your knees behind my desk with your mouth stuffed full of my cock?"

"You know I did," she said. She arched her back and tried to entice him to suck on her nipples.

"I want you to say it," he said before bending his head and licking the tip of her right nipple.

"Oh God – yes, I liked giving you head in the office!" She muttered. "Fuck me, Luke!"

"I think I'm going to add it to your job description," he said teasingly before sucking hard on first one nipple and then the other.

Pleasure was crashing through her, drowning out rational thought as he sucked and teased her nipples with his hot mouth and rubbed her clit with his cock.

"Every morning you'll come into my office, get on your knees and suck my dick. Is that clear, Ms. Smith?" He murmured against her breast.

She made a low keening noise as he released her hands before reaching between them and guiding his cock to her wet opening. "I'm waiting for your answer."

"I – what?" She gasped.

He slid the head of his cock into her and stopped. She whined in protest and smacked him on the back. "Keep going!"

His arms were trembling now and she could see the way he was fighting for control. "Sucking my dick every morning, Ms. Smith. New job duty, beginning – oh fuck!"

She had bucked her hips upward, taking almost half of his dick and he made a hard thrust in return, sheathing himself entirely.

"Oh God," she whispered. "Yes, just like that. Fuck me, Luke."

"Do you agree to your new – oh hell, honey, don't squeeze like that – job duty?"

"Yes, for God's sake! Yes!" She hissed at him.

"Excellent," he gasped out before fucking her hard and deep.

She buried her face in his neck to muffle her cries of pleasure and held on for the ride. She flung her arms around his back, feeling the large muscles rippling and contracting beneath her hands as he worked her into a frenzy of heat and need and desperation.

When he reached between them, pressed the heel of his hand against her clit and rubbed hard, she bit back her scream of release as she climaxed around his thick cock. He groaned harshly and buried his face in her neck, muffling his own moans of release as he thrust deep before he shook and twitched against her soft body.

He slipped off of her and disposed of the condom then collapsed on his back on the bed. "Fuck," he muttered almost to himself, "it gets better and better."

She wanted to agree, wanted to ask him if he thought there was some way they could keep doing this without it starting to be a major problem, but that was just her post-orgasmic glow happening. She knew perfectly well that this couldn't continue. Her stomach churning, she said, "It's late. You should probably leave."

She winced. God, that came out sounding much harsher than she meant, especially since what she really wanted was for him to stay the night.

Rather than being hurt, he grinned at her. "You're really going to make me leave your warm bed and drive home in the cold and the snow, Ms. Smith?"

"No," she said as she clicked off the lamp and plunged them into darkness. "I want you to stay, but I didn't want you to think you *had* to stay."

"I want to stay," he said before pulling her into his embrace. "Now go to sleep because I'm really tired and I have to work in the morning."

She smiled as he kissed her forehead and stroked her warm back. He was asleep in minutes but she stared sightlessly into the darkness. What the hell was she doing? She couldn't keep sleeping with Luke, she couldn't and she knew that. She had already made this mistake once before and it had cost her. Jeremy had changed her work schedule to punish her and if it hadn't been for this new job and her pay raise, Mama J would be kicked out of the care home by now. If things soured between her and Luke and she lost her job, she was risking Mama J's safety. Amy had said she wouldn't let Luke fire her but Jane wasn't foolish enough to actually believe that. Amy was sweet and kind but Luke was her brother. She would take Luke's side when push came to shove and Jane couldn't blame her for that.

There could be something more with him, Janie. You see that, don't you?

No, she didn't. That was just her foolish heart talking again. She had thought Jeremy loved her and she was dead wrong. Jeremy had said and did all the right things in the beginning too but when she broke it off with him…

She shuddered all over. She couldn't afford to lose her

job. Christ, she sounded like a broken record even to herself but she needed to do the right damn thing. If that meant she needed to keep reminding herself not to be an idiot, so be it.

He mentioned the weekend, her inner voice said. *Take the weekend with him and then end it, okay? He's not invested in you emotionally yet so he won't be angry that you don't want to keep sleeping with him if you end it on Sunday. It's been so long since you've had sex and isn't it nice to have him in your bed? Please, Janie? Just a few more days. Please.*

It was easy enough to agree to her inner voice's begging. A few more days was probably a good idea. If they screwed enough over the weekend, it would ease the sexual tension between them and going back to normal would be easier.

She curled a little closer to Luke. He stroked her back in his sleep and muttered something she didn't understand before growing quiet again. She rested her head on his chest, closed her eyes and tried to sleep.

෬ ෭

"I know, I'm late. I'm sorry," Jane said as she hurried into the kitchen the next morning and made a beeline for the fridge.

She hadn't fallen asleep until almost five and she'd forgotten to set her alarm on her phone. She normally woke at six and she and Amy left for the office at quarter after seven. She jerked awake at seven, sitting up with a gasp and reaching across the bed to shake Luke awake. His side was empty and he wasn't in the bathroom either. Obviously, he had already left. Trying not to be upset that he hadn't said goodbye to her, she had raced through her morning routine but it was seven thirty when she ran down the stairs.

Now, she whipped open the fridge and grabbed a juice. "Can you grab me an apple? Oh, and can you zip me up?"

She turned around and cracked open the juice. With no time to style her wet hair, she'd piled it into a bun on top of her head. She took a sip of juice and nearly spit it all over the floor when Amy grasped the zipper of her dress and then pressed a kiss against the exposed nape of her neck.

She choked down her swallow of juice as Amy's voice called from the hallway, "Luke, have you seen my keys?"

Jane stared wide-eyed at Amy when the blonde poked her head into the kitchen. "Lukie? My keys? Did you – oh, hey, Jane. You ready to go?"

"She's almost ready." Luke's velvety deep voice spoke behind her and he pressed another warm kiss against the nape of her neck before he zipped up her dress. "I found your keys on the kitchen floor last night. I hung them on the key hook by the front door."

"Thanks, Luke," Amy said as she pushed by them and grabbed her own juice from the fridge. "Jane will be a little late this morning. We're leaving later than we normally do and we're out of coffee so I'm swinging by Starbucks on the way to the office."

"All right," Luke said as he swung Jane around to face him. He slipped his arm around her waist and studied her. "Did you get enough sleep last night?"

"Gross," Amy said.

Luke rolled his eyes at her as Jane blushed. "Yes, I – I'm fine."

A small frown line appeared between his eyebrows but he nodded. "Okay. I'll see you at the office?"

"Yes. I won't be late," she said. "We'll get coffee at the office."

"Like hell we will," Amy said cheerfully. "The office coffee tastes like shit. We'll be late, Luke."

"That's fine," he said absently as he continued to study Jane. "In fact, why don't you take the day off, Jane? You've been working hard and - "

"No," she said. "I'm not taking the day off."

She gave him a furious look and he blinked a little at her ire before nodding. "Okay. See you in a bit."

Before she could turn her head, he pressed a gentle kiss against her mouth and stepped away. "We have that telephone meeting with the Board at nine, Amy."

"I know," she said. "Just us, right?"

"No. Mark will be there too," he said

Her face darkened and he shrugged. "The Board wants all three of us at the meeting."

"Yeah, fine," Amy said a bit sullenly.

"I'll see you both in a little bit," Luke said.

He left the kitchen and Jane waited until she heard the front door close before turning to Amy. "Amy, I'm sorry, I…"

She trailed off as Amy shrugged and said, "You have nothing to be sorry about, Jane."

"You okay?" Jane asked.

Amy nodded before picking at one brightly-polished nail. "Fine. I need caffeine. Are you okay?"

"Yes." She wasn't. She was furious at Luke for trying to make her take the day off. It was irrational, she knew it was irrational, but the old Luke would never have given her the day off because she looked tired. If Amy thought she was getting special treatment because she was sleeping with him…

"I'm not expecting special treatment because I slept with him," she said as she followed Amy to the front door.

Amy gave her a look of surprise. "I know that, Janie."

"I wanted to make sure," Jane muttered. "I know I told you this was a one-time thing only but…"

"You came home last night and Luke was in your bed," Amy said.

Jane nodded and Amy sighed before stopping in the hallway. "Janie, I love Luke to death but he has a way of bulldozing his way into a situation. Especially if it's something he really wants. I know you're kind of shy and not very assertive. Someone like my brother could take advantage of that without meaning to. You're not continuing to sleep with him because you think you have no choice, are you?"

"No," Jane said. "I want him just as much as he wants me."

"Good," Amy said. "I only want to be clear that you don't have to have sex with my brother in order to keep your job."

"I know," Jane said. She decided she sounded like she believed it.

"Do you?" Amy asked bluntly.

"Yes. C'mon, let's go. I need a coffee as much as you do."

෯ ෯

"Good morning, Jane."

Jane smiled at Mark. "Hello, Mr. Stanford."

He gave her a good-natured grin. "Call me Mark. How are you enjoying working for Luke? Is he playing nice?"

Jane hesitated. Did Mark know about her and Luke? Probably. He was Luke's best friend, no doubt Luke had mentioned to him that he was banging his damn secretary. Her cheeks bright red, she said, "Uh, yes, it's good."

"Did I say something wrong?" Mark asked.

"No, of course not," Jane replied. "Mr. Dawson has been very, uh, good to me."

Mark looked a little embarrassed. "Sorry, I didn't mean anything by my comment. I meant that there's always a spot for you in finance if you decide you don't want to work for the boss anymore."

She gave him a look of surprise. "Oh, that's very kind of you. Thank you."

"You're welcome," he said.

"Mr. Dawson is in his office if you want to – hi, Amy."

Jane watched as the smile dropped from Mark's face.

He turned and gave Amy a stiff nod. "Hello, Amy."

"Mark," Amy said coolly.

There was awkward silence that Jane hurried to fill. "Mr. Dawson is in his office and the Board is scheduled to call in," she checked her watch, "three minutes."

Mark and Amy continued to stare at each other. Jane had an idea that they had completely forgotten she was there.

"Amy?" She said. "The meeting?"

"What?" Amy said as she tore her gaze from Mark.

"The meeting with the Board," Jane said. "It's starting in a couple of minutes."

"Right, of course," Amy said. She hesitated and Mark made a small gesture with his hand toward Luke's office.

"After you."

"Thanks," she said.

She walked toward Luke's office and Mark's gaze dropped to her ass. When he realized that Jane was watching him, his cheeks turned red and he hurried after Amy.

∂∾ ∾∾

"Jane? Can you scan and email these documents to Kyra?" Luke asked.

Jane took the documents without looking at him. "Do you need me to pick up lunch for you?"

"No, I'm having lunch with Mark," Luke said.

She turned to leave and he frowned. "Jane, wait."

"What is it, Mr. Dawson?" She asked without turning.

He stood and moved around his desk to slip his arm around her waist. "What's wrong?"

"Now isn't the appropriate time to talk about it," she said.

He kissed the nape of her neck. He liked it when Jane wore her hair down but there were benefits to when she wore it up.

"Please don't do that," she said.

"Come to lunch with me," he said.

"You're having lunch with Mark."

"He'll understand if I bail."

She made an angry little noise and he turned her around, curving his arm around her waist again when she tried to step away. She gave him a furious look and pushed at his chest. "Let me go."

"Come to lunch with me," he repeated.

"I can't," she said before giving him a look of frustration. "I don't want special treatment from you."

He blinked at her. "I can take my assistant for lunch, Jane. I had lunch with Elaine once or twice a month."

"Did you blow off Mark to have lunch with her?" Jane said angrily. "Did you zip up her dress in the morning and tell her to take the day off because she looked tired?"

He didn't reply and she said, "Things are different now, Luke. We – we slept together and now it's even more important that I don't look like I'm getting special treatment. If others in the office find out that I slept with the boss..."

She trailed off and then said, "We need to be very careful. All right?"

He nodded and released her before stepping back. "Yes, I'm sorry. So, this means it's done. Is that right?"

Shit, why did he say that? What the hell did he do if she said yes? As fucked up as it was to be sleeping with his assistant, he didn't want it to be over. Not yet.

$\approx$ $\approx$

Jane studied Luke. The look on his face was one of careful detachment. She worried at her bottom lip for a moment. Did he want to continue having sex? Earlier this morning she would have said he did but she had just been irritable with him and snapped at him. That might have been enough to change his mind. Jeremy hated when she acted like a bitch and she'd learned to swallow her annoyance with him very quickly.

He was still waiting for her answer. God, why hadn't she asked the question first. She took a deep breath to steady her nerves and smiled tentatively at him.

"I was thinking about that earlier. I'd like to continue for a while if you do. But it's probably best if we have, um, an expiry date on this."

"An expiry date," he repeated. "That's a new one."

She blushed a little. "Look, we both know that we can't have an actual relationship but the," she glanced behind her at the closed doors but lowered her voice anyway, "sex is pretty amazing. I – I wouldn't mind a few more days to, um, enjoy you."

Oh Jesus, she sounded like a complete moron.

"We can get this out of our system and then go back to normal," she said. "What do you think?"

"A few days," he said.

She nodded. "Yes, I think if we, uh, spend the rest of this week and the weekend, that should be more than enough time. Don't you?"

He didn't reply and she swallowed down the painful lump that had appeared in her throat.

"I'm sorry," she said, "I think I've misread what you wanted. Ending it now is fine."

"You didn't misread," he said before returning to his desk. "Until the end of the weekend works for me."

"Are you sure?" She asked uncertainly.

"Yes." He sat down behind his desk and stared at his computer screen. "If you tell me what club you work at, I'll pick you up tonight when you're finished so you don't have to take the bus home."

"Oh, that's okay. I don't mind taking the bus."

He gave her an impatient look. "I'd prefer if you didn't take the bus so late. Besides, I know you're tired. You'll get more sleep if you let me pick you up. What's the name of the club?"

She shook her head. "No, thank you."

"Jane," he said irritably, "I don't mind."

"I do," she said. "You aren't missing out on sleep because of my second job. I've never had a problem on the bus at night."

He opened his mouth to argue and she said, "No special treatment, remember?"

"I remember," he said. He stared at his computer screen again and frowned before making a few clicks with the mouse. He leaned in to read the screen as he rubbed absently at his forehead. A muscle in his jaw ticked and he muttered, "Shit."

"What's wrong?" She asked.

"Can you ask Mark to come to my office?" He said.

She nodded and hurried back to her desk.

∂⊂ ⊃∂

"Wait, so these French guys are here because they've changed their minds and want to invest in the company?" Mark gave him a confused look. "But we haven't even begun to update the website. Didn't you tell me that Maria just did the ad for the new marketing people?"

"Yes. I don't have any idea why they're in the city," Luke said. "Pierre's email said they would be arriving tomorrow and could they meet with me and Amy Friday afternoon."

"They want to meet Amy?" Mark said.

"Unfortunately, yes," Luke sighed. "Think I can convince her to meet with them?"

"You're going to have to," Mark said.

"I know she hates doing this kind of stuff but if it means they invest in the line, then she's going to have to do it. Going international is the right move, Mark."

"I don't disagree," Mark said, "but Amy's not going to be happy with you."

"Probably not," Luke said. "Listen, make sure you're

available on Friday afternoon in case they want to meet with you as well."

"Sure," Mark said.

"Really?" Luke said.

"Yes, why?"

"Didn't think you'd come to the meeting if Amy was there," Luke said. "The meeting earlier today was," he paused, "tense."

"I didn't notice," Mark said as a muscle in his jaw began to twitch. "Do you think I can't do my job anymore, Luke? Is that what you're saying? You think I should quit?"

"Whoa," Luke held up his hands, "where is this coming from? You know I don't think that."

Mark glared at him before sitting back in his chair. "Sorry."

"Mark, we need to fix whatever's happened between you and Amy," Luke said. "Both of you are miserable."

"Maybe it has nothing to do with Amy," Mark said. "Did you ever think of that?"

"No," Luke admitted. "But that's because normally you tell me everything."

Mark gave him a guilty look. "I'm sorry. I know I've been a shitty friend lately."

"No," Luke said, "I'm being the shitty friend. I've been preoccupied with other stuff."

"Preoccupied with your assistant," Mark said. "You ever going to admit to me that you're fucking her?"

Luke glanced at the closed doors. "Keep your voice down. Fine, we had sex on Saturday night. We both said that was it and I meant it, I did. Only she walked into my office on Monday and I..."

He trailed off and then said. "Let's just say that my no sex at the office rule is null and void now."

"Shit, man," Mark said. "You need to be careful. Screwing your assistant in your office is a bad idea. Hell, screwing your assistant is a bad idea, period. What if she sues you for sexual harassment when you end it?"

"She wouldn't do that," Luke said. "You don't know Jane the way I do. She's sweet and kind. Besides, who said I'm going to end it?"

Mark shrugged. "Your last serious relationship was in University. You've never dated a woman for longer than a month since then."

"I've been concentrating on building the company," Luke said defensively. "Besides, you're one to talk. When was *your* last serious relationship?"

"Francine," Mark said. "We were serious."

"University girlfriend," Luke said.

"No, she wasn't. She was..."

Mark trailed off and Luke leaned back in his chair. "Face it, buddy, we're idiots when it comes to women. Neither of us have had a serious relationship in years. There's something wrong with the both of us."

"I'm serious about you, Lukie," Mark said solemnly.

Luke rolled his eyes. "Yeah, thanks."

"If you think we need couples therapy, I'll do it. I'll do whatever you want me to do to keep you happy, my little snugglebunny."

"Shut up, you ass," Luke said.

Mark grinned at him as Luke stared out the window for a minute. "Do you ever get tired of being alone, Mark?"

"You thinking you want something more with your assistant?" Mark asked.

"Maybe. I don't know," Luke said. "I haven't known her very long but there's something special about her. Not that it matters much how I feel. She wants to end it by the weekend. It's only sex for her."

"So, tell her you want more and see what she says," Mark said.

"Yes, because working together after she rejects me won't be awkward at all," Luke said.

Mark laughed. "You're just afraid of being rejected in general."

"She doesn't want more," Luke said. "She needs her job and she's afraid she'll lose it if things go bad."

"She makes a good point," Mark replied.

"Yeah, I know," Luke sighed. "Anyway, let's go for lunch early. You can help me figure out how to convince Amy to meet with the investors on Friday."

Chapter Thirteen

Jane stopped outside of her bedroom.   After her conversation with Luke, he had left early for lunch with Mark.   When he returned, he locked himself in his office and she hadn't seen him at all. She didn't have the courage to knock on his office door and say goodbye before she left for the day.

She sighed and rested her forehead against the door. Her visit with Mama J had gone horribly tonight. Mama J didn't know her and she had cursed repeatedly and thrown whatever items she could reach. Somehow, hearing sweet, soft-spoken Mama J cursing loudly and vehemently was the worse part.   The staff finally sedated her and Jane spent the last half hour of her visit trying not to cry while she watched her foster mother sleep.

Her lack of sleep last night had left her exhausted. Working at the club was the last thing she wanted to do and she was almost tempted to say screw it and call in sick. Instead, she had taken the bus to the club. She rubbed at her ass and winced slightly. The pinching and squeezing was over the top tonight and she was pretty sure the guy at table five had left a bruise.

She rubbed her aching back then gripped the door handle.   Luke wouldn't be in her bed - of course he wouldn't. He was angry with her earlier over her refusal to tell him the name of the club. It was better that he wasn't here, anyway. She was tired and needed sleep.

Are we going to bed or just going to stand in the hallway? Her inner voice asked grumpily.

She opened the door and, despite her belief, squinted at the bed in the darkness. Her breath caught in her throat and she hurried across the room and flicked on the bathroom light. Luke was a quilt-covered lump in the bed and a rush of happiness went through her. She closed the bathroom door and quickly showered and scrubbed the makeup from her face before brushing her teeth. She dropped her towel and slid into bed next to Luke. He was breathing deeply and she pressed a kiss against the back of his shoulder. He didn't move and she hesitated before turning her back to him and curling on her side.

It was enough that he was here with her, she thought happily. He was probably as tired as she was but he was still in her bed. She scooted backward until her back touched his warm back. She yawned and pressed her head into the pillow. The bed was toasty warm thanks to Luke's body heat and she smiled again. There was nothing bad about having Luke in her bed.

He turned and molded his body against hers, throwing his arm over her and cupping her breast. He kissed the back of her shoulder before mumbling, "I like finding you naked in my bed."

She smiled in the darkness. "You're naked in *my* bed."

"Tomato, tomahto," he mumbled again. "Work okay?"

"Yes," she said as he yawned. "I asked one of the other girls to take my shift tomorrow night so we could have an extra night together."

She shouldn't have taken tomorrow night off but she couldn't resist.

"S'good," he muttered. "Ready to be fucked?"

She giggled. "You're half-asleep."

He squeezed her breast as he yawned again. "Too tired, honey?"

"Yes," she said. "Go back to sleep, Luke."

He pulled her even closer and kissed her shoulder again before his body relaxed and he began to snore. Her smile widened as she snuggled into him and closed her eyes.

ॐ ॐ

"Luke? What time is the meeting with the investors tomorrow?" Amy stuck her head into his office.

"Three o'clock."

"Okay, thanks."

"Thanks for being so agreeable to meeting with them," he replied.

She shrugged. "It's my company too and I agree with you that it's time to go international with the clothing line. I'll do whatever is needed to make that happen."

"I know," he said. "But you were just saying that you hated the business side, remember?"

She shrugged again before saying, "Can you do me a favour? I told Jane I would give her a ride to see Mama J tonight but Valerie texted me. She got some last-minute tickets to see the Florida Georgia Line concert and I really want to go. But I need to leave to meet her right now. Can you give Jane a ride to the care home? It's so cold out and I hate thinking about her waiting for the bus in this weather."

"Yes," he said. "That's not a problem."

"Great!" Amy said. "Also, I'll be in late tomorrow."

"I figured," he said.

She grinned at him. "Can I assume you'll give Jane a ride to the office in the morning?"

He cleared his throat. "Yes."

"Have a good night, young Skywalker."

"You too, Yoda."

Amy flipped him the bird and left his office. Luke checked his watch. It was half an hour before the office closed for the day but he closed his laptop and stood up.

They could leave a little early. He would take Jane to see Mama J and then take her out for dinner. After, he'd take her home, undress her and spend the rest of the night touching her and making her come. Amy would be gone so there was no concern about keeping quiet. He grinned at the thought of making Jane scream his name again.

He'd woken at a little after four this morning with Jane's small body plastered against his. She was snoring softly and it was ridiculous how adorable he found it. He'd studied her sweet face and ignored his temptation to wake her for morning sex. She was tired and needed her rest. He'd never been much for cuddling but there was something comforting about waking up with Jane in his arms.

He grabbed his jacket and walked out of his office, checking his cell phone as he did. "Jane, I'm giving you a ride tonight and I think we should leave a little early so..."

"Mr. Dawson," Jane's voice was too loud and anxious, "I finished the documents you needed."

He glanced up. Maria, the head of HR, was standing in front of Jane's desk.

"Hello, Luke."

"Hello, Maria. What brings you up to this floor?"

"I had a meeting with Mark and thought I'd stop by and see how Jane was enjoying her new position. But seeing as you and Jane have plans, I'll head back to my office and - "

"We don't have plans," Jane said.

Her face was turning red and Luke said, "Amy asked if I could give you a ride to your appointment tonight as she's had a sudden change in plans. It's on my way home so I said yes."

Jane gave Maria an anxious look. "That's very nice of you, Mr. Dawson, but I can take the bus."

"Don't be ridiculous," he said. "But I do need to leave a bit early so..."

He trailed off as Maria studied Jane's red face.

"Yes, of course. Thank you," Jane said.

"Good to see you, Maria," Luke said.

"You as well. I'll need to book a meeting with you next week. I've already got a few potential resumes for the website upgrade."

"Good. You can book it with Jane. She has my schedule."

"You bet. Good night, you two."

"Night."

Maria walked away as Jane busied herself with closing her laptop and grabbing her purse. She gave Luke a look of panic as soon as Maria disappeared and Luke said, "It's fine, Jane."

"It isn't fine. I can't lie worth shit."

"That's for sure," he said with a small grin. "You need to work on not looking so guilty."

She glared at him. "It's not funny."

"It's kind of funny," he said. "Don't worry, she didn't suspect anything."

Jane pulled on her jacket. "I think she did."

"She didn't," Luke said. "Amy said you were going to visit Mama J, is that right?"

"Yes," she said. "Is everything okay with Amy?"

He nodded. "She just had the chance to go to a concert."

"I really can take the bus," Jane said. "I'm not expecting you to - "

"I don't mind," he interrupted. "After we visit Mama J's, we'll go for dinner. Do you like Thai food?"

"I do," she said.

"Good," he replied.

She was giving him an odd look and he arched his eyebrow at her. "What's wrong?"

"Nothing," she said.

"All right. Let's go visit with Mama J."

❧ ❦

"Is she sleeping?" Luke whispered.

"I'll check," Jane said.

Mama J was sitting in her chair by the window with her eyes closed. Her frail body was slumped over and he followed Jane as she hurried across the room.

"Mama J?" Jane said in a low voice. She touched the old woman's shoulder. Josephine lifted her head and squinted blearily at her.

"Hi there," Jane said as she pulled up a second chair and sat in front of her foster mother. Their knees were pressed together and Jane stroked Mama J's thigh as Luke sat on the edge of the bed.

"Did you have a good day?" Jane asked.

"Who are you?" Mama J said in a quavering voice.

Sorrow crossed Jane's face and Luke suddenly wanted to pick her up and carry her out of the room. She didn't deserve this kind of hell.

"It's Janie," she said. "I'm your daughter."

"I don't have a daughter."

"I'm your foster daughter."

"I wouldn't foster kids. I hate kids. I hate you. You're ugly!"

"Jane, maybe we should go," Luke said.

Jane rubbed Josephine's knee. "You don't mean that, Mama J. You love kids. You fostered a lot of them and everyone loved you. In fact - "

Quick as a snake, Josephine slapped Jane viciously across the face. "My name is Josephine! Not Mama J!"

"Jane!" Luke rushed over and placed his hand protectively on her shoulder.

Jane shook her head at him before smiling at Mama J. "I'm sorry, Josephine. I didn't mean to upset you."

"Who is that?" Josephine glared at Luke. "Is he here to steal my jewelry? Where's Walter? Walter knows what to do with fucking no-good jewelry thieves!"

"He's not a thief, Ma – Josephine," Jane said. "His name is Luke and - "

"Are you his whore? Is that it? You're his ugly little whore?" Josephine spat at her.

"No," Jane said. "Luke is my friend. He's not - "

Josephine tried to slap her again but Jane caught her hand.

"Don't do that, my love," she said in a low, grief-filled voice. She kissed the old woman's knuckles as Josephine's face crumpled and tears flowed down her wrinkled cheeks.

"What's wrong with me?" She moaned as she slumped in her chair again. "What's wrong with me? I'm so tired."

"I know," Jane said soothingly. "Why don't you lie down, Josephine? I'll help you into bed."

Josephine stared blankly at her. "I'd like that. I am very tired. What did you say your name was?"

"Jane."

"You're a good girl then, aren't you, Jane?"

Jane helped her stand. "Let's get you into bed, my love."

The old woman shuffled to the bed and Jane helped her lie down before tucking the covers around her. Luke stood at the end of the bed and watched as Jane smoothed back the old woman's thinning white hair.

"Is that better, Josephine?"

"Yes," she said. "Where's Walter?"

"I'm not sure," Jane said.

Mama J yawned as her eyes closed. "Can you find him? Tell him I'm waiting for him."

"I can do that," Jane said as she stroked Mama J's hair. "Go to sleep now."

"Find Walter?" Mama J mumbled.

"Yes, I'll find him," Jane said. She continued to stroke Mama J's hair until she fell asleep. She sat and watched her thin chest rise and fall for a few minutes before leaning forward and kissing her forehead. "I love you, Mama J. I'll see you later."

She stood and Luke watched as she discreetly wiped her cheeks before turning and smiling at him. "Ready to go?"

He stared at the red mark on her cheek as she gathered her purse and stood next to him. "Jane, are you all right?"

"Fine," she said. "But would you mind if we skipped dinner and just went home? I'm not very hungry."

"I'll pick up something on the way home," he said.

She shrugged. "Sure."

With a final look at Mama J, she started toward the door. Luke hurried after her and took her hand.

∽ ∾

"Jane, you should eat more," Luke said worriedly. He had stopped and picked up a pizza before driving Jane home and he watched her pick at the slice on her plate.

"Right," she said. She ate a couple of bites before putting the slice down and dropping her napkin over her plate.

Luke frowned but didn't have the heart to berate her about not eating. Hell, he barely had an appetite himself. He'd only met Mama J once and seeing her tonight was upsetting for him. He could only imagine how Jane was feeling.

Not that she would tell him anything. He had tried twice in the car to bring up what happened but she had changed the subject both times. He watched as she carried her plate to the counter and tossed the slice into the garbage before putting her plate in the dishwasher.

"Do you want any more?"

He shook his head and she closed the pizza box and stuck it in the fridge. Her face was pale except for the lingering red mark on her face. She drank the rest of her water as he said, "Jane, I'm sorry about what happened tonight."

She shrugged. "I'm used to it."

"You should talk about it," he said. "It'll help."

She shook her head and turned away but not before he

saw the glint of tears in her eyes. She stared out the small window over the kitchen sink. "I'm fine."

"You're not," he said. "It's okay that you're not. Talk to me, honey."

"Talking isn't what you want from me," she said bitterly.

He didn't reply and she made a choked sound before glancing over her shoulder at him. "I'm sorry, that was unfair and I – I didn't mean it. I'm just…"

She trailed off and he gave her a look of sympathy. "I know, honey. It's okay."

Her lower lip trembled and he tugged her into his lap as she burst into tears. He pressed her face into his neck and rocked her gently. He rubbed her back and whispered low words of comfort as she cried.

When her sobs trailed off after a few minutes, he grabbed a napkin from the table and pressed it into her hand. She wiped her eyes and blew her nose before sitting up and giving him a watery smile. "I'm sorry."

"Don't be," he said.

"Your shirt is soaked." She stared at his dress shirt. "There's makeup all over it."

"I don't care. Do you feel better?"

She nodded and dabbed at her eyes again. "Yeah, actually I do."

"Good. I'm sorry about what happened tonight." He ran his thumb over her cheek. "You'll probably bruise."

"She didn't mean to do it," Jane said defensively.

"I know," he said. "I know, honey. How often is she like that?"

Jane sighed and didn't object when he pressed her against his broad chest again. She rested her head on his shoulder as he rubbed her lower back. "It's happening more and more. The disease is progressing rapidly now. She used to have more good days than bad but the last month or so…"

She trailed off and made a soft sob. Luke kissed her

forehead. "I'm so sorry."

"Me too," Jane said. "I wish you could have known her before, Luke. She was the most amazing woman. She and Walter fostered over fifty kids. Did I tell you that?"

He shook his head and she snuggled in a little closer to him. "She did. She had pictures of all of them in a big photo album. She kept in touch over the years with at least thirty of them. They would email her pictures of their kids and it made her so happy. Up until she went to the care home, a bunch of them would still visit her."

"Do any of them visit her at the care home?" Luke asked.

Jane shook her head. "Not anymore. They did at first. It helped her to remember, I think. Seeing all those familiar faces visiting her. But then it stopped helping and the others they – they just drifted away."

He muttered a curse under his breath. Knowing that Jane had to deal with this all by herself made him sick to his stomach.

"I don't blame them," Jane said. "It's horrible to watch what's happening to her. I wish every day that I could just remember her the way she was. Does that make me an awful person, do you think?"

"No, honey. Not at all." He pressed a kiss against the top of her head.

"She had this way of making you feel special, you know? You could have the worst day in the world and Mama J would find a way to make you smile and make you feel better about it. She had a gift that way. I wish – I wish she'd been able to have kids of her own. If anyone deserved children, it was Mama J."

"She had you and the other kids," Luke said.

"It's not the same," Jane said. "She gave so much to us but never got what she wanted the most."

"I don't think she believes that," Luke said.

Jane didn't reply and he continued to rub her back as they sat silently. After a while, Jane sat up and gave him a small smile. "What time will Amy be home?"

"Late," he said. "She's also coming in late tomorrow. I said I'd give you a ride to work in the morning."

"I'll take the bus," Jane said.

"I'm going to be here, it makes sense for you to drive in with me," he said.

She blinked at him. "You – you're staying the night?"

"Yes. I've spent the last two nights here, why would tonight be different?"

"I don't look great and I've spent the last half hour sobbing into your shirt. My eyes are puffy and my nose is swollen and bright red. That's not exactly a sexy look," she said.

He pressed a kiss against the tip of her nose. "I find you sexy no matter what."

She smiled. "Spoken like a man who is looking to get laid tonight."

He shook his head and gave her a solemn look. "No, I'm being honest. You're the sexiest woman I've ever met, Jane Smith."

She swallowed and licked her lips before her gaze dropped to his mouth. He cleared his throat and tried to think of a reason to get Jane off his lap before she felt his rapidly hardening cock. She'd had a horrible evening and she wasn't interested in having sex. He knew that and was more than happy to just sleep in the bed with her again but his damn dick had different ideas.

The problem was solved when she slid off his lap. "I know it's early but do you mind if we go to bed?"

"No, of course not," he said. "I need to grab my bag from the car. Go to the bedroom, I'll lock up and be upstairs in a few minutes, okay?"

"Okay," she said.

She stood on her tiptoes and pressed a quick kiss against his jaw. "Thank you, Luke."

"You're welcome."

❧ ❦

Jane stared at the ceiling of the bedroom. She kept the covers pulled to her chin. She was naked and she wondered for a moment if she was being too bold. She knew Luke thought she wanted to go to bed early to sleep but the truth was, she was unbelievably horny for him.

A part of her knew she was using her lust for Luke as a coping mechanism. If she was fucking him, there was no room for sorrow or fear.

She's getting worse, Janie. You know she is. Maybe she'll never remember you again now. Maybe she'll –

She cut off her inner voice as fear skittered down her back. She didn't want to think about her sorrow at losing the Mama J she knew and loved – not tonight.

The bedroom door opened and Luke, carrying a garment bag and a leather overnight bag, slipped into the room. She had left the bedside lamp on and she watched as he hung the garment bag in the closet next to her clothes and carried the overnight bag into the bathroom.

She stared at the ceiling again and thought of nothing but how good it would feel to touch Luke. She would give him another blowjob, she decided. She loved his reaction and this time she could take her time. She didn't have to worry about someone walking in on them.

The bathroom door opened and Luke appeared wearing a pair of sleep pants and nothing else. They hung low on his hips and a surge of desire went through her as she stared at his v-line. God, his body was perfection. The narrow line of dark hair below his belly button made her mouth water. She had the sudden urge to pull on the drawstring of his sleep pants with her teeth. She stifled her nervous giggle as he shut the bathroom light off and crossed the room to climb into the bed beside her.

He reached for her and made a grunt of surprise when he felt her smooth skin. "Jane," he said cautiously, "why are you naked?"

"Why are you not naked?" She asked.

Boldly, she threw back the covers and straddled his hips. She could feel his erection against her core and she ground against him as he groaned and cupped her breasts. He kneaded them gently as she traced small circles across his chest.

"Jane," he whispered, "are you sure this is what you want tonight?"

"Yes," she said. "I need you. I need this."

He jerked under her when she pinched one flat nipple. "I want to make you feel good."

She leaned over him and kissed him. He immediately deepened the kiss, pushing his tongue past her lips to sweep inside her mouth until she was dizzy from her need for him.

"I want you so much, Luke," she whispered against his mouth.

"I want you too," he replied. "Let me make this about you tonight."

"No. I want to taste your cock again." She smiled at him before kissing her way across his chest. She admired the defined muscles of his abdomen, scratching her nails across them until he moaned. She kissed his chest and tasted his warm skin with her tongue before sucking on his flat nipple.

"Fuck!" He muttered as his hands clenched around the sheet.

She licked at his nipple before continuing downward. She nuzzled his belly button, tracing a circle around it as she pressed her breasts against his cock through his pants. She traced his v-line with her tongue and he made a low moan of need.

"Please, honey," he whispered.

She pulled on the waistband of his sleep pants with her fingers before grinning at him and grabbing the drawstring with her teeth. She tugged, undoing the neat bow he'd tied, as he panted harshly and his fingers fisted into the sheets again.

She wiggled back until she was straddling his shins and curled her fingers into his waistband. "Lift your hips."

He lifted and she pulled his pants down. He kicked them off his feet, nearly knocking her off his legs and onto the floor in the process and she giggled. "Careful, Mr. Dawson."

"Please," he said as she stared at his erect cock.

"Please what?" She said innocently as she ran her fingers over his balls.

"Please suck my cock," he groaned.

"Yes, Sir," she said before leaning over and taking his cock into her mouth.

He moaned and his fingers threaded through her hair as she sucked. He smoothed her hair back from her face and held it in a loose ponytail as he watched her suck.

"Such a good girl," he said hoarsely. "Do you have any idea how beautiful you look right now?"

She traced her tongue along the vein that ran along the underside of his cock and he shuddered all over. She swallowed his precum and pulled away before licking her lips. "You taste good, Mr. Dawson."

"Oh God," he whispered. "Keep sucking, Jane."

She bobbed her head up and down, sucking firmly as he moaned and pleaded and thrust his hips against her mouth. God, she loved his reaction. It made her so damn hot, she thought her lower body would catch on fire.

When she couldn't stand the throbbing in her pussy any longer, she released his cock with one slow, long lick and straightened. He reached down and fisted his own cock with a desperate look of need. She pulled on his wrist.

"Stop."

"Please," he moaned but released his cock. "Fuck, I was so close."

She grinned at him. "I know but I want to fuck you."

"I want that too."

She reached into the nightstand drawer and produced a condom. He raised his eyebrow at her and she said, "Always be prepared."

He made a sound that was halfway between a laugh and a groan. His hips arched when she rolled the condom onto his dick.

"Fuck me," he said through gritted teeth.

"Patience, Mr. Dawson."

She squeaked in surprise when he sat up and grabbed her around the waist. He lifted her and she gasped when his cock dragged along her clit before sliding into her tight entrance. She sank down on him, moaning as he cupped her shoulders and held her against him.

Without speaking, he thrust in and out rapidly. She tipped her head back and he kissed the column of her throat as she clung to his shoulders and rode him.

His fingers found her clit and rubbed as she ground her pelvis against him.

"Jesus," he muttered before rubbing her clit harder.

Her orgasm rolled through her, unexpected and shocking in its intensity. Beneath her, he groaned as her pussy tightened around his dick and held him deep inside of her. His hips bucked and he climaxed, thrusting so roughly that she would have fallen off his lap if he wasn't holding her in a tight grip.

He collapsed on his back, dragging her down with him. She rested her head on his chest as he stroked her back with the tips of his fingers.

"Did I hurt you?" He asked.

She shook her head. "No. It was really good. Thank you, Luke."

He squeezed her ass. "You're welcome, Jane. We should get some sleep."

"Hmm," she said sleepily. He eased her off of him and she watched blearily as he disposed of the condom before curling up behind her. He cupped her breast and kissed the back of her shoulder.

"Night, Luke."

"Night, Jane."

Chapter Fourteen

Jane walked into the reception and smiled at the two men standing at the reception desk. "Mr. Durand and Mr. Morel? My name is Jane. I'm Mr. Dawson's assistant."

The men gave her identical flirty grins. The taller of the two – he was blond with dark brown eyes and the bulky build of a football player stepped forward. He took her hand and brought it to his mouth before pressing a kiss against her knuckles.

"It's a pleasure to meet you, Jane. You must call me Pierre."

She supposed if she wasn't so obsessed with Luke, Pierre's good looks and French accent would have done something for her. As it was, she didn't feel a thing when Pierre blatantly looked her over before squeezing her hand and kissing it again.

"This is my associate, Julien."

"Hello, Mr. Morel," Jane said. Her other hand was taken by the dark-haired man and kissed as well.

"Julien, please" he said. He had gorgeous green eyes and he was a few inches shorter than Pierre with a leaner build.

Both were dressed in expensive suits and she was happy she was wearing a Dawson suit when Julien's gaze drifted over her. "That suit is exquisite, Jane."

"Thank you."

"Is it a Dawson?"

"Of course," she said. She pulled both of her hands free and tucked them behind her back. "Mr. Dawson is finishing up a phone call but he's asked me to bring you to the boardroom."

"Lead the way, Jane. We'll follow you wherever you go," Pierre said.

She led them down the maze of hallways to the boardroom. They followed her into the room and she smiled at them. "Mr. Dawson will be right with you. Could I get either of you a coffee or a glass of water?"

They shook their heads as Julien smiled at her. "But you must stay and keep us company until your boss arrives, Jane."

She hesitated and Pierre pulled out a chair. "We insist. We're here for a few days and need someone to tell us where the best tourist spots are."

She smiled and sat down in the chair. "Of course."

৵ ৶

Luke hurried into the boardroom. The phone call had gone longer than he thought and he hoped to God that Amy had been on time to the meeting. He opened the Boardroom door and froze in the doorway. Jane was sitting at the table and Julien and Pierre were flanking her.

Anger burned in his belly when Pierre picked up a lock of Jane's hair and rubbed it gently as Julien leaned in closer and let his arm brush against hers.

"Jane, you must accompany us tomorrow," Pierre said. "We cannot do tourist things without a tour guide."

"I'm afraid I have other plans," Jane said. A little of Luke's jealousy abated when she pulled her hair free of Pierre's hand and crossed her arms so that Julien wasn't touching her. "If you'll excuse me, I need to get back to my desk. I'm sure that Luke and Amy will be here shortly."

Both men stood as Jane pushed back her chair and rose gracefully to her feet. She turned and Luke was mollified when she saw him and a warm smile crossed her face. "Mr. Dawson, hi."

As the two men stood, Luke strode forward and stood closer than necessary to Jane before holding out his hand. "Pierre, Julien, it's good to see you again."

"You as well, Luke," Pierre replied. "Thank you for meeting with us."

"It was my pleasure," Luke said.

"We were just trying to convince your lovely assistant to be our tour guide this weekend," Julien said with a small grin at Jane. "Perhaps you can convince her?"

"I'm afraid Jane has work this weekend," Luke said.

"What a shame," Julien said.

"Jane, will you go to Amy's office and see what's keeping her?" Luke asked.

"Of course," Jane replied.

"I'm right here. I'm sorry I'm late." Amy rushed in, the bracelets around her wrists jingling, and smiled apologetically.

Luke watched as Julien and Pierre glanced at each other before stepping around him and Jane.

"Ms. Dawson," Julien said before taking her hand and kissing her knuckles. "It is a pleasure to meet you. My name is Julien Morel and this is my associate, Pierre Durand."

Pierre made a short bow as Amy tugged free of Julien's grip and held out her hand. Like Julien, he kissed her knuckles and then continued to hold her hand.

"It's nice to meet you both," she said.

She glanced at her hand before raising her eyebrow at Pierre. He gave her an appreciative smile before kissing her knuckles again. "Forgive me, Ms. Dawson. A woman as beautiful as you – I find difficult to let go."

More anger flooded through Luke. It was bad enough

that they were hitting on Jane but watching them hit on Amy was making his need to protect his little sister come roaring to life. He took Amy's arm and pulled her away from Pierre.

"My sister is a very busy woman. She's agreed to attend this business meeting, let's keep this business like. Shall we?"

Amy elbowed him discreetly as Pierre and Julien exchanged looks.

"Forgive my brother," Amy said. "He sometimes forgets that I'm a grown woman who's capable of taking care of herself."

She gave Luke a pointed look that he ignored. He didn't care if Amy didn't find the investors' flirting annoying, there was no way in hell he was letting his baby sister be groped by either of them.

Pierre smiled at her as Julien's gaze drifted over Amy's body. Luke clenched his hands into fists as Amy said, "Let's get started, all right?"

"Very good idea," Luke said stiffly. "Jane, would you mind bringing in some glasses and water?"

"Not at all," Jane replied.

As she left the boardroom, Luke waited until the French men were seated at the table before taking Amy's elbow and steering her toward the table. Keeping an empty chair between her and Pierre, he pulled out the chair for her and she rolled her eyes at him before sitting down.

☙ ❧

"You okay?" Luke asked Amy. It was two hours later and after walking Pierre and Julien to the elevator, he had followed Amy back to her office.

She collapsed in one of the beanbag chairs in her office. "I'm fine. I don't need you to protect me, Luke."

"They were blatantly hitting on you the entire meeting,

Amy!"

"So? They're good looking guys and I'm single. What's the harm?"

"The harm? Forgetting that they're not good enough for you, they're thinking of partnering with us. No mixing business with pleasure," Luke said.

"Are you kidding me? You're banging your secretary, Luke."

"That's different," he said. "Jane is…different."

"Jane is a sweetheart and you need to lock that shit down before she figures out that she's too good for you," Amy said with a laugh.

"We're not talking about me and Jane. We're talking about you. Don't sleep with Pierre or Julien," Luke said.

"You don't get to tell me what to do. Besides, a little flirting never hurt anyone. It might even help convince them to hand over their money."

His jaw dropped. "Amy, you don't think you have to sleep with them to get this deal, do you? The company is fine, the Board is happy with sales – we don't *need* to go international," Luke said.

"Of course I know that. I don't mind flirting with them but I'm not going to fuck one of them just to get an account with them," she said.

"Gross," he said.

She rolled her eyes. "You started this conversation. What time is dinner again?"

"We're meeting Pierre and Julien at seven," he said.

She glanced at her watch. "I'm going to work from home for a bit. Text me if you need anything before dinner. Okay?"

"Sure," he replied. He hesitated before saying, "I'm going to bring Jane to dinner tonight."

"Sounds good," Amy said absently as she scrolled through her phone.

"For work reasons," he said. "I'll pay her overtime. If we do more negotiations over dinner or they want to discuss work, I might need her to take notes or something."

"Mm, hmm." Amy was still staring at her phone.

"We're not dating," he said.

Amy glanced up. "Who's not dating?"

"Nothing, never mind," he said. "I'll see you at seven."

He left her office and headed back to his. Jane was sitting at her desk and smiled at him when he stopped beside it.

"How did it go?"

"Fine," he said. "We talked a lot about our plans for the new website design, how we would incorporate a more seamless shopping experience for our customers. They still haven't given us a final answer but that's probably because they were too busy flirting with Amy."

Jane laughed and picked up a stack of file folders on her desk. "They are very handsome and charming. I was with them for nearly twenty minutes before you showed up and they were a little relentless in the flirting. Hey, would it be all right if I filed these in your office or do you want me to wait until you're out?"

"Go ahead and file them now," he said shortly. Jealousy had flooded through him the moment she said Pierre and Julien were handsome and charming.

She hesitated at his tone but walked into his office. He followed her and shut the doors as she opened up the top drawer of his mahogany file cabinet. She had finished stacking the folders on top when he turned her around and yanked her into his embrace. He took her mouth in a hard kiss, squeezing her ass with one big hand as he pushed his tongue past her lips. She moaned and returned his kiss. The taste of her, the feel of her ass filling the palm of his hand perfectly, made his cock harden and he ground it against her. He pulled back and stared at her swollen mouth and flushed cheeks.

"What was that for?" She said.

"Did you like it when they flirted with you?" He asked

a bit sulkily.

"You're jealous," she said.

"No, I'm not."

"Yes, you are."

"No, I'm not."

She didn't reply and he scowled at her. "Fine, I'm jealous. But in my defense, women love a man with an accent."

She giggled. "You think I'm going to drop you for Pierre and Julien just because they have an accent?"

"Pierre *and* Julien?" He said.

She shrugged. "They share women and won't have sex without each other."

His mouth dropped open. "How the hell do you know that?"

"You can learn a lot about a person in twenty minutes. Especially when it's two men who delight in talking about themselves. Now, let me go – I really need to get this filing done."

"Jane," he said anxiously, "are you interested in them? Do you want to, uh, sleep with two men at once?"

Now it was her turn for her jaw to drop. "Did you just ask me if I wanted to have a threesome?"

"Do you want to sleep with Julien and Pierre?" He said.

"Of course I don't," she said. "Luke, what has gotten into you?"

He pulled her closer and pressed a kiss against her mouth. "Nothing. I only wanted to make sure you remembered that you have plans with me for the weekend."

"I haven't forgotten," she said.

"Good." He nuzzled her throat. "I'll make you forget all about those French bastards."

He thought that would make her laugh but she cupped his face and gave him a serious look. "I don't want to sleep with them. I know it's not serious between us and I

218

know we're done after Sunday, but I still wouldn't sleep with another person while I'm sleeping with you."

His stomach churned and he was surprisingly hurt by her statement that it wasn't serious between them. He swallowed down his disappointment and said, "I wouldn't either, Jane."

"I know," she said. "I really need to get this filing done or I'll end up staying late."

He shook his head. "You can't. Amy and I are meeting Pierre and Julien at seven for dinner and you're coming with us."

"I can't do that," she said. "it's not appropriate and besides, I'm going to visit Mama J after work."

"I'll drive you to see Mama J. We have plenty of time to visit with her before dinner," he said.

"It's not appropriate, Luke," she said. "I'm your assistant not…"

She trailed off and he reluctantly let her go and took a step back. "Exactly. You're my assistant and I might need you at this work dinner. If they want to discuss work stuff, you may have to take notes. I'll pay you overtime."

"It's work related," she said. Her face suggested that she didn't quite believe him.

He nodded. "Yes, so bring your laptop. All right?"

"All right," she said.

"Good." He returned to his desk and checked his email as Jane filed. He tried to concentrate on his work but his gaze kept flickering to Jane. God, she smelled so good and her ass looked fucking amazing in that skirt. He glanced at the couch before checking his watch. He hadn't fucked Jane on the couch yet and today was his last chance. Both Wednesday and Thursday, he'd had multiple fantasies about bending her over the back of the couch, lifting up her skirt and sliding into her while she moaned his name.

His dick was as hard as a rock again and he was about to lock the doors and coax Jane into a quickie when Mark walked into his office.

"Hey, Luke."

He tried not to glare at his best friend as Jane slid the last folder into the cabinet and smiled at Mark as she headed for the door.

"How are you, Jane?"

"Good, how are you?" She replied.

"I'm good." Mark sat down on the couch and stretched his long legs out as Luke watched Jane cross his office. She shut the doors and he sat back in his chair before turning to Mark.

"What's up?" He said. He could hear the irritation in his voice.

Mark raised his eyebrow at him. "I wanted to see how the meeting went. I'm assuming not well or are you pissed for some other reason?"

"I'm not pissed," Luke said.

"You sound pissed," Mark replied.

"I was thinking of convincing Jane to have a quickie in my office until you came strolling in," he said.

Mark laughed. "Bad timing on my part. Sorry, man."

"It was a bad idea anyway. I need to be professional," Luke said.

"Boring," Mark said. "Anyway, how did the meeting go?"

"They still haven't fully committed."

"Then why the hell did they come to the office?" Mark said.

"Honestly, I have no idea what's going on in their heads and they're easily distracted."

"What do you mean?"

"They were flirting with Jane and when I walked into the boardroom, both of them were touching her." Luke's face darkened with anger as Mark grinned at him.

"Beating up potential investors because they flirt with your woman is bad business practice."

"She's not my woman," Luke said as his email dinged.

He turned and stared at his computer screen. "Besides, the minute Amy walked in, they forgot all about Jane. It was more than a little disgusting to watch them hit on her. She didn't seem to mind all that much but - "

"They were hitting on your sister?" Mark interrupted.

"Yeah," Luke said as he clicked on the email. "They were all over her. I'm surprised they even invited me to dinner tonight. Pretty certain they'd rather spend all their time with Amy."

"They're having dinner tonight with Amy?"

Mark's voice sounded strange and Luke swivelled in his chair. "What's wrong?"

"Amy's having dinner with them tonight," Mark repeated.

"Well, we're having dinner with them – I'm taking Jane in case I need her to take notes or something - but I won't be surprised if they try and convince Amy to go back to their goddamn hotel room with them. Jane told me that they told her they share their women. That they won't even fuck a woman unless both of them are - "

"I'm going to dinner with you," Mark snapped.

"What?"

"What time and where?" Mark said.

"You want to have dinner with us?"

"Yes," Mark said irritably. "If it's a business dinner, I should be there. Don't you think?"

"Uh, sure," Luke said.

"Good." Mark stood up and stalked toward the doors. "Text me the time and address."

He left the office and Luke shook his head in bewilderment before turning back to his computer.

❦

"Amy, you look amazing," Jane said.

Amy was standing next to the coat check when they'd arrived at the restaurant. Luke took Jane's coat as Jane stared at Amy. The blonde was wearing a form-fitting dark green dress that hugged her curves and showed off a generous amount of cleavage.

"Thanks, Janie." Amy handed her jacket to Luke before smiling at Jane. "You look lovely as well."

Jane laughed. "I'm still wearing my work clothes, but thanks."

As Luke took their jackets to the coat check, Amy said in a low voice, "Do you think it's too much?"

Jane shook her head. "No, that dress is beautiful on you. Julien and Pierre won't know what hit them."

Amy blushed softly. "I didn't wear it specifically for them."

"Did you wear it for Mark?" Jane asked.

Amy stared at her. "Why would you say that?"

"Well, Luke mentioned that Mark was coming to dinner tonight and I thought…"

Jane trailed off and chewed at her bottom lip. "I'm sorry. I'm being an idiot. Forget I said that."

"Mark's coming for dinner?" Amy's face had paled.

"Yes. You didn't know?"

"Luke didn't mention it."

"Luke didn't mention what?" Luke had joined them and Jane suppressed her shiver when he rested his hand on her lower back and rubbed gently.

"Why is Mark coming to dinner?" Amy said sharply. "And why didn't you tell me?"

Before Luke could answer, Julien and Pierre had joined them. They stared in frank appreciation at Amy in her green dress before Pierre hurried forward and took Amy's hand, kissing the knuckles. He smiled at her and said, "Tu es belle, Amy."

"Thank you," she said as Julien crowded in on the other side of her. "Your dress is stunning, mon ange."

"Angel is very fitting for her," Pierre said before stroking a strand of Amy's blonde hair.

"Oui, très approprié," Julien murmured.

"I hate to interrupt, but we haven't met yet."

Amy paled at the sound of Mark's voice. She took a step back from Pierre and Julien and gave Mark an odd look that was half defiance and half guilt. Mark's face was dark with anger as he stepped forward and held out his hand. His nostrils flaring, he shook Pierre's hand and then Julien's. Jane wondered if he was deliberately avoiding looking at Amy.

"Mark Stanford. I'm the CFO of Dawson Clothing."

"It's nice to meet you, Mr. Stanford," Julien said. "We did not realize you would be joining us for dinner this evening."

Mark gave him a tight smile that didn't reach his eyes. Julien stared coolly at him and Amy said, "Mark often joins us for client dinners and meetings. He would have been there this afternoon but he had a previous meeting. Isn't that right, Mark?"

"Yes," Mark said.

There was an awkward silence and Jane lightly elbowed Luke in the ribs. He was studying his sister with a faint look of confusion. She elbowed him again and he said, "Well, now that everyone's here, let's ask the hostess to take us to our table."

☙ ❧

"Amy, these are magnificent," Pierre said. Both he and Julien leaned closer and studied the screen of her phone. When they were shown to their table, both men had snagged the seats on either side of Amy. They were outrageous flirts and both men were using their considerable charm on her. Jane had sat between Mark and Luke and spent most of the dinner wondering who would snap first and punch the French men. Her money was on Mark. Luke was obviously angry by the way the men were flirting with his sister but Mark's rage was palpable.

She watched with growing alarm as Julien's gaze dipped to Amy's cleavage and Mark's body stiffened. His hand tightened around his wine glass and Jane said hurriedly, "So, is anyone having dessert? Something sweet might be good."

"I do enjoy something sweet after dinner," Julien said in a low voice. He traced one finger across Amy's collarbone. Jane grabbed Mark's forearm with her right hand and Luke's thigh with her left hand and squeezed hard when they both started to stand.

Luke relaxed in his chair but Mark jerked in anger and stared at her hand before raising his gaze to her. She gave him a pointed look and he flushed before saying, "No dessert for me."

Jane released his arm as Luke said, "Me neither."

Pierre was studying Amy's phone again. "Seriously, ma chérie, these are incredible. Have you thought about starting a line with these?"

Amy shrugged. "Our clients want business clothes. A casual line doesn't align with their interests and I'm not wasting company money on a line that won't give us a return on investment."

"I think it would," Pierre said. "We should talk more about this casual line. Perhaps you'd like to come back to our hotel room after dinner? We can have some wine and talk business."

Jane thought Mark was going to have a stroke. His face was bright red and he was squeezing his wine glass until his fingers were white. She elbowed him discreetly and he glared at her before clearing his throat. "If you want to talk business, then it's Luke or myself you should direct questions to. Amy doesn't like to be involved in the business side. Isn't that right, Amy?"

She gave him a cool look as she tucked her phone into her purse. She sat back as Julien laid his arm across the back of her chair and played with her soft blonde hair. "I'm considering becoming more involved in the business side."

"Since when," Mark snorted. "You just want to make the pretty things, remember?"

She scowled at him and crossed her arms over her chest. The motion made her ample breasts push against her dress and both Julien and Pierre stared in unabashed delight at her pale skin. Jane wondered if she was the only one who heard Mark's low snarl.

"It's good to try new things," Amy said. "Life is boring if you're doing the same old things repeatedly."

Mark raked his hand through his hair as Pierre smiled at Amy. "Julien and I do love adventurous women who are up to trying new things."

"So, that's a no on dessert for everyone? Because it's getting late and I think we should call it a night," Luke said. Jane could hear the anger in his voice.

"Trying new things isn't always what it's cracked up to be," Mark said through clenched teeth. "Sometimes it's the biggest mistake a person can make."

"Amy?" Luke leaned forward. "Ames, are you all right?"

Amy's face had turned deathly pale and for one moment, Jane thought she was going to burst into tears. Desperate to help her friend, she said, "I need to use the ladies' room. Amy, how about you?"

Amy shook her head. "No," she said in a low voice as she stood up and grabbed her purse. "I need to go. Pierre and Julien, I'm afraid I can't meet this evening but if your earlier offer is still open, I'll be your tour guide tomorrow and perhaps we can talk about the new line then."

All four men stood and Pierre grinned delightedly at Amy before leaning forward and pressing a kiss against her cheek. "We would be honoured, mon ange."

Julien leaned in and kissed her other cheek. "Tell us the time and place and we'll be there, ma chérie."

"Let's say ten at the art museum on sixteenth avenue," Amy said. "That way I have plenty of time to," she paused and her gaze flickered briefly to Mark, "play tour guide."

"Perfect. We'll be there, mon ange," Pierre said.

"Good," Amy said.

She walked away as Mark slowly sank back into his chair. His hands were in tight fists and he stared at the top of the table as Julien said, "I believe we will call it a night as well. Are you available to meet with us on Monday, Luke?"

"Yes," Luke said.

"Bien," Julien said. "We will discuss our possible investment with your company. Say around three on Monday?"

"Fine" Luke said. "Enjoy your weekend and if there's anything you need, let me know."

"Oh, I am certain Amy will be able to help us with anything we need," Pierre said.

Mark inhaled sharply and Jane grabbed his thigh under the table, squeezing as hard as she could, when he started to stand. He glared at her and she subtly shook her head as, with a mild look of distaste, Luke shook first Pierre's hand and then Julien's.

"Mr. Stanford, it was a pleasure," Julien said before holding out his hand.

Mark stared at his hand before giving it a brief shake. "Pleasure," he muttered as a muscle ticked in his jaw.

Pierre smiled at Jane. "So lovely to meet you, Jane. Perhaps you would care to join the three of us tomorrow and," he paused and glanced at Julien, "try new things as well."

Before she could reply, Luke said, "I need Ms. Smith to work tomorrow."

"What a pity," Pierre said as Julien grinned at him before taking Jane's hand and kissing it lightly. "Bonne nuit, Jane."

"Good night," she said.

The two men left and Luke blew his breath out in a low rush. "Christ, that was awkward as hell. The way they were hitting on Amy was uncomfortable to say the least."

He trailed off and then jerked in surprise when Mark slammed his fists down on the table. The silverware rattled and Jane's empty wine glass tipped over.

"What the hell is going on with you tonight?" Luke said. "You insist on coming to dinner but barely say two words. What's your problem with Julien and Pierre?"

"What's my problem?" Mark snapped. "Those two assholes were practically humping Amy at the goddamn table and you didn't do a fucking thing about it. You're her brother for fuck's sake."

Luke blinked at him. "I didn't like it anymore than you did but she's a grown woman, Mark. Besides, she obviously didn't mind. She's going out with them tomorrow, isn't she?"

Mark's face turned bright red and he stood up abruptly. "I have to go. Good night."

He stalked away and Luke stared at Jane before rubbing at his jaw. "Mark is acting crazy tonight."

"Maybe it has something to do with Amy," Jane said delicately.

"Yeah, probably," Luke said. "It pissed me off, not to mention grossed me out, to watch them hitting on her. Mark thinks of her as his sister too so I shouldn't be surprised it pissed him off as well."

"Right," Jane said. "That must be it."

He gave her a curious look as he signalled the waiter for the cheque. "What?"

"Nothing," she said.

Luke smiled at her. "Have I mentioned how beautiful you look tonight?"

She grinned. "You don't have to sweet talk me, Mr. Dawson. I'm going home with you tonight."

He leaned in and nuzzled her neck. "Of course you are. Why wouldn't you?"

She rolled her eyes before rubbing his thigh. "Reign in the arrogance or I'll withhold the sexy times."

He burst into laughter and she shushed him when the couple at the table next to them glanced over curiously.

"You won't," he whispered into her ear. "You can't resist me, Jane Smith."

He sucked on her earlobe and she shuddered with pleasure. He was right – she couldn't resist him and didn't want to.

"I'll take you home first to grab some clothes and then we're spending the rest of the weekend in my bed. Any questions, Ms. Smith?"

"No, Mr. Dawson. No questions at all," she said sweetly.

Chapter Fifteen

"You really didn't have to come with me, Luke," Jane said as he drove toward the care home.

"I want to," he said.

"No, you wanted to spend the weekend in bed," she said.

"Only if you were with me," he replied with a wink.

She bit at her bottom lip. It was after three on Saturday and she and Luke had spent all morning in bed together. Luke was sleeping deeply when she had slipped out of bed and had a quick shower. She always went to see Mama J on Saturday and despite her desire to stay in Luke's warm bed, she wanted to see her foster mother.

She'd only been in the shower for a few minutes when Luke had joined her. As soon as he found out her plans, he had insisted on coming with her. She was both surprised and happy by his insistence.

As he pulled into the parking lot, she said, "Are you sure? You could drop me off and I'll take the bus back to your place when I'm finished visiting."

"I'm sure," he said. "I like Mama J and enjoy visiting with her. Unless you don't want me there?"

He gave her an uncertain look and she shook her head. "No, I want you there."

"Good. Let's go see Mama J," Luke said.

They climbed out of the car and she didn't object when he took her hand as they walked to the home. What was happening would be finished by tomorrow night and just because Luke was affectionate and sweet, didn't change anything. She needed her job.

She tried to let go of his hand when they entered the home but he refused to let go. He smiled at Bev at the front desk. "Good afternoon, Bev. It's good to see you again. You're looking lovely."

The older woman giggled like a school girl. "Nice to see you too, Luke."

"Hello, Bev," Jane said.

"Oh, hi, hon. How are you?"

"Good. Is Mama J in her room?"

"She is," Bev said. "She's having a good day today."

Jane breathed a sigh of relief and hurried down the hall as Luke followed her. She knocked on the door and opened it. Mama J was sitting next to the window and she smiled at Jane.

"Hello, my sweet Janie."

"Hello, Mama J." She dropped Luke's hand and leaned over the old woman, kissing her soft cheek before giving her a gentle hug.

Mama J returned her hug before smiling at Luke. "Hi there, young man."

"Hello, Josephine. My name is - "

"Luke," Mama J interrupted. "I remember. Your Janie's boyfriend."

"That's right, I am," Luke said. "It's good to see you again."

"Good to see you too," Mama J replied. "What are you two kids up to today?"

"Not too much," Jane said. "How are you feeling?"

"I feel good. My hip hurts a little but Bev gave me some meds earlier," Mama J said. "Luke, you should take my Janie out for dinner. She spends too much time here. She's young and shouldn't be spending all her time with an

230

old woman like me."

"Stop that, Mama J," Jane scolded gently. "I love spending time with you."

"I love spending time with you too," Josephine said. "But my Walter used to take me for dinner every Saturday night. There was this little diner on Westwood Street and we would go and sit in the last booth. I would order a vanilla milkshake, large of course, and Walter would roll his eyes and tease me because he would always have to finish it."

She patted Jane's face. "I miss Walter."

"I know, Mama J," Jane said.

"I'll see him soon," Mama J said briskly before wiping away the tears on Jane's cheeks with her thumbs. "Luke, take Jane out to dinner."

"Actually," Luke said. "I was wondering if both of you beautiful young ladies would accompany me for dinner this evening."

Jane pressed her lips together and tried not to burst into tears as a look of pure joy crossed Mama J's face. The old woman clapped her hands like a small child. "It's been so long since I've gone out for dinner."

She paused and then shook her head. "But I can't intrude on your Saturday night date."

"I insist," Luke said. "I'm taking Jane to a little diner on Westwood Street and we would both love it if you joined us. We need someone to tell us what's good on the menu."

"Please, Mama J," Jane said. "We want you to join us."

Mama J's smile widened. "I would love to come for dinner. Janie, help me to get dressed and put on my face, would you?"

Luke headed for the door. "I'll wait for you in the common room."

"Thank you, Luke," Jane said.

He paused in the doorway and gave her the grin she had grown to love. "You're welcome, Jane."

છે ન્

"How is the milkshake, Josephine?" Luke asked.

The old woman smiled at him. "Delicious, Luke. Thank you."

"You're welcome." He squeezed Jane's hand and leaned back in the booth as Mama J stared at the two of them. She hadn't eaten very much of her burger and fries but she'd drank a fair amount of her vanilla shake.

He studied the diner as Jane urged her foster mom to eat more. The diner wasn't his usual type of place. The red leather of the booths was old and faded with rips and butt imprints firmly worn into the seats. The restaurant wasn't very big, the waitress not very friendly and he was pretty certain the place would fail its next health inspection, but the food was surprisingly good.

Of course, he wouldn't be surprised if he and Jane ended up with food poisoning tomorrow. He grimaced inwardly. Not exactly the way he wanted to spend his last day with her but the look on Jane's face, and on Mama J's face, made the possible food poisoning worth it. He'd never seen Jane look so happy and as she smiled up at him, he leaned down and placed an impulsive kiss on her mouth. He could taste the chicken pot pie she was eating on her lips and he kissed her again before straightening.

Josephine was grinning at them and Jane flushed a little as the old woman leaned forward and said, "Your husband is a real sweetheart, Janie."

"He's not my husband, Mama J," Jane said.

Josephine frowned at them. "Why, of course he is. Don't speak so foolishly."

Jane took Mama J's hand and squeezed it lightly. "I think you're a bit mixed up. Luke and I aren't married."

Josephine yanked her hand away and scowled at Jane. "Don't lie to me. You know I don't like it when you lie to me!"

"I'm not," Jane said. "Calm down and - "

"Don't lie to me!"

Mama J's voice was rising and the few other customers in the diner were starting to look their way. "Why would you lie about not being married! I was at the wedding!"

"You're right, Mama J," Luke said. "Jane and I are married. You were at the wedding."

Mama J smiled triumphantly. "I know. For goodness sake, Janie, you shouldn't be ashamed of being married."

"I'm not," Janie said.

Josephine leaned forward and gripped his hand. "You love my Janie, don't you, boy? You love her and you're going to treat her well. Right?"

"Yes," Luke said.

"Say it," Mama J said agitatedly. "Say you love my Janie right now."

"Mama J," Jane said, "Why don't you have some more of your vanilla shake before it melts?"

"Say it," Josephine snapped at him. "Say you love my Janie."

"I love her," Luke said.

Jane twitched against him as Mama J continued to glare at him. Before she could grow more upset, Luke turned to Jane.

"I love you, Jane." He kissed her lightly.

Jane stared up at him, her cheeks red and her eyes bright. He kissed her again and said, "I love you."

It was his turn to twitch when Jane whispered, "I love you too."

Her cheeks flamed even more and she looked at the table as Mama J smiled at the two of them. "You're the sweetest couple ever. When are you going to make me a grandma?"

Luke barely heard her. His pulse was pounding in his ears and his head was reeling. Did Jane mean what she said? Hell, did he mean what he said?

"Luke? When are you going to make me a grandma?"

Mama J prompted. Her agitation had disappeared and she was sipping contently at her shake again.

"Uh, soon," he said, making Jane jerk against him again.

"Good," Mama J said happily. "Janie, eat some more of your dinner. You're too thin."

❧ ❧

Jane followed Luke into his bedroom. He'd been quiet and withdrawn since they took Mama J back to the care home. She was very tired and starting to mix up her words and Jane had quickly tucked her into bed before kissing her goodbye. To her relief, Mama J hadn't asked Luke about marriage or babies again and had just given him a weary goodbye.

"Luke?" She said as he stared out the window of his bedroom.

"Yeah?" He didn't look at her.

"Thank you for tonight. I know the diner isn't your type of place but it meant a lot to Mama J to go there again."

"You're welcome."

He didn't say anything else and she chewed on her bottom lip for a few minutes before crossing to the bathroom. She gathered her toiletries and carried them back into the bedroom before dumping them into her suitcase. She zipped it up as Luke said, "What are you doing?"

"I'm going to head back to my place," she said. She kept her voice upbeat. "Thank you again for tonight. I'll see you at work on Mon - oh!"

Luke had taken her arm and he pulled her into his hard embrace before scowling at her. "Why are you leaving?"

"You're upset with me," she said.

"I'm not upset with you. Tonight was just," he hesitated, "weird."

"I know and I'm sorry. I know it was awkward when Mama J made you say, uh, what she did, and I apologize for that. Thank you for playing along. It helps when she's starting to get agitated like that."

"Why did you say it?" He asked.

She blinked at him. "I – what?"

"Why did you say it back? Josephine didn't tell you to say it."

"Well, I – because I thought it would help calm her down," Jane whispered.

He studied her closely before releasing her. "Right. Well, it worked."

"It did," she whispered. She rubbed a shaking hand across her forehead as Luke turned and walked back to the window.

She stared at her suitcase for a moment. She should have told him the truth. The moment the words "I love you" had crossed her lips in the diner, she knew they were true. She groaned inwardly and chewed again at her bottom lip. She was in love with Luke.

She took a deep breath and picked up her suitcase. Best to get the hell out of here before she made a fool of herself and did tell him the truth. She could only imagine the look on his face if she told him that she really was in love with him. He didn't love her. He liked her a lot and obviously wanted her but he wasn't in love with her. Why would he be? They came from two different worlds and she was certain part of his fascination with her was because she was so different. But the fascination would eventually wane and he'd find someone who was in the same damn social class as he was. Lust wasn't love. She'd learned that the hard way with Jeremy. She wouldn't make the same mistake again with Luke. Not when Mama J's life depended on it.

"Thank you again, Luke," she said. "I really enjoyed our time together."

He turned and stared at her. "You promised me until

Sunday."

"I know but - "

"I don't want you to leave," he said.

The naked and raw pleading in his voice had her dropping the suitcase and crossing the bedroom to his side. "I don't want to leave either."

"Then don't. Stay with me, Janie," he said as he put his arms around her and buried his face in her neck.

"Okay," she whispered.

He lifted her up and carried her to the bed. He stood her next to it and they undressed each other before climbing into the bed. He stretched out on his side next to her and stroked his thumb across her cheekbone. "You're so beautiful."

"So are you," she said.

He smiled at her and kissed her sweetly, tasting her mouth as she clung to him. When his big hand cupped her breast, she arched into him and he smiled against her lips.

"I love your reaction to me, sweet Jane."

"I want you so much," she moaned.

"I want you too," he said. He teased her nipple with his thumb and trailed kisses across her upper chest. She reached between them and wrapped her fingers around his thick cock, rubbing urgently as he groaned into her ear.

"Keep doing that and I'm going to fuck you right now," he muttered.

"Yes," she said. "Please."

He studied her for a moment before pressing his hand between her legs. She widened her thighs and he cupped her pussy.

"Please, Luke," she said and tried to urge him between her legs.

"You're not ready yet," he said.

"I don't care. I need you!" She was suddenly dying to have him inside of her.

He shook his head. "No, I don't want to hurt you. Patience, Jane."

She glared at him and he gave her a sweet smile before beginning to rub her clit with slow, firm strokes. "When you're nice and wet for me, then I'll fuck you. It won't take long."

She spread her legs wide, arching repeatedly into his touch until she was soaking wet and moaning for him.

"See," he said arrogantly before sucking hard on her nipple. She cried out, her pussy clenching around his finger when he pushed it into her.

"Luke," she begged, "please."

"Whatever you want, sweet Jane," he replied. She watched as he rolled on the condom before kneeling between her legs. He slid into her with one hard thrust and she moaned happily as he rested on his forearms above her. She rubbed her tight nipples against his chest, watching desire dance across his face as she put her arms around his shoulders. He was sliding in and out in a slow, deep rhythm and she closed her eyes as he thrust.

"Look at me."

His low voice made her eyes pop open and she stared up at him as he continued to move in her. He rolled his hips in and out, grinding his pelvic bone against her clit as she made low gasps of pleasure.

"Keep looking at me," he demanded when her eyelids began to drift shut. "Don't look away, Jane."

"Yes, Luke," she whispered.

She stared at him as he moved faster. He was beginning to pant now and she dug her hands into his back as she met each of his thrusts. Their hips slapped together and she squeezed him tightly with her inner muscles.

He groaned and moved harder. He didn't tear his gaze from her and she whimpered low in her throat. "I'm so close, Luke."

"Me too," he gasped.

He reached between them and rubbed her clit. "Look at me when you're coming," he whispered.

He tugged on her clit and keeping her gaze on him, she climaxed with a shudder-inducing cry. Her body arched under his as she tightened around him. He made a soft mutter for mercy before thrusting deep and groaning her name. He stared intently at her as he came deep within her, his body shaking and twitching against hers. When he collapsed against her, she rubbed his back and kept her legs wrapped around his waist.

"That was so good," he muttered.

"Hmm," she agreed.

He lifted his head and stared at her. "Jane, I…"

She gave him an encouraging look when he trailed off. "What, Luke?"

He pressed a kiss against her mouth. "Nothing."

He rolled off of her and disposed of the condom before pulling her into his embrace. She snuggled into him, throwing her thin thigh across his thick ones as he rubbed her back with his warm hand.

He was quiet for so long that she was starting to fall asleep when his low voice came floating out of the darkness. "It's good between us. Isn't it?"

"Yes," she said sleepily. "So good."

He pressed a kiss against the top of her head. "Good night, Jane."

"Night, Luke."

☙ ❧

"Hello, sweetheart." Clara kissed Luke's cheek before folding Jane into her embrace. "Hi, dear."

"Hi, Clara," Jane said. She took off her jacket and Luke hung it in the closet for her as she slipped out of her boots.

"When Amy showed up without you, I was afraid you weren't coming to family dinner. But Amy said Luke was bringing you because he made you work today," Clara said. She gave Luke a gentle disapproving look. "You work too much, sweetheart, and now you're making Jane work too much."

"I didn't mind," Jane said. "It doesn't happen very often."

"You're looking gorgeous tonight, mom," Luke said cheerfully before kissing her cheek with a loud smacking noise.

Clara pinched Luke's cheek. "Aren't you in a good mood today. Your dad is in the garage tinkering with his car. He said for you to join him."

"Sure," Luke said. He disappeared as Clara put her arm around Jane and squeezed affectionately.

"Dearest, can you do me a favour?"

"Of course," Jane said.

"Can you go and talk to Amy? She's in the living room and she's been in a real mood since she got here. Something's upsetting her but she won't tell me what it is. You two have grown close so I thought maybe you could try talking to her."

"Sure," Jane said as guilt coursed through her. She had meant to text Amy this morning but Luke had kept her occupied.

Damn straight he did, her inner voice whispered. *How many times have you had sex today, Janie? Six? Seven? What do you think Luke's mother would say if she knew Luke was in such a good mood because you gave him a blowjob right before you left for family dinner?*

She gave Clara a distracted smile. Luke had woken her at seven this morning and they'd been in bed for pretty much the entire day. Her thighs ached as did her pelvis but she didn't regret their marathon of sex. After dinner, Luke would drive her back to her place and she would never again feel his warm body wrapped around hers or hear his deep voice whispering in her ear. The thought sent depression coursing through her and she shook it off immediately. Amy was upset and she needed to stop being such a bad friend and help her.

"I'll talk to her right now," Jane said.

"Thanks, dearest," Clara said.

Jane pressed a kiss against Clara's cheek. She was very fond of Luke's parents and she would miss them terribly. But she couldn't keep going to family dinners after tonight. It would be bad enough to see Luke every day at work, she wouldn't torture herself on the weekends as well.

She walked into the living room. Amy was sitting on the couch staring at the flickering flames of the fire burning in the fireplace. Jane sat down beside her and when Amy didn't look at her, said, "Hi, Amy."

"Hi, Jane."

"How was your day with Pierre and Julien yesterday?"

"Fine," Amy said.

"Friday night was a bit intense."

Amy sighed and said irritably, "I'm not talking to you about Mark. Don't bother asking."

"Okay," Jane said.

"Fuck. I'm being such a bitch," Amy said. "I'm sorry, Janie."

"It's fine," Jane said. "I'm just worried about you."

"So is my mom. I heard her telling you to come in and talk to me."

"I would have talked to you anyway. I mean to text you yesterday but Luke…"

She trailed off and flushed when Amy said dryly, "Yeah, I don't need the details."

"Sorry."

"Don't be. You know I like that you and my brother are together."

Jane thought about correcting her and decided now wasn't the moment. Amy was upset and she had a feeling she was trying to change the subject.

"Did you have fun with Pierre and Julien?" She asked.

"I didn't fuck them if that's what you're asking," Amy said as she stared into the fire.

Jane blinked at her. "I – that isn't what I meant."

"I was going to," Amy continued on as if she hadn't spoken. "I fully intended on ending yesterday in their hotel room and in their bed, with both of them. Why not, right? They were obviously interested in me, I'm single, they're single. What's wrong with having a good time with two handsome guys who want you?"

"There's nothing wrong with that," Jane said.

"Then why couldn't I do it?" Amy said angrily. "Why couldn't I just forget about – about him?"

"Because I think you love him," Jane said. "You should tell him, Ames. I think he loves you too."

"He doesn't!" She spat.

"You don't know that," Jane said.

"Do you love my brother?" Amy asked.

Jane hesitated and Amy stared at her. "Do you?"

"Yes," Jane whispered.

"Are you going to tell him?"

"No, but this is different. He's my boss and he's not in love with me."

Amy scoffed loudly. "Bullshit."

"He isn't," Jane said. "But Mark, he - "

"You really need to help me convince your mother that I need that car," Luke's father said as he and Luke wandered into the living room. "Hi, Jane."

"Hi, Gary," Jane said as Amy stared at her hands. "How are you?"

"Can't complain," he said as he sunk into his chair with a soft sigh. "How's work going? Luke keeping you busy?"

"Yes," Jane said.

"That's nice," Gary replied. He turned to Luke. "Amy says you might be going international with the line."

"We're trying," Luke said.

"Good, good," Gary said as Clara stuck her head into the living room.

"Dinner's ready."

"Thank you, lovie," Gary said. "C'mon, kids. Let's eat. I'm starving."

They followed him into the kitchen and sat down at the table. Clara gave Amy a worried look before smiling at Luke. "Luke, why don't you - "

She stopped as the doorbell rang. "Now who could that be?" She shook her head when Gary started to stand. "I'll get it, honey. Start dishing out the food."

She left the kitchen and Gary handed the rice to Jane. "Take lots, Jane."

She murmured her thanks and dished out some rice onto her plate before handing the bowl to Luke. As he took some, Clara swept back into the kitchen.

"Look who's finally joining us for family dinner!"

Mark appeared in the doorway. He was unshaven, his eyes were bloodshot and he looked tired and miserable.

"Mark!" Gary boomed. "Good to see you, son. Sit next to Luke."

Mark sat beside Luke as Clara grabbed a plate and silverware. She set it in front of Mark before leaning down and kissing his forehead. She ruffled his hair affectionately. "You look tired, dearest. What have you been up to this weekend?"

"Nothing," he said. "I'm sorry I showed up without calling."

"Nonsense," Clara said. "You know you're always welcome."

Jane glanced at Amy. The curvy blonde was staring at her plate and she didn't look up when Gary held out the platter of chicken to her.

"Ames?" He said before poking her in the arm. "Take some chicken."

She took the platter from her father and stabbed a small piece of chicken before passing the platter to Jane. Jane took it from her and gave Luke a quick glance. She couldn't be the only one feeling the tension between Mark and Amy, could she?

Apparently, she was, because the rest of Amy's family were acting oblivious to the way Amy was hunched over her plate and the tenseness in Mark's shoulders.

"So, Mark, honey, how are things?" Clara asked.

Jane stole another glance at Amy before reaching under the table and patting her knee. Amy gave her a strained smile before her gaze flickered to Mark. Jane took the bowl of cooked vegetables from Luke. God, it was going to be a long dinner.

∼ ∽

"Where did Luke get off to?" Clara asked as she loaded the last of the dishes into the dishwasher. "I wanted him to put the recycling out on the back porch."

"I think he and Mark are back in the garage with Gary. I'll do it," Jane said as she finished wiping the table. Amy had disappeared after helping her mother load the dishwasher. Jane had a feeling she had escaped to her old room and would be leaving any moment now. Dinner was beyond awkward and she couldn't believe that no one else felt the tension between Amy and Mark.

"Oh, that's fine, dearest," Clara said. "I'll have Gary do it tomorrow."

"I don't mind," Jane said. She took the blue bag and headed for the door that led to the back porch.

"Thank you, honey," Clara called. "Throw it in the big bin next to the freezer."

Jane stepped out onto the porch, letting the door shut behind her. It was a nice porch, screened in so during the summer months, they could sit and enjoy the weather without being eaten by mosquitoes. She hurried to the bin and lifted the lid before throwing the bag of recycling into it. The wooden floor was cold on her sock feet and she ran back to the door, groaning when she tried to turn the handle.

"Dammit." The door had locked behind her and she knocked loudly on it as she shivered in the cold air. She waited a few minutes before knocking again.

"C'mon," she muttered. She glanced at the other end of the porch. There was no porch light and it was hard to see in the dim light coming from the one window but she thought there was a door at the other end. She could go through that one and run around to the front of the house. Clara would hear the doorbell. Of course, she wasn't wearing any shoes and the snow was deep. She weighed her options before starting toward the other door. She'd run around to the front. She could always borrow a pair of socks from Clara if she had to.

Before she had taken two steps, the far door swung open and Amy stomped in. Her cheeks were bright red with the cold and her jacket was undone and her boots unlaced. Mark was right behind her. He was wearing his boots but no jacket and Jane sunk back into the shadows as he said, "Just stop and listen to me for a minute."

"Why should I?" Amy whirled around and glared at him. "I'm nothing but a big mistake to you, remember?"

"That isn't what I meant and you know that," Mark snapped at her. "Tell me what I want to know."

"No, it's none of your goddamn business!"

Jane opened her mouth to announce her presence as Amy tried to storm past Mark. She shut her mouth with a snap, watching with wide eyes when Mark grabbed Amy and pushed her up against the side of the house. He pinned her arms above her head and threaded his other hand in her long blonde hair, yanking her head back before kissing her hard on the mouth. Amy froze against him for a moment before returning his kiss eagerly.

Jane pressed her body against the door and stared at the ceiling of the covered porch. Shit, what did she do now?"

"Tell me, Amy."

Jane's eyes widened. Mark sounded...different. Hell, the demand and raw power in his voice had her suddenly ready to confess everything to him. She had no idea how Amy resisted him as the blonde said in a low voice, "It's none of your business, Mark. You don't get to tell me what to do or ...oh God."

Her voice trailed off into a low moan of pleasure as Mark said, "Did they take what's mine, Amy?"

Feeling like a voyeur but unable to resist looking, Jane lowered her gaze. She clapped her hand over her mouth. Her old boss, the by all accounts sweet and easy-going Mark, was still pinning Amy to the wall with one hard hand around her wrists. His other hand was shoved down the front of her pants. Amy made a low groan of need and spread her legs wide before arching into his hand.

"Did they touch my little slave's pussy?" Mark said. "Did she give them what belongs to me?"

"No," Amy whispered as Mark nuzzled her neck before licking his way to her jaw. "No, I didn't let them touch me."

"Good," Mark said. He kissed her again before sucking on her bottom lip. "You'll be a good girl and come for me right now. Do you understand?"

His arm moved and Amy moaned again as Mark said, "When we're done here, you're going to come back to my place and accept your punishment like a good little slave, aren't you?"

"Yes," Amy whispered.

He bit her throat and she gasped.

"What did you say to me?" Mark said.

He bit her throat again and she arched against him before whispering, "I mean, yes, Sir."

"Better. Your punishment will be dropping to your knees and sucking on my cock until I come in your mouth, little slave."

"Yes, Sir," she repeated.

Oh Jesus. Jane clenched her hands into tight fists. Listening to Mark call Amy his little slave was way fucking hotter than it should have been. She really needed to say something before things went too far.

Too far, Janie? It's a little too late for that, don't you think?

Her inner voice said with a gleeful little grin.

The door suddenly opened behind her and she just managed to catch her balance to keep from falling on her ass. She whirled around and stared at Luke who was standing in the doorway.

He gave her a puzzled look as he started to step out onto the porch. "Jane? What's wrong?"

She launched her small body at him, propelling him backward into the house in a desperate attempt to keep him from seeing his sister and Mark.

"Whoa! What the hell?" He said. "What's wrong?"

"Nothing," she said. "Nothing's wrong. I got locked out on the porch and was freezing my butt off."

He studied her for a moment. "Are you sure that's it? You look weird."

"I'm cold," she said before taking his hand and tugging him toward the kitchen. "Come on, let's see if I can get a cup of tea from your mom."

"Sure," he said before following her down the hallway.

She breathed a sigh of relief and forced herself not to look back at the porch door.

ॐ ॐ

Jane stared at Amy's house and tried not to cry. Luke had driven her home after dinner and knowing this was it for them made her feel nauseous. Luke shut off the car and opened his door.

"Luke, what are you doing?" Jane asked.

"Coming inside." He arched his eyebrow at her. "I'm spending the night."

"I – what?" She gave him a confused look. "But it's Sunday."

"Exactly. You said we had until Sunday, it's still Sunday," he said. "Is that a problem?"

"No," she said as she climbed out of the car. She tried to hide her excitement as they entered the house and took off their jackets and boots. Light was shining out from the kitchen and she glanced in as they walked down the hallway. Amy was sitting at the table staring into a cup of tea and Luke stuck his head into the room.

"Hey, Ames. I'm spending the night."

"Yeah, sure, okay," Amy said. Her cheeks reddening, she said, "Janie, could I talk to you for a minute?"

"Can it wait until tomorrow?" Luke asked. His big hand was rubbing her lower back and Jane smiled up at him.

"I'll only be a minute. I'll meet you upstairs, okay?"

"Sure," Luke said. "Night, Amy."

"Night, Luke."

Jane sat down across from Amy. When she heard her bedroom door shut, she reached across and squeezed Amy's hand. "I'm really sorry about earlier."

"No, I'm sorry. I – I needed to get some fresh air and Mark followed me outside. I didn't mean for you to hear or see what you did. I thought you were in the kitchen with mom."

Jane squeezed her hand again. "You don't need to apologize. I took the recycling out for your mom and got locked out. I was about to say something when things got um..."

She trailed off as Amy blushed. "Oh God, I am so embarrassed."

"Don't be," Jane said. "I knew something was up with you and Mark so it wasn't that surprising. Why aren't you, uh, at his house?"

Now her cheeks flushed and Amy glanced up at her before groaning. "Oh fuck. Did you hear everything?"

"Yeah, I'm sorry," Jane said. "Listen, I'm not judging you, all right? It was kind of hot actually. I had no idea there was that side to Mark."

"Jane, you can't say anything to Luke, okay?" Amy said urgently. "Promise me you won't say anything to him."

"I won't," Jane said. "I promise I won't."

Amy searched her face before nodding. "Okay, thank you and thanks for keeping Luke from seeing us earlier. I'm sorry. I didn't mean to drag you into this mess."

"You didn't," Jane said. "There seems to be a lot of, um, attraction between you and Mark so why aren't you with him?"

Amy blinked rapidly before rubbing at her forehead. "It's a long story. Listen, my brother's waiting for you and honestly, I don't want to talk about what happened. I wanted to apologize for it and ask you not to say anything to anyone about what you saw and, um, heard."

"I won't, Amy. I promise," Jane said.

"Thanks, Janie."

"You're welcome. And listen, if you do want to talk about it, I'm here, okay? Sometimes it's better if you talk about it."

"Yeah, okay. Thanks, Jane."

"You bet. Good night, Amy."

"Good night."

Chapter Sixteen

Luke was already in bed and waiting for her. She brushed her teeth and washed her face before climbing into the bed beside him. He brushed her hair back from her face and she smiled at him.

"Are you sure you don't mind me staying the night?" He asked.

"No, I want you to stay," she said.

He traced his hand over her bare shoulder and down her arm. Goose bumps broke out on her skin and he leaned over her and kissed her collarbone. "We had sex a lot today."

"We did," she confirmed as he cupped one small breast and stroked her nipple.

"Are you sore?" He asked.

She was a little sore but she shook her head. "No."

He rested his hand on her hip and kneaded the flesh. "Are you sure?"

"Yes," she said. "Make love to me, Luke. Please."

She was suddenly on the verge of tears. This would be the last night she would spend in the arms of the man she loved and she fought back the wave of depression. She wouldn't spend this last night feeling sorry for herself. She would enjoy her final night with Luke and not let herself dwell on the future.

She kissed him hard on the mouth. "I want you."

"I want you too, sweet Jane," he whispered.

He pushed her onto her back and as his mouth began a slow path of kisses down her body, she closed her eyes and concentrated on nothing but how good he made her feel.

∂‿∞

"Wake up, Jane." Luke kissed the back of Jane's shoulder.

She rolled over to face him and smiled at him in the dim light. "I'm not sleeping."

"You should be, it's really early."

She glanced at the alarm clock. "Why are you awake so early?"

He didn't want to tell her that he had spent all night awake. This was his last night with Jane and he wasn't going to waste it by sleeping. He rubbed her hip. "I need to leave early. I didn't bring work clothes with me."

She gave him a small smile. "Right, of course. Thank you for spending the night with me, Luke. Thank you for everything."

He kissed her gently. "Thank you. I had a really good time."

"I did too."

He waited for her to tell him she didn't want it to end but he was being an idiot. They couldn't keep sleeping together. He didn't want to be known as the boss who banged his secretary and it wasn't like she was going to quit so they could have a relationship. It was obvious that most of her paycheque went to Mama J's care. She needed the money and he couldn't blame her for that.

So transfer her back to Mark's department at her current pay. Problem solved.

His mouth gaped open. Holy shit – could it be that simple?

"Luke? What's wrong?"

He stared at her and blurted out, "You don't need to work for me."

"What?"

"You don't need to work for me," he repeated.

She froze and a look of fear crossed her face. "Are you firing me?"

"What? No, of course not!" He said. He sat up and ran his fingers through his thick hair. "But you could transfer back to finance. You could work in Mark's department again and then we could - "

He stopped abruptly and she gave him a curious look. "We could what?"

"Date," he said. He had almost blurted out that they could get married. Fuck, what was wrong with him?

"You want to date me?" She said.

"Yes," he said. "I do. There's no policy on inter-office dating and I get that people will talk if we date, even if I'm not your direct boss, but I don't care what they say. Do you?"

He hurried on before she could reply. "I know you need your current wage to take care of Mama J and I understand that. But, you could transfer back to Mark's department at your current wage."

"I was a data entry clerk. They don't make that much," she said.

"I'll talk to Mark about it," Luke said. "You're intelligent and a fast learner. You could learn to do more than data entry."

She stared silently at him and he said, "Unless you don't want to date me and then, uh, forget everything I just said."

She burst into laughter and he grinned nervously at her. "Is that a yes or a no to dating me?"

"I want to date you," she said.

"Yeah?" He knew he sounded like an eager little kid but he couldn't help it. "Really?"

"Yes," she said. "But only if I transfer back to Mark's

department."

"I'll talk to him today," Luke said. "You can be back in his department by tomorrow."

"You might want to wait until you find a replacement for me," Jane laughed.

"I'll talk to Maria and get her to put out a job listing right away. We'll put you back in Mark's department and I'll maybe borrow you for urgent stuff while we're waiting for the new PA to start."

She sat up and he pulled her into his lap, kissing her on the mouth as she tangled her hands in his hair.

"Let's have sex to celebrate," he said.

She laughed. "We don't have time. You need to go home, remember? Besides, we can't celebrate yet. Mark might not want me back in his department. I'm sure they've filled the position I left by now."

Luke shook his head. "He'll put you back in his department. Don't worry about that."

"You don't know that for sure," Jane said. She was a little worried about Mark's reaction to having her work for him again, especially since she knew his and Amy's secret.

"I do," Luke said confidently. "Now, stop talking and lie back so I can eat your pussy."

"We don't have time," she repeated.

"There's always time for pussy eating," he said solemnly.

Her laughter ended when he yanked back the covers, pushed her onto her back, knelt between her thighs and buried his face in her pussy.

"Fuck me!" The words burst from her throat in a harsh little moan as his tongue slicked over her clit.

He lifted his head and grinned up at her. "Whatever you say, Ms. Smith."

∂∘ ∘∂

"So, as you can see," Luke said as he tapped the screen

of his laptop, "we are fully committed to overhauling our digital presence and creating a brand new shopping experience for our clients."

Pierre and Julien studied the screen as Luke discreetly checked the time. It was already five thirty and Jane would have left for her second job by now. He tried to hide his irritation. He hadn't even had the chance to tell her the good news. Mark was perfectly willing to have Jane return to the finance department and was open to the idea of training her to do more. Hell, he had even suggested that if Jane was interested, she could take a few accounting classes. He'd wanted to tell her right away but Pierre and Julien were early for their meeting. He'd spent the last three hours, going over the company's finances with them for the third time and detailing their plan to change their website and digital footprint. Frankly, he was getting tired of their waffling and was ready to throw in the towel.

Pierre glanced at Julien and nodded before sitting back in his chair. "Congratulations, Luke. We would like to invest in your company."

"Good. You won't regret it, gentlemen. I'll have Mark draw up a contract and we can start negotiations."

"Perfect," Julien said. He glanced at his watch. "This calls for a celebration. You must go out with us this evening."

"I have quite a bit of work to do," Luke said. "In fact, I should probably - "

"We insist," Pierre said. "If we're going to be working so closely together, we should get to know each other better, don't you think?"

"Yes," Luke said. Jane was working late anyway. It wouldn't hurt to get to know the two French men better. "I know the perfect place for dinner."

"Bien," Pierre said. "And we have heard of the perfect entertainment for after dinner."

He grinned at Julien as Luke said, "What are you thinking of?"

"There's a place called "Teasers". Have you heard of it?" Julien asked.

Luke nodded and kept the dismay from his face. "I have."

"Perhaps you have visited this fine establishment?" Pierre said.

"No," Luke grunted.

Julien raised his eyebrows. "You have an issue with us going?"

"Not at all," Luke said.

"Bien," Julien said. "So, you will join us then?"

"Of course," Luke said. "I'll invite Mark as well."

"The more the merrier," Pierre said. "Now, if you will excuse us, we would like to say hello to your delightful sister before we leave."

"She's not here today," Luke said. Amy had called in sick this morning.

"What a shame," Julien said. "Give us the name of the restaurant and we will meet you and Mark there in say," he glanced at his watch, "an hour?"

"Sure." He gave them the name of the restaurant and shook their hands before walking them to the elevator. When they were headed downstairs, he walked to Mark's office and knocked before sticking his head into the room.

"Hey, what are you doing?"

Mark looked up from his desk. "I'm about to head home."

"So, no plans?" Luke said.

Mark gave him a suspicious look. He didn't look as tired as he had Sunday night but he still looked out of sorts. "Why?"

"Julien and Pierre have agreed to invest with us," Luke said.

"That's good," Mark replied.

"You don't sound that excited."

Mark shrugged. "I am. I just don't like those guys. Or trust them for that matter."

Luke sighed. "I don't know what you want me to say. Working with them will be good for the company despite how we feel about them personally."

"I know," Mark said. "Ignore me, I'm tired today."

"About that – I need you to go out with me tonight."

"What are we doing?" Mark asked.

"We're having dinner with Julien and Pierre and then going to Teasers."

"No," Mark said as he closed his laptop and stood up. "No fucking way."

"Come on, Mark," Luke said. "I need you to help me out with this."

"I'm not going to a goddamn strip club with those two assholes," Mark said.

"C'mon, man," Luke said, "it's one night of your life."

"They don't even like me."

"They were fine with you coming along. I can't go to a strip club with only them," Luke said. "You know I can't."

Mark sighed. "Fine. But you fucking owe me."

"I know," Luke said. "Thanks, buddy."

঻ ঻

"This place is disgusting," Mark muttered into Luke's ear.

"It could be worse," Luke said. They followed Julien and Pierre to a table and he sank into the chair as the two French men stared eagerly at the stage. A woman wearing bikini bottoms and nothing else was gyrating against a pole. She was an excellent dancer and her body was lean and well-toned with high, firm breasts but he felt nothing when he stared at her. He wanted to be at home with Jane. He checked his watch. He wondered how long it would take before he could call it a night.

Julien and Pierre were still watching the woman dancing and when the waitress approached them, Luke smiled politely at her. "We'll take four whiskeys. Thanks."

She nodded and walked back to the bar. She wore a tiny pink skirt with a white satin bustier. A white kitten ear headband was perched on her head and her thigh high stockings had tiny white bows at the bands. Luke studied the club as Mark leaned forward in the chair next to him.

The place wasn't very full, although there were more men than he would have thought for a Monday night. One of the tables across the club was crowded with eight men in business suits. Their faces bright red, they were talking in loud voices as they watched the woman dance.

"Luke," Mark nudged him in the side, "let's get out of here. Now."

Luke frowned at him. "We just got here."

"We should go," Mark said. He was staring at the table of drunk men with an odd look on his face.

Luke studied the table of men as well. "Look, I don't want to be here anymore than you do, but we need to stay at least an hour before we bail. We'll have a couple drinks and make some small talk and then we'll..."

He trailed off as he caught sight of the waitress who was serving the table of eight men. She was dressed in the same outfit as their waitress, her dark hair was in a high ponytail and her perfect skin was covered with a thick layer of makeup but he still recognized her.

"What the fuck?" He said.

"Luke, let's go – you can talk to her tomorrow," Mark said as he glanced at Pierre and Julien. Both men's gazes were glued to the woman on the stage and Mark grabbed at Luke's arm when he stood.

"Let me go!" Luke yanked his arm free and strode across the club. He took the waitress' arm and without looking at him, she said, "No touching, please."

"No touching," he repeated and she froze before looking over her shoulder.

"What are you doing here?" She said in a low voice.

"What am I doing here? What am I doing here?" His

voice was rising and she made a shushing motion before glancing nervously at the bar. "Jane, what the fuck are you doing here?"

"Hey, are you gonna take our order or not?" One of the men slurred.

"Be right with you, sugar," Jane said. Luke's gut tightened when the man studied her small breasts and licked his lips.

Jane pulled free of his grip and glanced again at the bar before heading toward the corner farthest from it. Luke followed her and glared at her.

"What are you doing here, Jane?" He studied the kitten ears on her head and the way her small breasts were nearly busting out of the tight bustier. She wore dark eyeshadow and false eyelashes and her lips were painted a dark red.

"Working, obviously," she said. "Why are you here?"

"Julien and Pierre insisted we come here," he snapped. "Why didn't you tell me you worked at a goddamn strip club?"

"Why do you think?" She retorted before glancing at the bar. A dark-haired man wearing a knit cap and a vest without a shirt was leaning against the bar and staring at them. Both arms were covered in tattoos and he raised his eyebrows at Jane in a silent question.

She waved at him and stared up at Luke. "I need to get back to work. Can we talk about this later?"

"Do you dance?" He asked.

"What?"

"Do you dance on stage as well?"

"No. I just waitress."

He tried to hide the relief on his face but he must have done a piss poor job because she immediately bristled. "The women who dance here are good people and if you're going to look down on them, I - "

"I don't," he interrupted. "I don't look down on them, Jane. I just don't like thinking that other men watch you dance or see your naked body, okay? I won't apologize for that."

She sighed as his gaze travelled over her uniform. "They don't. I've never danced, just waitressed. I really can't talk about this right now. My boss is here and he's not the most," she paused, "reasonable guy. I'll text you later, okay?"

"I'm not leaving you here alone."

"Luke, I've been working here for a long time. Please trust me that I'll be fine."

He didn't reply and she chewed at her bottom lip before glancing at the bar again. "I need to go back to my table. I – I'll try and make sure that Pierre and Julien don't see me."

She slipped past him and walked back to her table. Trying not to notice the way the men were staring at Jane's ass, he returned to his table and sat woodenly next to Mark.

"You okay?" Mark said.

He nodded then shook his head. "Fuck, I don't know."

Their whiskeys had arrived while he was talking to Jane and he drank his in two big gulps, wincing at the burn. Julien leaned over and grinned at them. "What do you gentlemen think of getting some private dances?"

"No," Luke and Mark said at the same time.

Pierre rolled his eyes and finished his own whiskey. "Americans, they don't know how to have a good time."

"You two go ahead and get your private dances," Mark said.

Julien shrugged before downing the rest of his whiskey. He stood and ambled toward the bar. He spoke to the bartender who directed him to the dark-haired man who still leaned against the bar. They spoke briefly before Julien turned and waved at Pierre.

Pierre stood. "Gentlemen, it's been a pleasure. We head back home tomorrow but we'll be in touch about our new partnership."

Luke didn't reply. His gaze had wandered to Jane. She was standing with her back to them as she spoke to the men she was serving.

"That sounds good," Mark said. "Enjoy your evening."

"You as well," Pierre said.

He joined Julien and the two of them followed Jane's boss past the stage to an unmarked door. They disappeared into a private room as a dancer stopped in front of their table. She leaned over and Mark eyed her cleavage as she purred, "Care for a lap dance, handsome?"

"No thanks," Mark said.

"How about you?" She turned to Luke who shook his head. He was still staring at Jane and the dancer made a low laugh.

"You don't want her, sweetheart. Her tits are way too small and she don't dance nearly as well as I do."

Luke glared at her and she took a step back before glancing at the giant of a man who was standing near the stage.

"We're not interested," Mark said. "But thank you."

"Whatever." The woman shrugged and, hips swaying, walked away.

"Time to go, Luke."

"No," Luke said.

"It's not a good idea to stay," Mark said.

"Then go," Luke said.

Mark sighed. "This is such a bad fucking idea."

Before the words were even out of his mouth, Luke was standing and stalking across the club. One of the men had stood, grabbed Jane's ass and squeezed it hard. She tugged his hand away but he grabbed her ass again as Luke stopped beside her. With an angry growl, he grabbed the man's hand and twisted it. The man howled with pain and fell to his knees as Luke leaned over him and said, "Touch her again and I'll break your arm."

"Luke, no!" Jane said. "Stop it, right now!"

"Do you understand?" Luke said to the man on his

knees. "Repeat what I just – "

He grunted with pain when one of the man's friends jumped on his back. He hooked his arm around Luke's neck and Luke let go of the other man and staggered back. He grabbed the man's arms and bent over quickly. The man sailed over his head and landed on the table with a splintering crash. Glasses exploded and the other men made hoarse cries of surprise as Luke punched the man twice in the face.

"Stop it!" Jane shouted. "Tony, no! It's okay – don't hurt him!"

Another arm was wrapped around his neck, this one was thick as a goddamn tree trunk and Luke's air was immediately cut off when it squeezed tightly.

"Tony! Stop!" Jane said pleadingly.

"Let him go, you asshole."

He could hear Mark's angry voice as Jane appeared in his rapidly diminishing vision. "Please, Tony. He's a friend. Please."

The vice around his throat relaxed a little and he dragged in a lungful of air as Tony half-carried him across the club. He dropped Luke into a chair and Luke stared at the giant standing in front of him. Tony had to be close to seven feet tall and he weighed at least three hundred pounds. He stared down at him as Jane put her small hand on his forearm and said softly, "He won't cause any more trouble, Tony. I promise."

"You sure?" Tony's voice was a rumbling truck. "I don't want him hurting you, Janie."

"I'm her fucking boyfriend, you jackass," Luke said hoarsely.

Jane made a low moan of dismay as Tony rolled his eyes. "Your boyfriend always this much of a dick?"

"He's had too much to drink," Jane said. "Don't tell Jeremy, okay?"

"Don't tell Jeremy what?"

Jane turned white as the man in the knitted cap

materialized next to Tony. He stared at Luke before turning his gaze to Jane. "What's going on, Jane?"

"Nothing, Jeremy," Jane said. "Just a misunderstanding, that's all."

"Misunderstanding?" Jeremy said. "I've got a customer with a busted nose and another one screaming that his hand is broken. You call that a misunderstanding?"

Luke stood and stared at Jane's boss. He was nearly half a foot taller than Jeremy and he studied the man's face as Jeremy gave him a cool look.

"You know this guy, Jane?"

"Jeremy, I..."

She trailed off as Jeremy reached out and put his hand on the back of her neck. He started to tug her toward him and Luke knocked his hand away from her and pulled Jane against his body.

"Don't fucking touch her," he said as Mark rested his hand on his arm.

"Be cool," Mark muttered into his ear.

He ignored his best friend and stared at Jeremy. "Don't touch her again."

"So you do know him," Jeremy said to Jane.

"He's just - "

"I'm her boyfriend," Luke snapped at him.

"Luke, hush," Jane said anxiously.

He gave her a confused look as a grin crossed Jeremy's face. "You know the rules, Jane."

"I'm sorry," Jane said. "I – I didn't tell him and he - "

"Not my problem," Jeremy said. "You're fired. Get the fuck out of here."

"Jeremy!" Jane gave him a desperate look but Luke tightened his grip around her when she tried to wiggle free. "Please, let me explain."

Jeremy shook his head. "No. Shelly, get your fat ass over here!"

"What you want?" The chunky Asian woman who

ambled over from behind the bar glared at him. She was missing her front teeth and the overwhelming smell of tuna hung over her like a thick cloud.

"Get Jane's things from her locker and bring him out. And move your fucking ass for once, would you?"

She shuffled off as Jane said, "Jeremy, please. I need this job. You know I do."

"Then you shouldn't have let your boyfriend come in here and start punching my paying customers," Jeremy drawled.

Jane glanced at Luke. "Luke will apologize to the customer and buy him and his friends a round of drinks. Okay?"

"No, I won't," Luke said.

"Luke!" Jane gave him a desperate look that he studiously ignored. As far as he was concerned, Jane being fired from this hellhole was a good thing.

"Here's your stuff." Shelly had returned and she shoved Jane's coat and her bag at her before belching loudly. The scent of tuna mixed with beer wafted over them and Mark made a low grunt of disgust.

"Jesus," he muttered as Shelly grinned at him, revealing the gaping hole where her teeth should have been.

"You want a private dance, sexy?"

"Get lost, fat ass," Jeremy said dismissively.

Shelly flipped him the bird before wandering away. Jeremy rolled his eyes before pointing at the door. "Get out, Jane. You can pick up your final paycheque on Friday."

"Jeremy..."

"Get out. Tony, walk them to the door."

"Let's go, Jane," Luke said. He kept his arm around Jane's waist as they followed Tony to the door. The big man opened the door and Luke ushered Jane out into the cold.

"Janie?" Tony touched her arm and Jane pulled free of Luke and let the big man pick her up and hug her. "I'm sorry, girl. I'm going to miss you."

"Thanks, Tony. I'll miss you too. I'll see you around, okay?"

"Yeah. Candy's having her birthday party next month. You'll be at that, right?"

Jane nodded. "Wouldn't miss it."

Tony kissed her cheek and set her on her feet before staring at Luke. "Take care of my girl, dickhead."

Luke didn't reply and Tony grinned at him before returning to the club. Mark rubbed his hand over his forehead.

"Christ, that was a fuck up."

Jane tugged her jacket on and picked up her bag before walking away.

"Jane!" Luke chased after her and pulled her to a stop. "Where are you going?"

"The bus stop," Jane said.

"I'll drive you home," he said.

"No thank you," she said. "I want to be alone."

"I'm driving you home, no arguments," Luke said angrily.

She glared at him before shrugging. "Fine, let's go."

✿ ✿

"Jane, will you just talk to me for God's sake?" Luke said as he followed her into the kitchen. She dropped her bag on the floor and glared at him.

"Keep your voice down. Amy is sleeping."

"We need to talk about what happened," Luke said as she yanked open the freezer door. She pulled out a bag of frozen peas and threw them at him.

"Put this on your hand."

He sat down and rested the bag of peas on his hand as Jane paced back and forth in the kitchen.

"Are you going to apologize for getting me fired?" She asked.

"No," he said. "You shouldn't be working there. You're better than them, Jane. You - "

"No, I'm not," she said. "I'm not better than them, Luke. The people who work there – Tony, Candy, Selena – they're good people. Yeah, there's some real garbage people there but that's true at every job. Don't look down on them because of what they do to keep their families fed."

"I'm not," he said.

"You are."

He sighed. "Okay, you're right. I am and I'm sorry. I'm being an asshole. But, Jane, why are you working there?"

"Why do you think?" She said. She yanked at the tiny pink skirt and then suddenly pulled the kitten headband off her head and tossed it into the garbage. "I need the money."

"Not anymore," he said. "You make more money working at Dawson Clothing now and your rent isn't as high living with Amy."

She sighed and rubbed at her forehead. "You can't possibly understand."

"Try me," he said.

She sank into the chair across from him. "Mama J's care is very expensive, all right? Yes, I make enough now to not need the second job but what happens if – if things don't work out between us? You think Amy's going to let me keep living here? I'll have to find a new place to live and I'll be right back where I was. I've been putting the money I make at the club in a nest egg."

"You act like we're not going to work," Luke said. "You don't know that."

"We're very different," she said gently.

"So?" He gave her an angry look. "If you don't want to even try in this relationship then - "

"I'm not saying that," she interrupted. "I want to be with you and I hope it works but I have to be realistic. I don't have the luxury of just pretending you're my Prince Charming and I'll never want for anything again. I need to take care of Mama J. She's the most important thing in my life, Luke, and I won't do anything to jeopardize her care. Do you understand that?"

He did understand. He hated it but he knew how important taking care of Mama J was to Jane. "Yes, I understand."

She gave him a searching look. "Do you?"

"I do," he said. "I'm sorry I got you fired."

"Thanks," she said. "I'm sorry that your clients saw me working at the club."

"They didn't," Luke said. "They didn't notice you when they first got there and they were in a private room when," he paused, "everything else happened."

"Good, that's good," she said.

They sat in silence for a while before he said, "Should I go home?"

She shook her head. "No. I want you to stay with me tonight."

Relief flooded through him and he stood and tossed the frozen peas back into the freezer as she gave him a nervous look. "Unless you don't want to stay?"

"I want to stay," he said.

She gave him her sweet smile and he pulled her into his arms and kissed her. "I'm sorry, I just hated seeing that guy touching you."

"I know," she said. "Thank you for coming to my rescue. It was very Prince Charming-ish of you."

He held her tightly and kissed her forehead. "I'll always take care of you, Jane. I promise."

She didn't reply and he kissed her again before leading her to her bedroom.

Chapter Seventeen

Luke drummed his fingers on the steering wheel as he stared at the strip club. It was Tuesday afternoon and he was vacillating between going in to speak to Janie's disgusting former boss or just driving back to the office.

He squeezed the steering wheel. He owed it to Jane to at least try and get her job back. He hated the idea of her working here, hated it more than he thought possible, but Jane was a grown woman. Not having the money from the club was worrying her, he could see it in her face. She'd already transferred back to Mark's department this morning but he'd dropped by before lunch on the pretense of getting her to type a quick document for him. The pinched and worried look was still on her face even though she had smiled at him and assured him that everything was fine when he'd asked in a low voice if she was okay.

So help her get a second job somewhere else, his inner voice argued. *Working here is dangerous for Jane. You'll never fucking relax again if you know she's here.*

No, he probably wouldn't and he could have suggested that Jane get a job somewhere else but it was more than just the job thing. He'd fucked up by going off like a hothead and he didn't want Jane thinking he was trying to control her.

That asshole Jeremy probably won't give her the job back anyway. But you'll have at least tried and showed Jane that you feel bad about what happened.

That thought got him moving and he reached for the door handle as someone knocked on his window. He jumped but managed not to shriek like a scared little kid as Tony bent and stared at him through the glass.

His heart thudding in his chest, Luke stepped out of the car as Tony gave him an assessing glance.

"Hey, dickhead."

"Hello, Tony."

"What are you doing here? Club don't open for another hour."

"I came to apologize to Jeremy and see if he would give Jane her job back."

Tony frowned. "You want your woman working here?"

"No," Luke admitted. "But I want it to be her choice."

"Fair enough," Tony said. "C'mon."

Luke followed Tony into the club. The chairs were up on the tables and the stage was dark. Jeremy was sitting at the bar drinking a beer and studying a tablet.

"Janie's guy is here to see you," Tony said.

Jeremy stared at Luke. "What do you want?"

"To talk," Luke said.

Jeremy glanced at Tony. "Take this back to my office." He handed Tony his tablet, who nodded to Luke before leaving.

"What can I do for you, Mister…"

Jeremy trailed off and Luke said, "Dawson. Luke Dawson."

Jeremy looked him up and down. "Jane got herself a real fancy boyfriend, didn't she?"

"I'm here to apologize for starting a fight in your club and to ask you to give Jane her job back."

"We got rules at this club. The girls know them. Always tell the customers you're single even if you ain't, and never let your man come to the club."

"I didn't know Jane worked here and she didn't know I would be there last night," Luke said. "If I had known the rules, I would have followed them."

Jeremy laughed. "Oh yeah? Why would I believe that? I saw the way you looked at her. You don't like other men looking at your woman, let alone touching her."

"It's my fault, Jane shouldn't be punished for that," Luke said.

Jeremy took a swallow of beer. "How'd Jane meet someone so fancy anyway?"

"She works for my company."

Jeremy's eyes widened and Luke stared at him in surprise when he burst into loud laughter. "You are fucking kidding me – you're her goddamn boss?"

"Technically yes," Luke said. "She doesn't work directly for me."

Jeremy laughed again and Luke gave him a cold look. "What's so funny?"

"You have no idea how sweet little Jane has snowed you. You with your goddamn fancy suit and your fucking Rolex. You've got more money than God, I bet, and yet a little golddigger like Jane can sink her claws into you."

"It isn't like that," Luke said through clenched teeth. He was holding onto his self-control by a thread. It was a mistake to come here.

"Why the fuck are you with her? She ain't that good looking and she's a fucking cold fish in the sack so what is it?"

Cold washed over Luke as nausea rolled through his stomach. "What did you say?"

Jeremy grinned at him. "She didn't tell you. You're not the first boss that Jane has slept with. It's what she does, man."

"You're lying," Luke said in a low voice.

"Like fuck I am. I might be a bastard but I'm not a lying bastard," Jeremy said cheerfully. "Jane started coming on to me not even a month after she started working here. We were fucking within two months."

"No," Luke said through numb lips. "No, she wouldn't sleep with someone like you."

"What's wrong with me?" Jeremy gave him an indignant look before laughing. "Jane didn't have any complaints, trust me."

He took another drink of beer as Luke stared at him. "She start asking you for money yet?"

Luke shook his head and Jeremy tipped his beer bottle to him. "She will soon, trust me. She'll start talking about that foster mother of hers, about how sick she is and how much it costs to take care of her. She'll act like she ain't got nothing. That she ain't got no food and can't make her rent because all her money goes to her foster mom. You start to feel sorry for her, maybe buy her a few groceries, pay her heat bill one month. Next thing you know, she's taking all your green and living the high life just because she thinks sucking your cock on the regular gives her that right."

"Shut up," Luke said. "Shut the fuck up."

"Ooh, hit a nerve there, did I?" Jeremy said. "Listen, man, it's better for you that you know how Jane really is. She's got that sweet girl act down to perfection but she's using you for your money. It's what she fucking does. She don't care about anyone but herself. She's a snake who hides in the grass and bites you when you least expect it."

Luke stared at him and Jeremy shrugged. "Keep dating her – you'll find out. I was smart enough to kick her ass out of my bed before she got too much of my hard-earned money but you don't strike me as that smart. Jane's got a tight little pussy, I'll give her that, and men like you are always blinded by pussy."

Rage pulsing through him, Luke punched Jeremy in the face. The smaller man fell off the stool, landing on his back with a harsh thud as his bottle of beer smashed on the floor and splattered him with liquid.

"You fucking asshole!" Jeremy gasped as blood poured from his nose.

Luke bent over and grabbed the collar of his shirt. He lifted him until their faces were inches apart and said, "Go anywhere near Jane and I'll kill you."

"Get off me," Jeremy said as fear flashed in his eyes. "Get off me or I – I'll call Tony."

Luke barked harsh laughter and dropped him. Jeremy's head bounced off the floor and he winced before scrambling away from him. "Fucking asshole! Get out of my club!"

"Gladly," Luke snarled. He turned and stalked out of the club.

৵ ৶

Jane knocked on Luke's office door. Today was her first day back in Mark's department and even though Maria was obviously curious about why she was no longer working with Luke, she hadn't pushed too much for the reason. Kyra had welcomed her back with no questions asked and Jane was thrilled to discover that Mark was arranging to have her take some accounting classes. She was still worried about losing her second job but she'd hidden it from Luke when he'd popped by before lunch to ask her to type a quick document for her.

Right before the end of the day, he'd sent her an email asking her to come see him. She smiled happily to herself. Maybe he would go with her to see Mama J tonight and then spend the rest of the evening with her. It was worrisome not to have the extra money from the club and she knew she would have to find another second job, but she'd maybe take a week or two and enjoy her extra time with Luke.

"Come in."

She opened the doors and stepped into Luke's office,

closing them behind her. Luke was sitting at his desk and he didn't look up as she approached his desk.

"Hi," she said.

"Hello, Jane."

Her smile faltered as he looked at her. She sank into the leather chair in front of his desk. "Is there something wrong?"

He sat back in his chair and folded his hands across his lean abdomen. He was acting so strangely – stiff and cold – and apprehension trickled down her spine.

"I went to see your old boss at the club today."

"What?" Her mouth dropped open. "Why – why would you do that?"

"I went to apologize and ask him to give you your job back."

Warmth flooded through her and she smiled at him. "You did? That's really nice of you, Luke. Thank you."

"It didn't work," he said.

"I'm not surprised. Jeremy isn't - "

"Did you fuck him?" Luke interrupted.

The colour drained from her face and she said, "Wh-what?"

"Did you fuck your boss at the club?"

She swallowed and nodded. "Yes. I dated Jeremy for a while."

Anger flashed in his eyes and he looked away from her before standing and pacing back and forth in front of the window. "I didn't want to believe him."

"What did he tell you?" She asked cautiously as she stood.

"Did he help you with money?" He asked.

"I – well, he bought me some groceries once or twice when I was really low on food," she said.

He laughed bitterly and she gave him a defensive look. "I didn't ask him to do it. He offered."

"Of course," Luke said. "So, is this what you do, Jane? You sleep with your boss? It's some kind of game to you?"

"No!" Jane said. "Luke, I tried not to sleep with you because of what happened with Jeremy. I realized it was -"

"Tried not to sleep with me, huh?" Luke said. "Guess that didn't work out so well for you. Although, I'll admit you put on a good show for quite a while. You did an amazing job of getting me all hot and bothered for you and worried that you were going to starve because of me. Getting your heat and electricity cut off because I *forced* you to buy better clothes was a nice touch. Very convincing."

"What are you talking about?" She whispered as Luke turned and glared at her.

"How did you manage the rent thing? Hmm? Or was that a lucky coincidence that you used to your advantage?"

"I don't know what you mean," she said. "Luke, calm down and tell me exactly what Jeremy said to you."

"It doesn't matter," he said. "It's over, Jane."

"What do you mean?"

"It's over between us. We're done," Luke said coldly.

"You're firing me?" She whispered as fear stabbed at her heart. How would she care for Mama J?

More bitter laughter exploded from his mouth. "Right, it's the money you worry about most isn't it?"

She chewed at her bottom lip and didn't say anything as Luke gave her a disgusted look. "No, I'm not firing you, Ms. Smith. But what's happening between us is finished. Don't contact me outside of work. Do I make myself clear?"

"Perfectly," she whispered.

"Good." He turned and stared out the window.

Her throat aching and tears sliding down her cheeks, Jane left his office and hurried away.

᠀ ᠀

Jane ignored the knocking on her bedroom door and continued to scroll through her phone. She wrote down a phone number before clicking on the next listing. She frowned. The apartment was in the Badlands and she had hoped to avoid that area but based on her budget, she didn't think she had much choice. She had applied for a few part time waitress jobs tonight but she didn't expect to hear back from them for at least a week and didn't know for sure that she would even get an interview. She needed to find a place to live that she could afford on her current salary. With the cost of Mama J's care, that meant the Badlands.

"Jane?" Amy knocked again. "Please let me in."

She sighed and rubbed at her forehead. "Come in, Amy."

Amy opened the door and peeked into her room before holding out the mug she carried in her right hand. "I brought you tea."

"Thank you." She scrolled through her phone again as Amy set the mug of tea on her nightstand and sat beside her on the bed.

"How was Mama J tonight?" Amy asked.

"Not great," Jane said. "She didn't remember who I was and she was very upset because she couldn't find Walter."

"I'm sorry."

"Me too," Jane said as she wrote a phone number down on her pad of paper.

"What are you doing?"

"Looking for a new place to live," Jane said absently.

"What?"

Amy's outraged tone had her looking up in a hurry.

"Why the hell are you doing that?"

Jane set her phone down and sipped at her tea. "Your brother broke up with me yesterday."

"I know that," Amy said. "He was in a foul mood this morning and he said you had broken up. I'm sorry, honey."

"Thanks," Jane said.

"I know it isn't any of my business but," Amy paused, "what happened? You two seemed perfect together."

"He didn't tell you?" Jane asked.

"He wouldn't give me any details. He just said that you were no longer together. What happened, honey?"

Jane sipped at her tea again, grateful that Luke hadn't told Amy that she was a whore who slept with her bosses on the regular. "I don't want to talk about it."

"Jane - "

"I respected your privacy when you said you didn't want to talk about Mark," Jane said gently.

Amy pressed her lips together. "You're right. I'm sorry and I won't pry again. But I don't understand why you're looking for a new place to live."

"I can't live with you anymore."

"Why not?" Amy said.

"Because your brother hates me and he's your brother." Jane wondered if Amy was being deliberately obtuse.

"I don't care," Amy said. "You're my friend and I like having you live with me. You don't have to move out. Yeah, Luke's my brother but it doesn't mean that I'm going to automatically agree with all of his choices. I don't know why he broke up with you but whatever it was, he's stupid for doing it."

Tears welled up in Jane's eyes. "I don't want to come between you and your brother. Family is what's important."

"You won't," Amy said. "I love Luke and I love you, and you being my roommate won't be a problem. I promise."

"It might be," Jane said. "If it does, I'll move out. Okay?"

Amy rolled her eyes. "Yeah, okay, but it won't be a problem."

Jane didn't reply and Amy rested her head on her shoulder. "I'm sorry it didn't work out with my brother, Janie. He's an idiot."

"He isn't," Jane said. "Besides, it's better this way. It would never have worked out between us – we're too different. I was a fun distraction for him and he just got swept up in the moment."

She forced herself to smile at Amy. "It's good that he realized how he really felt."

"Honey, did you tell him that you loved him?" Amy asked.

"No, and it's good that I didn't," Jane said. "I'm embarrassed enough and it would have been much worse if he had realized that I fell in love with him. I was an idiot to think I could have a relationship with him."

She wiped briskly at the tears that were sliding down her cheeks before sipping at her tea. "This is really good. Thanks, Ames."

"You're welcome, honey."

∽ ∾

"Mama J?" Adrenaline pulsed through Jane's body as she hurried into Mama J's room. It was Thursday evening, she had come straight from work to see her foster mother. It was just after dinner and it was unusual to find Mama J in bed rather than her chair by the window.

"Mama J? Are you all right?"

She breathed a sigh of relief when the old woman looked over her shoulder and smiled at her. "Hello, my Janie."

"Hi. Why are you in bed?" She asked as she dragged the chair over and sat down. "Are you not feeling well?"

"I'm feeling a little tired today," Mama J said.

"Do you want me to come back tomorrow?" Jane asked.

"No," Mama J said. "It's been so long since I've seen

you, Janie. Why didn't you visit me last night?"

Jane smiled at her. She had visited but wasn't surprised that she didn't remember. "I'm sorry. I was a little busy last night."

"Of course you were," Mama J said. "You have a new boyfriend. How is he? Did you bring him to visit me?"

Jane froze. She hadn't really expected Mama J to remember Luke without seeing him and sharp pain stabbed her in the chest. She had kept her emotions under control today – it had helped that she was on a different floor and didn't have to worry about running into Luke – but she was suddenly very close to crying. Luke had been so kind and sweet to Mama J and knowing that she would never see that side of him again made her want to burst into tears.

"Janie?" Mama J touched her hand and at the look of love and sympathy on her face, Jane began to cry.

"Oh, my Janie," Mama J said. She shifted over in the bed and patted the empty space. "Climb into bed with me, sweetheart. Come on now."

Blubbering like an idiot, Janie climbed into the bed next to Mama J and buried her face in her throat. She clung to her foster mother as Mama J stroked her hair and murmured soft words of comfort.

After a while, her sobbing eased to the occasional sniff and she took the tissue Mama J handed to her. She wiped her eyes and blew her nose before resting her head on Mama J's thin chest.

"Better, Janie?"

"Yes," she whispered.

"Did you and your man have a fight?"

"Yeah. He's really angry with me over something I did in the past."

Mama J snorted. "Men can be so foolish about things sometimes. He'll come around, Janie, I promise you."

"I don't think he will," Jane said.

"He will. I've seen the way he looks at you. He loves

you."

Jane didn't reply and Mama J put one finger under her chin and tipped her face up. "He loves you. He looks at you like Walter looked at me and if there was one thing I knew for certain about my Walter – it was that he loved me."

"I wish I could have met him," Jane said.

"Me too. He would have loved you," Mama J replied. She stroked Jane's hair as Jane rested her head on her chest again.

"Listen, sweetheart, your man will realize the error of his way and come back to you begging for your forgiveness. I guarantee it. I know I'm old and getting forgetful but I haven't forgotten what I've learned about relationships. Will you take a bit of advice?"

"Yes," Jane said.

"When he comes around asking for forgiveness, don't make him grovel too much. It can be hard for some men to admit when they're wrong. If he says he's sorry, if he asks you for your forgiveness, give it to him without much fuss. Love grows sweeter when you forgive easily. All right?"

"Okay," Jane whispered. It was easy to tell Mama J what she wanted to hear. Luke would never ask for her forgiveness. She had fooled herself into thinking that he might care for her despite who she was and what she had done. Men like Luke didn't fall for women like her.

"That's my good girl, Janie," Mama J said. She ran her fingers through Jane's soft hair. "Don't tell my other kids this but you were always my favourite. I remember the first day I met you. The last few years had been difficult ones for you – your social worker had told me all about it – but I could see the goodness and the sweetness on your face. I knew you were something special right away."

Jane smiled at her. "I'm not the special one. You are. You saved my life, and I will never be able to repay you for that."

Mama J kissed her forehead. "I love you, sweetheart."

"I love you too, Mama J," Jane said. "Always."

ॐ ॐ

Luke leaned back in his chair and rubbed at his eyes. They were burning and itching from lack of sleep and he stared blearily at his watch. It was the longest goddamn Friday of his life and he wanted to get the hell out of the office and go home. He planned on spending the weekend getting very drunk. Maybe then he would sleep. Maybe then he would stop thinking that he'd made the biggest fucking mistake of his life.

He closed his eyes and then popped them open almost immediately. Fuck, would he ever have a moment where he closed his eyes and didn't see Jane's face? He had promised her that he would always take care of her and instead, he'd ended it. God, the look of hurt and betrayal on her face when he had told her they were finished. It had nearly killed him.

So then why did you end it? His inner voice complained. *You miss Jane, I miss Jane – talk to her.*

There was a knock on the doors to his office before they opened and Mark walked in. He sat in the chair across from him and stared at him.

"What?" Luke said irritably.

"You look like shit."

"Unless you have something work related to talk about, I'm not interested in chatting."

Mark didn't reply and they sat in silence for a few minutes before Luke blurted out, "I broke it off with Jane."

"What? Why?" Mark said. "I thought you moved her to my department so you could date her."

"I did, but then I found out something…"

Luke trailed off and stared miserably at Mark. His best friend leaned forward and said, "Tell me what happened."

∂⊷ ⊷∂

Half an hour and a shot glass full of whiskey later, Mark put his feet up on Luke's desk and leaned back in his chair. "You're an idiot. You know that, right?"

"You're not helping," Luke said.

"I am," Mark insisted. "You need someone to be straight with you and I'm the asshole who's gonna give it to you straight."

"Fine," Luke said. "Get it over with."

"You're in love with Jane Smith. That's fucking easy to see and you went and screwed it up because you hate that she fucked that wanker from the club. You hate the fact that Jane had sex with someone you think is beneath her."

"That's not it at all," Luke retorted. "She sleeps with her bosses, Mark. That's what she does. She sleeps with them for their fucking money. I was just another boss for her to fuck and take advantage of."

"You asshole," Mark said. "Did you even listen to her side of the story?"

"No," Luke admitted.

"So, you're taking the word of that scumbag at the club over the word of the woman you love. A woman who is ridiculously sweet, who went so long without food that she passed out in your goddamn office. A woman who has worked two jobs for how fucking long to pay for the care of an old woman who isn't even her family. She lived in the fucking Badlands with no heat and no electricity in the middle of the goddamn winter. She bought clothes instead of food when you made fun of her wardrobe."

Luke winced but Mark continued on mercilessly. "She's a good person and you know that. Even if she did the stuff that the dillhole at the club said she did – people make mistakes. Don't condemn her for her past. She loves you for who you are, do the same for her. Do you have any idea how lucky you are to get the chance to be

279

with the woman you love? Don't throw that away, you fucking asshole."

Luke stared at his best friend in silent shock. Mark glared at him before dropping his feet to the floor with a loud thud. "You can still fix this with her. Get on your goddamn knees and beg for her forgiveness if you have to."

There was a moment of silence and then Luke groaned. "Fuck, I'm such an idiot."

"Yeah, that's what I've been saying," Mark said. "Where are you going?"

Luke had jumped up and headed toward the door. "I'm going downstairs to talk to Jane."

"She's not here today," Mark said.

"What? Is she sick?"

Mark shook his head. "No. She cc'd me on her email to Kyra. Her foster mother is in the hospital and she asked for a personal day."

Luke swore loudly and yanked his cell phone out of his pocket. He dialed Jane's number and cursed again when it went straight to voicemail.

"Did she say in the email what hospital?" He asked Mark.

"No."

"Shit." He thought for a moment before googling the number for the care home. He waited impatiently as it rang twice before Bev answered.

"Bev, it's Jane's boyfriend Luke."

"Hello, Luke."

Bev's voice was uncharacteristically solemn and Luke swallowed down the anxiety brewing in his chest. "Listen, I've been in meetings all day and just got Jane's voicemail about Mama J. But she was upset and forgot to tell me what hospital Mama J is at or even what happened."

"Josephine had a brain aneurysm this morning. It's not looking good for her. She's at St. Mary's in the ICU."

"Thanks, Bev," Luke said. He hung up the phone and

grabbed his coat.

"What happened?" Mark asked.

"Mama J is really sick. I have to go to the hospital," Luke said as he ran out of his office.

Chapter Eighteen

"Amy? What are you doing here?" Luke strode out of the elevator and stared in surprise at his baby sister. She was sitting in the small waiting room between Tony from the strip club and a woman wearing a micro skirt and a thin t-shirt that said "Teasers" on the front in flowery script.

"Hey, dickhead," Tony said.

"Hey, Tony," Luke said distractedly. "Amy? How did you know about Mama J?"

Amy frowned at him. "Jane woke me this morning and told me. I drove her to the hospital and have been here all day. You didn't notice I wasn't at the office?"

He shook his head as the woman next to her stuck her hand out. "Hey there. I'm Candy."

"Hi Candy. I'm Luke – Jane's boyfriend." He shook her hand.

"Nice to meet ya," she said. "Tony, I'm gonna get a coffee from the cafeteria. You want somethin', baby?"

"I'll come with you. How about you, gorgeous? Can I get you something?" Tony said to Amy.

"No thank you, Tony," Amy said.

He heaved himself up out of his chair and Luke sank into it as he and Candy headed to the elevator.

"Did Jane text you?" Amy asked.

"No. Mark mentioned that she took a personal day because her foster mother was in the hospital. I tried Jane's number but it went straight to voicemail so I called Bev at the care home. Where's Jane?"

"She's in the room with Mama J."

"How's she doing?" Luke asked anxiously.

"It's bad, Luke. She has a ruptured cerebral aneurysm and she's in a coma. They said she's not going to wake up and that she's brain dead."

"Shit," Luke said. "I need to see Jane."

"I'm not sure that's a good idea. Jane is - I think she's close to completely losing it. She hasn't cried and she's not showing much emotion at all. That isn't like her."

"What room is she in?" Luke said.

"Luke…"

"What room, Amy?"

Amy sighed. "Four. Buzz the door and tell the nurse you're here to see Josephine Radlin."

"Thanks, Ames."

"Luke?"

"Yeah?"

"Don't screw this up. If she wants you to leave, just leave. Okay?"

"I will."

৯৯ ৶৶

When he walked into Mama J's room, he could barely stop himself from pulling Jane into his arms. She was sitting next to the bed, holding Mama J's hand, and she looked so sad and broken that his chest squeezed painfully.

There was a second chair on the other side of the bed and he eased into it as Jane stared at Mama J's face. The old woman was hooked up to what seemed like a dozen machines that all beeped and squawked intrusively.

"Jane?" He said tentatively.

She glanced at him before turning her gaze back to

Mama J. "Hello, Mr. Dawson."

"Jane," he said, "I'm so sorry about Mama J."

"Thank you. What are you doing here?"

"Mark told me you took a personal day because Mama J was sick. I called Bev and she told me what happened."

"Right," she said. "Probably illegal for her to share that information but Bev has a crush on you." She gave him another of those brief glances before she stared at Mama J again. "You're probably used to that. Who doesn't have a crush on you, right?"

"What I said earlier? I'm sor - "

She held her hand up and shook her head. "No, not now. Please."

He lapsed into silence as Jane reached out and stroked Mama J's face with the tips of her fingers. "Thanks for coming, Mr. Dawson. Mama J liked you a lot. It would have made her happy that you came to see her."

"You should have called me, honey," he said softly. "You shouldn't go through this alone."

"I'm not alone," she said. "I have Amy and I texted Candy from the club. She and Tony are here. You said not to contact you if it wasn't work related and I said I understood."

He flinched at her matter-of-fact tone but hell, he deserved that. "I shouldn't have said that. I'm so sor - "

"Mama J has a DNR," Jane interrupted. "I knew she did, we talked about it when the Alzheimer's really started to take hold of her. She didn't want to be kept alive on machines, she said. She told me that death was only a transition and nothing to be afraid of. She said she would be with her Walter again and she couldn't think of anything she wanted more than that."

She lifted Mama J's hand to her mouth so she could kiss her knuckles. "The doctor talked to me about the DNR after he said that Mama J was brain dead. In a few minutes, they're going to come in here and shut off the machines and Mama J is going to die. And then I'll be all alone."

She spoke with an odd lack of emotion that frightened him badly. He stood and moved around the bed, crouching next to her chair and cupping her face. "You're not alone, honey. I'm here with you. Okay?"

"It's over between us. You said that yourself."

"I was wrong," he said. "I made a terrible mistake and I - "

"Jane?" A man stepped into the room. He was wearing a lab coat and there was another man and a woman with him.

Jane stiffened and a look of despair crossed her face. Luke took her hand as she said, "Hello, Dr. Wales."

"Hi. Are you ready?"

"Yes," Jane said in a low voice.

The doctor glanced at Luke and Jane said, "You don't have to stay."

"I want to," he said. "I want to stay with you, honey. Please let me."

"Sure, whatever you want," she said carelessly as she stared at Mama J's face.

෴

"Shit, Luke, I have never been so worried about someone in my life," Amy said.

It was almost two hours later. Luke had driven Jane back to Amy's house and Jane had excused herself to her room as soon as they walked through the door.

"She's not crying. Why isn't she crying?" Amy almost whimpered.

Luke hugged his sister. "I think she's in shock. She didn't cry when they shut off the machines and Mama J died."

"Oh Jesus, that poor girl," Amy said as tears dripped down her cheeks. "I don't know what to say or do. I feel so damn useless. Should I stay with her in her room tonight, do you think?"

Luke shook his head. "I'll stay with her."

"Does she want you to?" Amy said.

He swallowed heavily. "She hasn't asked me to leave yet."

"If she does?"

"Then I will. But I'm hoping she'll let me stay."

He hesitated and then said, "I love her, Ames. I love her and I hurt her so badly and I don't know if she'll ever forgive me for it."

Amy hugged him hard. "She will, Lukie."

"I hope you're right." He kissed his sister on the forehead before walking up the stairs to Jane's room. He knocked on the door and opened it. Jane was wearing her nightdress and standing by the window with her forehead resting against the glass.

"Jane? I'm going to stay the night with you. If you're okay with that."

"Sure," she said. "Whatever you want, Mr. Dawson."

He closed the door and crossed the room to stand behind her. He rubbed her lower back. "I'm so sorry about Mama J, honey."

"Thank you," she said. He could see her reflection in the glass and she remained dry-eyed as she said, "I went to visit her last night. She was tired but she was good. You know? She was Mama J. She knew who I was and she – she knew that I was upset. She comforted me and gave me advice and t-t-told me she l-l-loved me."

Her small body was beginning to shake and he wrapped his arm around her waist and pulled her against his chest as her face crumpled and she made a wailing cry that hurt his heart. He turned her and lifted her up. She wrapped her arms around his shoulders and buried her face in his neck as she sobbed brokenly. He carried her to the bed and she clung to him and continued to cry as he laid on the bed. He rubbed her back and whispered meaningless words of comfort as she cried. Almost half an hour later, her sobs had become the occasional watery sniffle.

"Better?" He whispered.

She nodded and gave him a desperate look of need before resting her head on his chest. "I'm sorry. Please don't leave me."

"I won't," he said. "Go to sleep, honey."

ॐ ॐ

Jane stared at the ceiling as the beams of light from the rising sun shone into the bedroom. Luke was snoring quietly and she resisted the urge to study his face in the dim light. She had only slept a few hours before waking. She'd spent the rest of the night thinking about Mama J and trying not to dwell on the bad memories. She wanted to only remember the good things and she knew that was what Mama J would want too.

She eased her body away from Luke's. She needed to start making arrangements for Mama J's funeral. Panic bit at her insides. Funerals were expensive and her little nest egg wouldn't be nearly enough no matter how cheaply she tried to do the funeral.

She cringed and wished bitterly that she could afford to give Mama J the funeral she deserved. She wiped at the tears that were threatening to fall and sat up before reaching for her phone. It was on the nightstand where she'd left it last night and she stared blankly at it for a moment. What did she want her phone for again?

She was tired and so sad and she wanted to curl up against Luke's warm body and think about nothing. She snuck a quick glance at him. His face was relaxed in sleep and she ignored her urge to run her fingers through his dark hair. God, she loved him so much.

He loves you too, Janie. He's with you now, isn't he?

Yeah, he was. She didn't know why but she assumed it was because he felt sorry for her, was maybe worried that she was going to off herself like her mother did because he broke her heart and Mama J died. When he woke up and she assured him that she wasn't suicidal, he'd leave and she'd be alone.

The thought sent despair through her and she fought back the wave of tears again before staring at her phone. She needed to make funeral arrangements. She would keep herself busy and not think about how much it hurt to not have Luke or Mama J. She would plan Mama J's funeral and…right, money. It was expensive and she needed to get another job asap. She was pretty sure that funeral homes had payment plans but she would need a second job to make the monthly payments.

Janie, stop. Mama J is dead and you don't have the care home expenses anymore. Stop and think about -

She ignored her inner voice. She *needed* a second job. If she had a second job she wouldn't spend her time thinking about how much she missed Luke or that with Mama J dead, she was truly alone. More panic rose in her and she pushed it down grimly. Using her phone, she checked the local job ads, searching with growing desperation for weekend waitress jobs. There had to be something out there.

"Jane?"

Luke had woken and he sat up in the bed beside her, rubbing his hand across the scruff on his jaw. She gave him a fleeting smile before scrolling through her phone again. "Hi, Luke."

"What are you doing?"

"Looking through the job postings for a second job," she said.

"Why?"

"Funerals are expensive," she said. She squinted at her phone. There was a posting for a waitress job at a night club on the west side. It would be a hell of a bus ride but beggars couldn't be choosers.

"Jane, stop."

Luke's hand closed around her phone and he tugged it away from her.

"Hey, give that back," she said.

"Just stop for a minute, honey."

"I can't," she said. "I need a second job for Mama J's funeral. She deserves a nice funeral!"

Her voice was rising and she made herself stop and take a few deep breaths. "Please give me back my phone."

"I'll pay for the funeral," Luke said.

She burst into loud and bitter laughter. "You're fucking kidding me, right?"

"No," he said. "I want to pay for the funeral, Jane."

"God," she said, "you really do think the worst of me, don't you?"

"No," he said. "Honey, I don't. I shouldn't have - "

"Here," she collapsed on her back and spread her legs, "climb on and have a go, Luke."

"Jane," he said. "Stop it."

"Why?" She said. "That's what girls like me do, right? We spread our legs for guys so that they'll buy us shit. I guess I'll probably be the first woman to fuck for funeral costs but hey, aim high in life, right?"

"Stop it!" He sat her up and gave her a gentle shake. "Don't say shit like that."

"You think I'm a whore," she said.

"I don't!" He shouted. "I don't think that and I'm sorry for what I said. I should never have believed that asshole and I don't know why I did. I'm so sorry, Jane."

She stared at him for a moment. "What did Jeremy tell you?"

"Does it matter?" He said. "I was wrong to believe him and I'm sorry."

"Tell me," she said. "It matters to me."

He sighed and she listened with a numb kind of disbelief as he recited what Jeremy had said to him. When he was finished, she stared at her hands and said, "You believed him."

"I shouldn't have. I was upset and surprised and acted like an idiot," he said.

She lifted her head and met his gaze. "When I started working at the club, I was a virgin."

He winced. "You don't have to explain anything to me, honey. Please, I don't - "

"I want to," she said. "I have to. Just listen, okay?"

"Okay."

"When I started working at the club, I was a virgin. I was also lonely and worried about Mama J. The Alzheimer's was starting to get bad and I was so afraid I was going to lose her. And I was tired of feeling alone, you know? Jeremy was, well, he had a certain kind of charm and I was stupidly naïve and believed him when he said he loved me."

She dropped her gaze to her hands that were twisting in her lap. "Shamefully, it didn't take him very long to get me into bed. I didn't know it at the time because he was my first but the sex wasn't very good. Jeremy didn't always take his time and didn't seem to notice or care if I had an orgasm. I – he used to tell me that my breasts were too small and was always hinting that I needed a boob job."

"Asshole," Luke muttered.

She shrugged. "I thought he loved me. I really did. I knew he wasn't always good to me but I thought I was in love with him. I know now that I was just tired of being alone. But at the time…"

She trailed off and gave him a small smile of regret. "I look back now and wonder how I could have been so stupid. I talked to him lots about Mama J. Told him how much she meant to me and yeah, I told him that her care was expensive and that it was tough financially but I never asked him for money. What he said about buying me groceries is true. There were a couple of times when he bought me some food. Both times it was when he was staying overnight at my crappy apartment and I think he only bought the food because he was hungry but whatever – I needed the food. I should have said no, he made me feel a little bad for accepting his charity, but I was hungry."

She could hear the shame in her voice and she pulled away when Luke tried to touch her. "A few months after I started sleeping with him, I stopped by his place unexpectedly and found him in bed with one of the dancers from the club. He'd been sleeping with a bunch of women at the same time. We, uh, we'd always used condoms but I went and got tested for STDs immediately. I was terrified that he had given me something. I was clean, thank God, but I couldn't believe he had betrayed me like that. I tried to talk to him about it, tried to get him to feel bad for what he had done but he laughed at me. Told me I was a stupid little girl if I actually believed that he would fall in love with someone as pathetic as me."

She stared at her hands again before saying, "I *was* pathetic for thinking he loved me. But I – it was so nice to have someone, you know? To not feel like it was just me against the world. It's stupid, I know, but I was blinded to the truth because I didn't want to be alone anymore."

She raised her gaze to him and stared unblinkingly at him. "I shouldn't have slept with him. Not because he was a bad person but because he was my boss and it was unprofessional even if I was just waitressing at a strip club. After we broke up, he took me off the weekend shifts and put me on week nights. It was to punish me. Tips aren't nearly as good during the week. It's why I applied for the job as your PA. The cost of Mama J's care had gone up and I didn't have enough money even with both jobs."

She smiled at him. "I was attracted to you but I told myself not to act on it. I had already made one mistake by sleeping with my boss and I couldn't afford to do it again. Not when Mama J was depending on me. Only, I was still so tired of being alone and you were so different than what I thought. You were kind and sweet and, god, the way it felt when you touched me. I'd only slept with Jeremy before you and I had no idea that sex could be like that, you know?"

He nodded and she patted his hand. "I swear to you that I didn't get my heat and electricity cut off to try and suck you into taking care of me. I really believed that you would fire me if I didn't wear better clothes and I needed my job. I was embarrassed by my lack of money and the day I fainted in your office was one of the most shameful moments of my life."

"I know you didn't do it on purpose," he said. "I'm sorry I said that you did."

"I shouldn't have slept with you and I shouldn't have taken advantage of your kindness, but you shouldn't have believed Jeremy over me," she said.

"I know," he said hoarsely. She watched in surprise as he slid out of the bed and dropped to his knees beside it. He took her hand in his and said, "I'm sorry, Jane. I was an idiot and I shouldn't have said those horrible things to you. I love you. I'm so sorry. I know I don't deserve it but will you forgive me?"

"Yes," she said.

He blinked at her and she almost laughed at the look of surprise on his face. "Yes?"

"Yes," she repeated.

"Just like that," he said.

She scooted to the side of the bed and swung her legs over the side. She tugged him between her legs and cupped his face before pressing a kiss against his mouth. "A very smart woman once told me that if you love someone, you forgive them when they say they're sorry. That love grows sweeter with forgiveness."

"You love me?" He said.

She kissed him again. "Yes. I love you, Luke Dawson."

"I love you too," he said.

She gave him an adorably cheeky grin. "Yeah, I heard you the first time."

He laughed and kissed her fiercely before hugging her so hard she couldn't breathe. She pounded him on the back and he released her before kissing her again.

"I want you to move in with me," he said.

"What?" Shock reverberated through her.

"I've been miserable without you the last few days. Come home with me. Please."

"I can't leave Amy alone," Jane said, "and what if it doesn't work out between us?"

"Do you really believe that it won't?" Luke asked.

She shook her head. "No, I don't."

He squeezed her hands. "Live with me. I want to fall asleep in my bed with you next to me and know that you'll be there when I wake up in the morning."

"But Amy hates living alone and she's been really good to me, Luke. I don't want to hurt her feelings."

"We'll talk to Amy but I know my sister and I guarantee you that she'll be nothing but happy for us," he said. "Trust me on this. All right? Move in with me, Janie."

"Okay," she said. "But I'm paying my half of the mortgage."

He laughed. "Honey, I own the house."

"Of course you do," she said. "Sometimes I forget that you're rich."

"Not just rich – stinking rich," he said.

She smiled. "At least let me contribute to groceries."

"Deal," he said. "I promise you won't regret moving in with me. I love you, Jane."

She touched his face before resting her forehead against his. "I love you. Always."

෧ ෨

Want to find out what the heck is going on with Amy and Mark?

Read "Undeniably Hers", Book Two in the Undeniable Series.

Interested in reading more about Jane and Luke? They make plenty of cameo appearances in "Undeniably Hers".

Please enjoy this excerpt from "Undeniably Hers".

෧෧ ෨෨

"Breathe, Amy."

"I'm breathing."

"Not enough," Valerie said as the elevator doors opened.

They stepped out into a small room with white walls. A man was standing beside a door and Valerie smiled at him. "Just give us a minute."

He nodded and Valerie led Amy to the far corner. "Take a couple deep breaths, babe."

She breathed deeply before smiling tentatively. "I'm good."

"Better than good," Valerie said. "You're about to have the best experience of your life."

"Right. Are you sure I look okay?"

"No. You look fucking amazing." Valerie eyed her dress before letting her gaze linger on Amy's breasts. "God, I wish I had your tits."

"Be thirty pounds overweight and you can have them too!" Amy said brightly.

Valerie rolled her eyes. "Men love your curves and you know it."

"Yeah, they really do," Amy said and Valerie laughed.

"There's my Amy. C'mon, girl, let's go and get you laid by a total stranger."

They approached the man standing at the door and Valerie held out her arm. A plastic blue wristband was around her slender wrist and the man scanned it before turning to Amy. Amy held her own arm out. Her waistband was green and she had found it on the nightstand in her room. Valerie had explained that the wristbands were required to enter the lower area of the club and that the colour represented her experience in the BDSM world. Green was for a complete novice and she was a little embarrassed by it. The man scanned her bracelet without saying anything then opened the door and ushered them through the doorway.

Amy stopped immediately and tried to keep a neutral look on her face. Scantily-clad women and men filled the room. Amy's eyes widened when a woman wearing leather pants and a leather bustier walked by. She had a leash in her hand that was clipped to the collar of a man wearing just a pair of tight jean shorts.

It was a large room – large enough that she couldn't see the far end of it past the people milling around – and it was painted a dark red. Dim light shone from sconces hung on the wall and there were a series of hallways that broke off from the main room.

"What's going on over there?" Amy whispered to Valerie.

There were about seven rows of chairs set up in front of a small stage. Dark curtains were drawn across the stage but the chairs were already nearly full. Each chair had a cushion beside it and she watched as a blond-haired man sat down. A slender woman wearing a collar and a gorgeous form-fitting dark green dress knelt gracefully on the cushion next to the chair. The man smiled at her and petted her dark hair before gently pushing her head to his thigh. She rested her cheek against his leg and stared adoringly at him as he spoke with the man sitting next to him.

"They're setting up for the show," Valerie said.

"Show?"

Valerie nodded. "They do some public exhibits."

"Public exhibits of what?"

"Depends. I think tonight there's a flogging and a forced orgasm scene."

Amy's eyes nearly bugged out of her head. "Flogging?"

Valerie squeezed her arm. "Stay calm, honey. Remember, everything that happens here is consensual."

The dull sound of a paddle hitting flesh and a sharp squeal of pain came from their left. Amy turned, her hand gripping Valerie's in a hard grip as she stared at the scene. A man with his pale skin glowing in the dim light was straddling a bench. His chest and stomach rested against the padded upper part of the bench and his arms and legs were placed on the padded arm and leg rests screwed into the sides of the wooden bench. Leather straps were attached just above the rests and they were wrapped around his upper thighs and biceps, holding him firmly in place.

As they watched, a woman wearing a beaded mask and a short red dress, spanked him on the right ass cheek with a wooden paddle. The man jerked and cried out then moaned happily when the woman rubbed his red cheek soothingly.

"It's called a spanking bench," Valerie murmured into her ear.

"H-have you ever tried it?" Amy asked.

Valerie nodded. "Yes, but not in public. I always ask my chosen Dom to take me to a private room."

Amy barely heard her. She watched in fascination as the woman set the paddle on a small table before slapping the man's ass repeatedly with her right hand. The man was moaning in pain but the look of pure bliss on his face was undeniable.

She wondered what it would be like to be strapped to a

bench like that. To be vulnerable and helpless while a man spanked her. As the woman gave the man a particularly vicious slap and the man squealed loudly, Amy decided it wasn't for her. She wanted to give up some control but not like that.

What if it was Mark doing the spanking?

The errant thought sent an almost painful cramp of pleasure deep in her belly. She made herself look away from the spanking scene. Mark was the most easy-going man she knew. He wasn't a pushover but he was always willing to accommodate and compromise both in his work life and personal life. Pretending he was a Dom, pretending he would like to spank her was utterly ridiculous. A man like Mark wouldn't set foot in a place like this and just the thought of him finding out that she did, made her cringe. Despite Valerie's assurances, she was still feeling very much like a freak and she'd die before she'd ever let Mark know that she liked the idea of being dominated.

An image of Mark hovering over her, of his hands clamping around her wrists and holding her still as he pushed between her thighs flickered through her. It sent more pleasure pulsing through her belly and an absurd desire to giggle. The thought of sweet, gentle Mark ever holding her down and forcing her to take his cock was so absurd it bordered on surreal.

Still, if it meant having Mark in her bed, she'd gladly give up all of her own timid desires to be dominated. She liked the idea of it but she wanted Mark. Wanted him exactly as he was – sweet and kind and undoubtedly amazing in bed but not dominant. Not him.

Valerie was pulling on her hand. She wanted to take a quick walk through the room – her initial shock was wearing off and she was fascinated by everything – but Valerie led her to the first hallway.

A woman, holding a tablet in one hand, was standing at the entrance wearing jeans and a golf shirt that said

"Secrets" over the right breast. She looked so normal and ordinary that it sent another wave of surreal through Amy.

"Hi, Kori. How are you?" Valerie asked politely.

"Fine, thanks," the woman said. "You have a private session booked tonight?"

"Not me but my friend. This is Amy. Amy, this is Kori. She works here."

"Um, hi," Amy said.

She tugged self-consciously at the hem of her short dress as Kori pushed the screen on her tablet. It lit up and she scrolled through it before smiling at them. "She's in the Blue Room. Come with me please, Amy."

Amy gave Valerie a nervous look and Valerie stood on her tiptoes and kissed her cheek. "You'll be fine. Have a good time, honey."

She disappeared into the crowd as Amy said, "Wait! What happens after? How do I find you?"

Valerie was already gone and Amy jumped a little when Kori touched her arm. "Miss Amy? Follow me please."

She followed the woman down the hallway. Unmarked doors lined the hallway and she bit her lip nervously when Kori stopped in front of one and opened it. She stepped inside tentatively and couldn't stop her sigh of relief. The room was small and painted a soft shade of blue. It had a warm kind of intimacy to it and she studied the king-sized bed and then the blue overstuffed armchair that was tucked into a corner.

There was a door on the left side of the room and a tall wardrobe against the wall next to it. Kori smiled politely at her before starting to close the door.

"Wait!" Amy said. "What, uh, what do I do now?"

"Someone will be in soon to give you instructions," Kori said before closing the door.

Amy bit at her lip again before crossing the room to the door. She opened it and peered inside. It was a small bathroom with a shower and she checked her reflection in the mirror over the sink. Her cheeks were red and her eyes were bright with anxiety.

She took a deep breath and closed the door before opening the door to the wardrobe. She stared wide-eyed at the contents. There were a variety of collars as well as handcuffs and leather cuffs. A whip and a flogger were nestled on a bottom shelf and a basket held a variety of different sized anal plugs. Brightly-coloured vibrators filled another basket and there were a few items that she couldn't even identify. She quickly closed the doors as the door behind her opened.

She spun around and stared silently at the woman who had entered the room. She was tall and curvy like Amy and stunningly pretty. Her hair was a rich black and hung to her waist in soft curls. Her burgundy dress clung to her curves and her lips were painted a bright red. Dark eyeshadow lined her green eyes and she moved with an effortless sway of her hips that Amy knew she'd never be able to mimic.

"Good evening."

Even the woman's voice was sexy and Amy cringed inwardly when her own voice squeaked out a "good evening."

"Your name is Amy?"

"Yes."

"I am Mistress Selene."

She drifted toward her and Amy took a step backward. "Oh, um, I think there's been a mistake."

The woman raised one perfectly groomed eyebrow at her before touching the ends of Amy's blonde hair. "What do you mean?"

"I, uh, was looking to book with a man."

Mistress Selene smiled. "Yes, I know. I am not playing with you tonight. Although, you are quite lovely."

Her fingers traced the soft skin just above Amy's breasts and sent a shiver down her back.

"I am simply here to help you prepare for your play session."

"Oh, okay," she said.

"You've signed all the paperwork?" Mistress Selene asked.

"Yes. Earlier in my room. We dropped it off at the, um, front desk," Amy said.

"Excellent. Now, my understanding is that you're asking for a bit of sensory deprivation with restraints and intercourse. Is that correct?"

Amy nodded and Mistress Selene let her fingers trace her bare upper arm. "Out loud, please."

"Yes. That's what I'm looking for."

"Good. Your safe word please."

"Magnolia," Amy said. It was her favourite flower.

"Pretty," the woman said. "If at any time you wish to stop, simply say your safe word and the play session will end immediately. Do you understand?"

"Yes, I understand."

"Perfect. Your Dom will be here shortly." She moved to the wardrobe and Amy watched as she selected a dark red piece of silk and two leather cuffs before returning to her. She held out her hand and Amy took it. She led her to the armchair and urged her to sit down. Her legs were already shaking and she collapsed more than sat in the chair as Mistress Selene smiled at her.

"Your hands, please."

She held out her hands and watched as Mistress Selene buckled the leather cuffs around her wrists. They were lined with silk and surprisingly light and comfortable. She studied the metal hoop that was embedded in each cuff as Mistress Selene moved behind her.

The red silk appeared in front of her face and she took a deep breath as Mistress Selene murmured into her ear. "Ready, my lovely?"

"Y-yes," Amy whispered.

She closed her eyes as Mistress Selene draped the blindfold across her eyes. She was plunged into total darkness and she gripped the arms of the chair tightly and willed herself not to hyperventilate.

The silk was tied tightly behind her head and Mistress Selene stroked the top of her head before whispering in her ear, "Stay where you are, my lovely. He'll be with you soon."

"Thank you," Amy said softly.

She heard the woman's footsteps cross the room and the door opening. It closed with a soft click and she stayed where she was, her heart thudding almost painfully in her chest.

ॐ ॐ

"Evening, Boss."

"Hey, Trent." Mark walked into the room they had nicknamed the 'control room'. It was dominated by a large table with multiple laptops. Several office chairs were tucked under the table and he sat down in the one next to Trent. There were twelve screens embedded into the wall above the table and he studied them idly. "How's it going?"

"Good," Trent said. He was tall and lanky with a pierced nose and he tugged absently at the chain that connected his nose ring to the hoop in his ear as he studied the laptop in front of him. "Full house tonight and nearly all of the private rooms are booked as well."

"Already? It's only ten," Mark said.

"What can I say – we're popular," Trent said. "The show starts in half an hour and the chairs are all full."

Mark studied the screen that showed the stage. Trent was right, all of the chairs were filled and a crowd had gathered behind them as well.

"Who's on tonight?"

"Richard."

"That explains it," he said.

"Explains what?" Another man, he was short with dark hair and a barrel-like chest entered the room and sat next to him. "Hey, Mark."

"Hi, Dave. Why there's such a big crowd tonight. Richard's working."

"They do love him," Dave said. "He has a waiting list of submissives. Did you know that?"

Mark nodded as he pulled up a spreadsheet on the laptop in front of him. He studied the numbers from the previous night as Dave said, "Of course, it doesn't help that you don't do shows anymore."

"It's not just shows," Trent said. "He's not doing anything. Hasn't for months now and the subs are starting to complain."

Mark rolled his eyes. "It hasn't been that long."

"Yeah, it has," Trent said. "Kori had seven different subbies asking if you would be playing tonight."

Mark didn't reply and Trent glanced at Dave who shrugged.

"Are you?" Trent asked.

"Am I what?" Mark asked.

"Playing tonight."

"No," Mark said as he scrolled through the spreadsheet. "Not tonight."

"What's going on with you, man?" Dave asked. "You used to play every weekend and now it's nothing for the last three months."

"There isn't anything wrong with me. I just decided to take a break for a while."

"Right," Dave said skeptically.

Mark gave him a look of exasperation. "Where's Selene?"

"She's getting a newbie ready."

"We have a newbie tonight?" Mark asked.

Trent nodded and pointed to the second screen from the left. "Yes, first time at the club. She's in the blue room."

Mark only half-glanced at the screen. Selene was standing in front of a tall, curvy blonde who had a truly spectacular body. He looked back at the spreadsheet in front of him. The blonde's body reminded him a little of Amy's, actually. If Amy ditched the flowing skirts and loose blouses she normally wore and poured herself into a little black dress. His stomach tightened and his cock twitched a little against the confines of his jeans.

Jesus, just thinking about his best friend's little sister was a mistake. For years, he'd kept his lust for her a secret, kept it firmly hidden under a tight fist of control but it was becoming more and more difficult to be around her. If he didn't figure out what the hell to do about his inappropriate desire to fuck her, he would have to quit his job at Dawson's Clothing. He made more than enough money from the Club, he didn't technically even have to continue with his job as CFO of Amy's clothing company.

If you quit, you won't get to see her anymore.

He scowled at the spreadsheet. That was the fucking idea. He couldn't keep seeing her. It was too difficult and too damn dangerous. Three months ago, he had stopped playing completely with the subs at the Club. Stopped when he realized he was deliberately choosing women who looked like Amy. Stopped when he realized that playing with them left him feeling cold and empty.

He glanced at the Blue Room screen again. Of course, this woman's body was making him reconsider –

His eyes widened as he finally took a good look at the woman's face. "Fuck me!"

Trent jerked, nearly spilling the cup of his coffee by his right hand as he twisted to stare at Mark. "Boss, what's wrong?"

"It can't be," Mark said as she stood and squinted at the screen. "It can't be her."

"Can't be who?" Dave asked.

Mark clenched his fists and muttered, "Move, Selene. Goddammit."

Selene was partially blocking the blonde's face and all the breath rushed out of him when she stepped away and walked to the wardrobe. "Holy fuck," he said faintly. Amy - his sweet Amy - was standing in the Blue Room.

"Boss, what's going on?" Trent asked cautiously.

"The newbie," Mark snapped. "What is she asking for?"

"Uh, I don't know," Trent said.

"Look it up!"

Trent grabbed a tablet and quickly scrolled through it. "Um, she's wanting some sensory deprivation, restraints and vaginal intercourse only. No oral sex or anal sex."

Mark watched as Selene led Amy to the chair and buckled the cuffs around her wrists. "Who's assigned to her?"

"Brandon's with her tonight."

"No, he isn't," Mark said.

"He isn't?" Trent replied.

"No, goddammit!" Mark said.

"We always use him for the newbies," Dave said.

"Not tonight. Let him know he can walk the floor instead."

"Uh, okay, but what do we do with the newbie?"

"She's playing with me," Mark said grimly before stalking from the room.

Trent stared at Dave who shrugged and said, "Guess his break is over."

☙ ❧

About the Author

Ramona Gray is a Canadian romance author. She currently lives in Alberta with her awesome husband and her mutant Chihuahua. She's addicted to home improvement shows, good coffee, and reading and writing about the steamier moments in life.

If you would like more information about Ramona, please visit her at:

www.ramonagray.ca

Books by Ramona Gray

Individual Books

The Escort
Saving Jax
The Assistant
One Night
Sharing Del

Other World Series

The Vampire's Kiss (Book One)
The Vampire's Love (Book Two)
The Shifter's Mate (Book Three)
Rescued By The Wolf (Book Four)
Claiming Quinn (Book Five)
Choosing Rose (Book Six)

Undeniable Series

Undeniably His
Undeniably Hers